MURDER IN
AN IRISH CASTLE

BOOKS BY VERITY BRIGHT

MURDER IN AN IRISH CASTLE

VERITY BRIGHT

bookouture

Published by Bookouture in 2022

An imprint of Storyfire Ltd.
Carmelite House
50 Victoria Embankment
London EC4Y 0DZ

www.bookouture.com

ISBN: 978-1-80314-828-1
eBook ISBN: 978-1-80314-827-4

To all the hopeless romantics in the world – I'm one of them!

1

      —————

'We are utterly, utterly lost!'

Lady Eleanor Swift's words cut through the monotonous rhythm of the windscreen wipers.

'If you say so, my lady.'

Eleanor's piercing green eyes swivelled to her butler as he steadfastly stared forward, steering the Rolls Royce along the inky-black ribbon of water-filled potholes that passed for a road.

'I do actually, Clifford. It's almost midnight, we've been driving for an eternity and, as I said, we find ourselves entirely lost.' She peered under the brim of his brushed bowler hat and into his eyeline. 'But do feel free to refute my observation.'

Taking one leather-gloved hand from the wheel, he mimed buttoning his lips. She laughed, her good humour restored. She'd inherited her late uncle's estate and staff a few years earlier, including his long-serving and ever-loyal, dry-witted butler.

'Oh, come on, Clifford, admit it. We're lost in the woolly wilds of drizzle-soaked Ireland and we last saw any sign of life hours ago.'

He mimed unbuttoning his lips. 'I was merely going to

observe, my lady, that to be "temporarily displaced" as we are at this moment, is not the same as being "utterly, utterly lost". While to "find oneself lost" is, in itself, a contradiction.'

He continued staring forward through the windscreen into the dark and drizzle as they bumped along the rough road. She shook her head.

'Clifford?'

'My lady.'

'I've got a good game. It's just sprung to mind. You can go first.'

He nodded. 'And my challenge?'

'To explain how on earth you and I are going to make it through an entire week together without my boiling your head for being so irritatingly precise!'

'Hmm. With a complete disregard for decorum as usual, I imagine.'

She tutted in amusement. 'I'm sure my uncle didn't have to put up with this level of insubordination. Especially when you were his batman for all the years of his commission in the army. But seriously I am so—' They hit a particularly deep pothole. She hung onto the dashboard with one hand and her late uncle's bulldog, who was sitting in the footwell, with the other. 'Sorry, Gladstone, old chum.'

The elderly, comfort-loving bulldog huffed loudly and plonked his heavy head back into her lap. She ruffled his ears and turned again to her butler.

'I was trying to say that I am grateful for you driving through the night from where we disembarked the ferry at Rosslare. Especially as all the while you've pretended you're not at all exhausted, which I know you must be. And also for accompanying me on my last-minute Irish odyssey. It means the world, genuinely. Particularly as it is the festive season and you normally spend it at Henley Hall along with the rest of the staff.'

He nodded. 'Nevertheless, it is my sincere pleasure, my lady. Sadly, as you know, his lordship, your uncle, never managed to visit Ireland as he inherited his Irish estate only a year or two before his tragic passing. He was too engaged during that period in his business endeavours to make the trip and neither could I. Thus, he entrusted the estate to the care of the staff already in situ, which, of course, you also inherited along with the baronetcy.'

Eleanor winced. 'That's a terrifying thought. Me, being an Irish baronetess. After my rather bohemian upbringing abroad, I haven't finished wrestling with the intricacies of being a titled lady of the manor in rural England yet.'

'Indeed, you have not,' he said, far too quickly to her mind. 'But in part, perchance, because "wrestling" is an uncouth sport fit only for backstreet dens of male iniquity.'

'Perhaps. But, along with some Bartitsu martial arts, it comes in jolly handy for fending off unwanted male attentions when travelling across the world alone, I can tell you. Anyway, I don't suppose I'll need either here. So for now, fingers crossed, I hope you're right about where we are, so that finally, our Christmas holiday might begin and— What?'

'Forgive me, my lady. I did not mean to let my face betray my feelings. But I might have unwittingly developed an aversion to... that word.'

'What, "holiday"?' At his firm nod, she groaned. 'Yes, I can see your point. Most of our previous holidays haven't quite gone according to plan, have they?'

He slowed the car to navigate a series of rubble-filled craters just visible through the drizzle obscuring the car's headlights. 'Most of?'

'Alright. None of. All of them have been a complete disaster. With a tragic turn of events in the form of an unwanted murder or two thwarting any chance of relaxing. But not this year. This year we're going to shamelessly kick our heels, Irish style, and enjoy Christmas.' She held up a finger. 'And it's "we" because that includes you too, Clifford. If I have to scrub every inch of starch from your impeccably stiff butler's shirt collars myself.'

He shuddered again. 'Too gracious, my lady.'

She laughed. 'Now look here, it's hardly my fault that I've got caught up in such things before.' She held her hands up. 'And dragged you into investigating them too, I admit. But, honestly, all I can say is that this time, we are going to prove him wrong.'

His lips quirked. 'You mean Chief Inspector Seldon? Who asserted that you attract, ahem, dead bodies rather readily, perchance?'

'"Like a spinster attracts stray cats", he had the dashed cheek to say!' She absent-mindedly fluffed out her fiery red curls as her heart skipped at the thought of her impossibly handsome and impossibly awkward beau who, unfortunately, was working on a high-profile case over Christmas. 'I've no idea why I still give him the time of day, you know.'

'Neither do I, my lady. Although we might need to work on the transparent signs that always betray you at the mention of his name.'

'Dash it! Am I that obvious? On second thoughts don't answer. Instead, concentrate on getting us to our destination as quickly as is safe.'

They bumped on through the rain-splattered darkness. He peeped sideways at her, his tone soft. 'I hope you find a little comfort in this initial, if brief, exploration of your family roots on the Gaelic side?'

His words caught her emotions unawares. She tugged a lock of her red curls out from under her sage cloche hat and stared at it. 'Is that why I came? To try and find some sort of connection after my parents' disappearance when I was a child? And then losing my last relative in Uncle Byron nearly three years back after I'd hardly known him?' She ran one hand down her emerald silk scarf. 'Mightn't it just have been because it seemed churlish to turn down such an effusive invitation?'

'It might,' he conceded in a kindly tone. 'It is not every day one's presence is formally requested by a committee.'

'Especially by the village committee of Derrydee in West Ireland. It's got quite a ring to it, I think.' She reached into her coat pocket. Pulling out a handwritten card, she tapped it thoughtfully. 'So tomorrow, after a simply enormous hearty Irish breakfast, we'll venture into the town – well, village, to meet the sender of this invitation.'

'A perfect suggestion. A Miss Winifred Breen, headmistress of the local school and head of the Derrydee Village Committee. She will no doubt be relieved to see you have arrived.'

A wave of panic washed over Eleanor at the thought of being met with a row of expectant faces. Making small talk of any nature had never come naturally to her.

'Umm, do you suppose they will have laid on some sort of welcome ceremony? A sort of flags and bunting type of affair?'

'I really couldn't say, my lady.'

'Yes, you jolly well could! Because if you know there will be but think it's better I don't know in advance, you won't tell me to save me from becoming anxious. However, you're wrong this time. I'd rather be forewarned.'

'Since you have pressed me into an answer, I imagine it unlikely for two reasons.'

'Go on. The first?'

'Irish people are known to be considerably less formal than their English counterparts in the main. Notably so in rural areas.'

'Good. And the second?'

'Unfortunately, not everyone in Ireland is an avid fan of their cousins from across the water. With, if you will forgive the boldness of the observation, possibly good reason.'

'But they would have loved Uncle Byron if he'd ever come, surely? You've given me the impression that he was always a champion of local ways wherever you travelled.'

'Unquestionably so, my lady. His lordship steadfastly maintained we were the visitors abroad, even when we were stationed at his majesty's request. And later, long after he retired, his view never wavered, no matter in what distant land his lordship and I found ourselves.'

'And right there, you've done it again, Clifford! Just when I've managed to contain my curiosity over what you and Uncle Byron really got up to after you both left the army, you stir it up like a hornets' nest.'

'My apologies.'

'Are all well and good, thank you, but unnecessary.'

'And insufficient, I detect. So, yes, my lady. It will be my pleasure to regale you with a few tales whilst we reside at Hennelly Towers. At least, those which discretion permits my revealing alongside a game of chess and a little too much port into the long hours, no doubt.'

'Perfect! Which reminds me though, Clifford. Why isn't the baronial home called "Henley Towers", like Uncle Byron's surname? After all, the house I inherited in England is called "Henley Hall"'.

'Because "Henley" is in fact the anglicised version of the original Irish derivation, namely "Hennelly"'.

'Ah!' She forced her heartfelt longing that her uncle could be with her back into the mental box of wishes that could never be.

'If his lordship could have been here,' he said gently, reading her thoughts, 'he would have been as excited as you are about revisiting his Irish roots. And all the more delighted to have been doing so with his beloved favourite niece.'

'Good try, Clifford. But I was his *only* niece.'

'Indeed, but no harm in accepting an easy accolade, my

lady.' He paused at her laughter. 'Particularly when it was as sincere a fondness as any gentleman could ever hold.'

'Thank you.' She shivered, tuning in to just how chilly the all-pervading damp was making her feel, even inside the Rolls. 'Anyway, I hope the welcoming committee, if there is one, isn't expecting me to appear as a genteelly dressed lady of the manor. Because if this weather continues, I shall have to greet them bundled up to the nines in my thickest winter coat down through to my many layers of unflattering woollen underthings.'

He let out a quiet groan. 'Rest assured, I will have strict words with your housekeeper on our return.'

'But Mrs Butters hasn't done anything wrong.'

'On the contrary. She has clearly omitted to pack you any sense of propriety whatsoever.' He ran a finger along his collar. 'Until then, if a special effort might be made to refrain from mentioning the, ahem, unmentionables?'

'Agreed. However' – she stared through the windscreen at the few feet of road visible in the Rolls' headlights – 'unless we become "temporarily un-displaced" soon, we're unlikely to arrive in time to take advantage of our host's generous invitation to join them for a traditional Irish Christmas anyway.'

He rolled his eyes good-humouredly and tapped a spot on the map, which was meticulously folded to fit into the holder mounted on the walnut dashboard. 'I would conjecture that we are but a few miles from our destination, my lady. According to my calculations, the turning should appear soon on our right. Then we will be on the final stretch to the village of Derrydee and Hennelly—*Brace!*'

He threw an instinctive arm across her while stamping on the brakes. The car slewed to a stop, spraying stones and mud into the undergrowth. The engine cut out. In the eerie silence, Eleanor glanced at her butler in confusion and then at the road ahead.

'Good lord!'

2

'My lady, please!'

But Eleanor was already halfway out of the car, swinging herself around the passenger door. She fell to her knees, the car's headlights illuminating the body they'd almost run over.

In a trice, Clifford was beside her, whipping up his jacket tails as he dropped to his haunches. He thrust a slim torch into her palm, beating her in pressing two fingers to the man's neck. She held her breath.

'Alive. But pulse is erratic and weak.' He checked the man's airway was clear, nodding at her questioning look.

Forcing her innate hasty nature to one side, she dug deep into the memories of her nurse's training during the war and swept the torch over the casualty. The weak light picked out the coatless man's coltish limbs clad in a once-smart shirt under a thick sleeveless woollen jerkin. A simple silver chain bearing what she thought must be some sort of religious medallion hung around his neck. His dark slim-fitting breeches, now soaked through, were buckled loosely at the knee where long woollen socks ran into stout leather boots. She gingerly swept back a lock of thick wet curls stuck to his forehead, and peered closer at his pallid, blue face. The man's eyes were glassy and empty.

'No sign of impact with a vehicle, which I first suspected to have been this poor chap's problem, Clifford. Limbs appear unbroken given they're not lying at awkward angles. No indication of a head wound, either.'

'And no blood on the visible parts of his shirt or breeches.' The torchlight picked up the confused flinch of her butler's brows.

'Drunk?'

Clifford sniffed the man's breath. 'No hint of alcohol, my lady.'

She nodded and bent down to the man's ear. 'Can you hear me? If so, grunt.'

No response. She tried again. Still nothing. Her brows knitted. 'There might be no sign of injury or overindulgence but he's unconscious with a weak pulse all the same.' She stared up at the drizzle and then at the puddle around the man's body. Her nurse's training was telling her something was wrong, but what, she couldn't pinpoint. She shook her head. 'I say we risk hauling the poor fellow onto the back seat of the Rolls. We need to get him to the nearest place where he can receive medical attention.'

'Agreed.' Clifford darted to the car and returned with two tartan travelling rugs. Together, they rolled the man onto his back on the first blanket. Holding the torch in her teeth, with Clifford's help she placed the second cover over him. They then each wound the corners of the makeshift blanket stretcher around their hands.

'One. Two. Three.'

With a grunt, she lifted her half, grateful, as he lifted the other, that her butler somehow maintained the strength and agility of a man half his age.

Probably all his years in the army, Ellie.

With the road surface muddy and perilously cratered, the short distance around to the back of the Rolls was tricky enough. She groaned at how hard it was to move a deadweight, before her natural positivity kicked in with a sharp reprimand.

He isn't dead, but his staying that way depends on us!

Having manoeuvred their casualty into the car, Clifford climbed into the front as she knelt in the back beside the unconscious man now laid along the rear seat.

'What is it?'

He shook his head as he started the car. 'Nothing, my lady. I merely noted a small patch of what looked like oil under the Rolls and feared we had a leak, but it's nothing. I'll attend to it later.'

'More urgently, where on earth do we go? I mean, who would have a telephone out here? Then again, is there anyone out here at all?'

Pulling the map from its holder, he studied the paper intently. Dropping it, he swung the wheel and reversed the car on the narrow road with well-practised precision. His ever-measured tone showed no hint of panic.

'A few miles back, my lady, there is a place where we might find someone with a phone.'

'Back? But we haven't passed through so much as a hamlet.'

'Indeed we have not, but the place is shown off the main road, which is why we did not see it. Hopefully, the gentleman will be cared for there until a doctor can be found.'

Progress was painfully slow. Clifford drove as fast as he could, but the ceaseless bumps and the car's repeated slides in the mud slowed their already painful progress to a crawl. Worse still, it threatened to throw their patient to the floor of the Rolls. With one hand bracing him, and the other keeping herself upright, Eleanor concentrated on monitoring his condition, allowing Clifford to focus on navigating the treacherous road.

With a muttered, 'Here or nowhere,' he turned off left down

a narrow lane that was little more than a cart track that rose steeply without warning. A few minutes later, he pointed through the windscreen. 'Lights!'

She glanced up. 'Clifford, you clever bean. What hamlet is that?' But even as she asked, the monolithic shadow set high on a steep promontory looked more like a castle than a collection of homes.

'This is not a hamlet, my lady. This is our, and certainly the gentleman's, best hope.'

Eleanor ran up the steps and hammered on the heavy oak door with all her might.

After what seemed an age later, the small wooden slot in the centre was drawn back. 'Yes?' a sharp female voice called. 'What is it you want at this hour?' Before Eleanor could reply, the voice came again, the Irish lilt all the stronger this time. 'Even the righteous need sleep, child.'

'No doubt, but sometimes they also need a doctor. And fast!'

The tiny window shot closed, nearly catching her fingers. A moment later, the door swung open to reveal a diminutive, bespectacled woman. She was dressed head to toe in black with a white wimple running under her black hood and fanning out around her neck, wisps of grey hair poking out. A pair of intense blue eyes scrutinised her.

Eleanor sighed in relief. 'Ah, thank goodness. You're a nun.'

'Sister Imelda Josephine. I am the Mother Superior. Where is this needy daughter of our Lord?'

Clifford materialised next to Eleanor and bowed from the shoulders of his wet overcoat, bowler hat in hand. 'Reverend Mother, please forgive our intrusion, but it is a needy *son*. The gentleman is unconscious with a failing pulse.'

'A man, you say. Oh dear, dear.' The Mother Superior pulled the door to behind her and followed him to the car where he shone the torch onto the back seat. She seemed to be about to say something, but on seeing their passenger, her hand shot to her mouth. She shook her head as if to herself and then looked at Eleanor and Clifford. For a moment she hesitated, then seemed to decide. 'I suppose you'll both be needed to carry him inside?'

'Only with your permission,' Clifford said with more patience than Eleanor could have conjured up.

'Very well. If it must be so. Please bring the person in. There's no sister with expert medical training here, but we have a telephone. As does the nearest doctor. I will arrange a call to be put through.'

Eleanor manhandled the bottom half of the prone figure out of the Rolls, her rain-drenched hands fighting the cold coursing through her body. She squared her shoulders.

'Ready?'

'Ready, my lady.'

As they started awkwardly up the first of the weak lantern-lit steps to the door, she hissed to Clifford, 'Where are we, exactly?'

'This is Ballykieran Abbey, my lady. Run, for the last hundred years, by a community of Benedictine nuns, I believe.'

Readjusting her grip on the blanket stretcher, she peered over her shoulder. 'Maybe it's on account of the recent troubles, or because our patient is a man, but she seemed rather reluctant to help, wouldn't you say?'

He shook his head. 'If I might be excused the need to render an opinion, my lady.' He lowered his voice even further. 'At least until we are alone.'

They carried their patient into the high-vaulted entrance hall lit only by three tall candles set in ironwork holders on one wall. Eleanor tripped on the enormous uneven flagstones, almost dropping the man. 'On that long red settle by the statue of Mary Magdalene, Clifford,' she grunted, her words booming off the high-vaulted ceiling and stone walls.

'Not there. Here, child.' The Mother Superior emerged from behind a carved wooden partition screen. Next to her was an older woman, also in full nun's habit, pushing an ancient-looking trolley reminiscent of those Eleanor remembered from her school kitchens. 'The only suitable place is on the other side of the abbey.' Glancing down at the unconscious man, the Mother Superior seemed to hesitate again. 'What exactly is wrong with your... your friend?'

Eleanor shook her head. 'Oh, we've no idea who he is. We found him in the middle of the road. In fact, if Clifford here hadn't been so alert, we would have' – she gulped – 'run him over ourselves.'

The Mother Superior stared between them. 'Not known to you at all?'

'Indeed not, Reverend Mother,' Clifford said.

They heaved the man onto the trolley and set off across the abbey, the Mother Superior leading the way. The 'suitable place' was eventually reached via more raised and sunken flag-stones along icy, barely candle-lit corridors, all heavily scented with beeswax and an unfathomable peppery aroma. The room itself turned out to be a simply furnished, high-ceilinged but narrow stone chamber. Flickering candlelight danced over the pale, hand-cut walls, picking out the figurine reliefs running halfway up which formed a fresco of women engaged in a raft of godly endeavours.

The Mother Superior nodded to a pile of cotton shifts and led Eleanor and the other nun from the room. They waited outside while Clifford changed the man into dry clothes, Eleanor realising it wasn't worth the trouble arguing. Once he'd finished, she rejoined him and helped heave their still uncon-scious burden onto the bed and then covered him with the woollen blankets provided.

The Mother Superior pulled a long brass key from within

the folds of her habit, waved them out, and locked the door behind her.

'He will be fine. The doctor will be here shortly.'

Eleanor felt a stab of anxiety, her nurse's training baulking at leaving the man alone.

'Oh gracious. Shouldn't we—'

But the Mother Superior was already walking swiftly down the corridor. Eleanor hurried after her, her brows knitted. Leaving the unconscious man felt wrong. *Even if it is prohibited for one of the nuns to sit with him, surely someone should look in on him every few minutes?*

A moment later, she admitted to herself that she had been hasty. As they passed an intricate and wide-arching stained-glass window, she caught the distorted form of a man on the other side hurrying back the way they had come. *The doctor, thank heavens.*

Another minute on, she was almost equally relieved that the enormous refectory they had emerged into, whilst not warm itself, did hold the promise of something to halt her shivering. A tall china teapot sending out tantalising swirls of steam awaited at the end of a long wooden table. The plate of hard-baked, honey-coloured biscuits alongside it looked like pure manna.

'You look exhausted, child,' the Mother Superior said, scanning Eleanor's face. 'Please avail yourselves. I shall return in just a moment.'

Clifford set about pouring her a generous cup. 'If we will be detained long, my lady, I will retrieve your overnight case that you might re-attire yourself in something less' – he looked her over in dismay – 'wet and muddy.'

She shrugged. 'Hardly important if I'm sporting a little of the local landscape about my person, Clifford, given that our poor, helpless friend isn't even conscious. Hopefully, we'll get good news regarding him soon, though.' She took several hearty gulps of her tea, which necessitated hastily fanning her tongue with half a biscuit.

They'd emptied the teapot and eaten the biscuits – well, Eleanor had – long before the echo of stout-heeled footsteps heralded the return of the Mother Superior.

'I have made all the arrangements.'

Eleanor sighed with relief. 'Thank you. I saw the doctor had arrived. Has he had a chance to—' She tailed off as the Mother Superior shook her head.

'Doctor O'Sullivan needs to travel from beyond the Crag. You must ferret out some patience, child. He'll not arrive for another pot's worth and longer besides.'

'Oh.' Eleanor felt crestfallen. 'My mistake. I thought the man I saw in the cloisters was him.'

The Mother Superior stiffened. 'Here in the abbey?' She pointed at Clifford. 'Save for your man, who would never normally be permitted, there is no one. I have, however, requested Father Quinn to attend. He'll be taking the back route since Tristan knows it best. It's shorter than the road.'

At Eleanor's puzzled look, the Mother Superior added, 'Tristan, his donkey, of course.'

Clifford gave a quiet cough.

Not everyone has a Rolls, Ellie. Most around here, it seems, don't even have a car. She nodded.

'Ah, a donkey. That must be tricky though. I mean, umm, in the darkness and rain.'

'Which are all of God's making,' came a rich-timbred voice from the doorway. She turned to see a stocky, white-haired man shaking a small lake's worth of water from the hood of his thick green worsted cape. Underneath he wore a black cassock, while scuffed brown leather boots with mismatched laces adorned his feet.

'Ah, Father Quinn, it is yourself.' The Mother Superior rose. 'I thought you'd be longer about the road.'

The priest coughed. 'Tristan felt our Lord's call to get here and fair danced his way.' He clapped his hands. 'Now, who is in need of prayer and where are they?'

The Mother Superior reached inside her gown and pulled out the long brass key. Father Quinn reached slowly for it.

'I see,' he said gravely. 'Then may God's will be done, good sister.'

3

Eleanor, failing to stifle another unladylike yawn, caught Clifford rolling his eyes behind his pince-nez. She shrugged. The austere refectory's only source of light was three suspended cartwheels, each holding nine lit candles, and she'd long bored of trying to count the number of wall stones from the flagstoned floor to the vaulted ceiling.

'It's been ages since the Mother Superior disappeared and it must be, what, one in the morning by now?'

He put down the slim leather notebook in which he'd been making some sort of meticulous list and consulted his pocket watch. He held up two fingers.

'Two! We arrived here, what, almost one and three-quarter hours ago? We're swimming in tea and' – she gesticulated down the corridor – 'the distant wheezy bellow of organ music, but absolutely no information about our poor casualty.'

'Quite.'

Her curiosity over what he was writing was interrupted by Gladstone's excited whimpers. They looked over to where the bulldog lay asleep on his back on the flagstones, evidently chasing dream rabbits as his paws twitched. 'Honestly, why do people say "It's a dog's life" meaning a miserable existence? He's living like the hairiest, greediest prince who ever existed.' As if to prove her point, Gladstone broke off whimpering and started snoring, the sound echoing around the vast hall. She turned back to Clifford. 'You do know you're breeding a monster, don't you?'

Her butler's eyes twinkled as he peered over his pince-nez. 'Just the one, my lady?'

She laughed. 'Yes, you terror!'

'Most remiss of me, then.' He turned to a new page and made a show of pretending to add a long note, reading aloud as he wrote. 'Required with immediate effect: significantly more strident endeavours in ensuring greater indulgence is lavished upon the mistress.'

She shook her head. 'Please don't. Work only on enjoying Christmas the minute we hear our poor fellow is alright and we're back en route to Hennelly Towers.'

They both looked up at the sound of two male voices answering the Mother Superior at the same time out in the corridor. Gladstone jerked to sleepy attention and rolled on to his front. His nose twitched towards where the voices had come from and he let out a low growl.

'So much for you being the only man in the abbey,' Eleanor whispered to Clifford as they rose together. She tapped her leg for Gladstone to join her, grabbing his collar as he did so.

'In there,' the Mother Superior's voice filtered in. 'Our guests are waiting.'

'What, all three of them?' came a languid retort. 'Because laying out the sick on the dining tables died out with the plague for good reason, you know?'

'I do,' the Mother Superior replied waspishly as she came into the room, followed by a short, beetroot-faced man. He had thinning ginger hair and the telltale edging of striped pyjama bottoms poking out from his police uniform trousers.

'The... the injured person is elsewhere, naturally, Constable Doyle.'

Behind them was an elegantly built, green-suited man carrying a doctor's bag. He took a deep breath and adjusted the unlit pipe in his mouth before striding over the threshold to join the other two. The man the Mother Superior had addressed as 'Constable Doyle' stared at Eleanor and Clifford.

'And you are?'

The Mother Superior looked questioningly at Eleanor. 'We haven't actually got as far as names, have we, child?'

'And yet your hospitality has been second to none,' Eleanor said genuinely as she passed Gladstone's lead to Clifford. She stepped over to the two men, offering a hand to either. 'Morning, I'm Ele—'

'Lady Swift,' Clifford interjected on reaching her side.

The policeman looked her over with poorly disguised disdain. 'And mustard cuts just as well with the backside of a tin teaspoon.' Any charm his Irish lilt had was lost to his snide tone.

She flapped a quieting hand at Clifford, who had taken a defensive step forward. The other man nodded at her and folded his long pale fingers over his jacket front. 'Sullivan O'Sullivan.' He gripped the stem of his pipe in his teeth. 'Doctor. Of house – and abbey – calls, it appears.' He looked sideways at the Mother Superior. 'Of all hours too, would you know?'

Eleanor glanced at Clifford, whose brows were threatening to break his golden rule of never showing any sign of displeasure. Knowing it was on account of the men's far from effusive response to her, she slapped on her best smile. 'Well, gentlemen, we're extremely grateful you've come out. Both of you, I'm sure. Especially on such a soggy night.'

The policeman snorted. 'Morning, you mean! Night ended long backwards. My blankets can tell the time just fine, 'specially when dawn's not far off her wake-up call. And that out there...' He whirled in an uneven circle as if looking for a window to point through. Finding none, he jerked to a stop. 'Out there is as filthy as it gets.'

The Mother Superior glared at him. 'Nothing our Lord sees fit to send is "filthy", Constable Doyle!'

The doctor snorted. 'Can I get to the business of tending to the patient? Or must I see what's left of the night through in pointless preambles first?'

Before the Mother Superior could respond, Eleanor thought it best to jump in. 'Oh, thank you, Doctor Sullivan... O'Sullivan, I mean. The poor fellow we found seems in a serious way. Although we couldn't fathom at all what is wrong since there's no actual sign of injury.'

The doctor smiled thinly. 'Then, the luck of the Irish be mine since I haven't entirely wasted my time in being summoned here.' He marched out of the refectory with the Mother Superior.

Left alone with the policeman, Eleanor and Clifford discreetly shared a puzzled look.

'You'll be taking a seat now. And without a word of protest,' Constable Doyle said sharply as he yanked a notebook from his breast pocket. Despondently watching the stream of water run from its cover down to the floor, he added, 'And don't be dreaming up any shenanigans. Now, your name?'

Eleanor swallowed hard. It had been a long night already. 'Oh, I see. You missed it the first time. Well, it's Lady Eleanor Swift. Of Henley Hall, Little Buckford. In Buckinghamshire. And Baronetess Derry of Ross, it seems. And this is Clifford, my butler.'

'English,' the policeman muttered, scribbling only half a line. 'Suspicious, you being so far from home, then.'

Clifford stared hard at the policeman. 'Her ladyship is visiting here for Christmas, Constable. And by formal invitation.'

'And that's supposed to explain why you took it upon yourself to as good as flatten a man under the wheels of her fancy car?'

She bit back the sharp riposte burning on her tongue. 'Clifford didn't run over the poor man! In fact, no one did. He hasn't a mark on him that we could find. We simply saw a fellow human in need of help and subsequently did all we could to aid him, as I'm sure anyone would have done.' She spread her hands on the table. 'Shall I just tell you exactly what happened?'

'And what purpose would that serve for delivering up the truth?' Constable Doyle said. 'I do the questions. You do the answers.'

'Got it, Constable,' she said, containing her exasperation. 'Next question, then?'

'Well, if your man wasn't run over by yourselves, then there is no crime and my bed's gone colder than a grave for nothing.' He shook his head as he stretched his legs stiffly. This left more of his pyjamas on show, which he tried to cover up by scraping his heavy boots down the back of his trousers.

Behind him, Clifford adjusted his grip on Gladstone's lead and tapped the policeman on the shoulder. 'If you wish to continue conversing with her ladyship, might I suggest that you try a more civil approach, Constable?'

Constable Doyle spun around. 'Threatening a man in uniform, are you?'

'Not a bit,' Clifford said nonchalantly. 'But Master Gladstone here...' During the last minute, the bulldog's quiet growling had grown in ferocity. Now, he squared up to the policeman, his hackles rising.

Constable Doyle opened his mouth and then shut it quickly. Backing away, he shoved his notebook and pen into his top pocket. 'I'm off to see what Sullivan has worked out, but I'll be right back.' He glared at Gladstone and pointed an irate finger at Clifford. 'And when I do, you'd better have that dog under control!'

He marched out in the direction the doctor and the Mother Superior had gone.

'Excellent work, Master Gladstone.' Clifford handed the eager bulldog a treat from his pocket.

Eleanor stifled her laughter. 'Clifford, you are a total scally-wag. And you too, Gladstone.'

After a calming sip of tea, she put her cup down and frowned. 'Now, I know I'm exhausted and perhaps a little tetchy, but that Constable Doyle seems to be of the opinion that we are the wrongdoers here! I appreciate no one likes to be dragged from their bed in the middle of the night – or early hours of the morning – but his manner is quite intolerable.'

'Indeed.' He held her gaze. 'Although, not just with us, did you notice?'

'I did. He was rather cutting to the Mother Superior as well, I thought.'

'Who parried back with equal frostiness, to my ears. Doctor O'Sullivan being only marginally more gentlemanly in his discourse with the lady.'

'It all feels decidedly odd. And wrong.' She sat back down on the bench. Running an anxious finger along the grain of the oak table, she sighed. 'Now I feel bad for momentarily laughing. There's a very sick man at the root of all of us being here at this hour of the morning. And the mystery of what exactly he was doing at such an ungodly hour in the middle of nowhere.'

He nodded. 'And what exactly is ailing him?'

'No matter.' Doctor O'Sullivan strode in, Constable Doyle hurrying after him. 'His troubles will soon be behind him.'

'Oh, thank goodness, he's awake!' Eleanor cried, leaping up.

Doctor O'Sullivan shook his head. 'No. Not awake. And not going to be. Father Quinn is saying the last rites.'

She gasped in dismay. *His manner seems so cold. But then*

again, Ellie, as a doctor, this would hardly have been his first time tending the dying, so it's not surprising.

Clifford stepped to her side, his tone edged with concern. 'My lady, you did all you could for the gentleman.'

'Although, as the doctor, one might say that was the role I have just played,' O'Sullivan said tartly. 'However, his condition was no surprise after a heart attack like that.'

'Heart attack?' she said, with a wobble in her voice. 'But—'

Clifford gave a discreet shake of his head.

He's right, Ellie. No point disputing with a doctor. These things happen.

She took a deep breath, but her distress clearly showed in her face. Clifford addressed the two men.

'Might her ladyship be permitted to know the gentleman's name, that a modicum of comfort may then be drawn when offering words for his passing?'

'His name?' Doctor O'Sullivan and Constable Doyle shared a look. The doctor shrugged. 'I couldn't say. He wasn't local.'

Constable Doyle nodded. 'We know our own kind here. And, like yourselves' – he gave them a pointed look – 'he wasn't one of them.'

They were joined by Father Quinn as Eleanor took the pristine handkerchief Clifford slid into her hand and pressed it over her mouth.

'He is no longer of this earth,' the priest said simply.

'Oh, that poor chap.' Her heart squeezed with sadness for the stranger. 'For it to end like that. On such a lonely road.' She blinked back the hot prick of tears. 'I hope he came to, even momentarily, so he knew he wasn't alone in his final moments.' She looked at the priest imploringly. 'Maybe he managed to say something before he passed?'

The priest cast his eyes down and busied himself adjusting the folds of his cassock. 'You probably want to be getting about your business. Good night to you both.'

Outside, they walked in silence to the Rolls. Clifford held Eleanor's door open but rather than climb in, she quickly glanced in the windows of the doctor's car parked nearby. She shook her head. *What were you expecting to see?* She really didn't know, she'd just been compelled to look. She went to step away, but something caught her eye. Turning back, she could see in the moonlight filtering into the car that the back seat was wet. Very wet.

Wrinkling her brow, she hurried to the Rolls and climbed in.

4

_____

Clifford eased the Rolls to a stop. In the car's headlights Eleanor could see two tall, scrollwork gates. At his questioning glance, she nodded.

'Yes.' She dodged Gladstone's fluttering jowls as he snored against her chin. 'Your wonderful company and artful distractions have worked their magic, thank you. I've sent my silent words of farewell to our tragic stranger.'

'Whom you did all that was possible to aid, my lady.'

'We both did. Now,' she said, nodding at the gates, 'we've finally arrived, have we?'

'Indeed. Hennelly Towers awaits.' His lips pursed. 'However, the retainer should greet us. But we are, to say the least, rather late in our arrival.'

'I should say so!'

Her gaze swept the gatehouse, visible in the pale moonlight that had appeared as the drizzle and clouds had rolled away. Not a single window was lit.

Clifford's brows knitted. 'Most unacceptable, my lady. My sincere apologies.'

'Clifford. It's ridiculous o'clock in the morning. He probably gave up on us and sensibly went to bed. You said yourself that Irish ways are more relaxed than English ones. Especially in rural areas.'

'It would seem so!' He stepped out and pushed the gates open. A few moments later, as the Rolls stopped at the end of the long, snaking driveway, she climbed out.

'Oh, my!' Her frosted breath drifted upwards as she stared at the castle she now owned. With the rain clouds having blown themselves out, the temperature had plummeted but, in the crisp, clear air, the moon hung behind the building's castellated roofline like a glittering orb. 'Clifford, it couldn't be more exquisitely fairy tale.'

Gladstone let out a woof from the passenger seat in agreement.

Above them rose a five-storeyed expanse of dark stone, each floor peppered with lead-latticed windows. Beyond the austere roof castellations, a raft of higgledy-piggledy chimneys ran between the two semicircular towers flanking either end.

Clifford took a step backwards to better scan the edifice. 'Hmm. An eclectic mix of styles. The painting of it that hangs in the west wing of Henley Hall hardly does it justice. However, all the better to enjoy in the daylight hours, perchance? Which, my lady' – he gestured up the steps – 'may well be upon you before you have managed to lay your head at all if we tarry any longer.'

'Now that you mention it.' She hugged her shoulders. 'I didn't know it was possible to be too tired to stand and too excited to sleep at the same time.'

'Really? Because I had come to believe that is the very definition of enjoying Christmas, Lady Swift style. For the moment, shall we meet' – his brow flinched again as he scanned the darkened windows – 'whichever, if any, of your skeleton Irish staff have been assigned to late night duty?'

He rapped the large circular brass ring on the imposing oak door and stood back. Silence. After a minute, he rapped a second time. Still silence. A faint prickle ran down her spine.

He shook his head and muttered, 'Is there anybody there?'

She broke off from scanning the building for any sign of light, or life.

'What did you say?'

'This reminds me of a poem, my lady. *The Listeners* by Walter de la Mare. A traveller comes to a moonlit door and knocks there on, but nobody answers. The only sound is that of his horse chomping on the grass of the forest floor.'

She grimaced. 'I know what you mean, but I'm not sure there's even anyone listening. Human or not!' She marched up to the door and gave it a shove.

It creaked open a few inches. No light came from inside. They exchanged a look. She pushed it again, and it slowly swung fully open. The prickly feeling returned. Stepping over the threshold, Eleanor jumped as Clifford's pocket torch clicked on. He swept the beam around the high, stone ceiling and dark-oak panelled walls. The light picked out an enormous fireplace at one end with two enormous settees either side and above the mantelpiece, *a pair of stuffed wolf's heads, Ellie?*

He sniffed. 'Whether there is, as you wondered, a welcoming committee in the village for your arrival or not, there is certainly not one here!'

She shook her head. 'Actually, Clifford, you're wrong.' She pointed downwards.

He swung the torch on to the floor. In the middle of the enormous hall sat the fluffiest ginger cat she'd ever seen. Gladstone's nails clattered against the flagstones as he skittered to a halt. He let out a low growl, his short hackles rising.

The cat merely yawned, rose and wandered over to sniff the now confused bulldog, its white-tipped tail twitching. Eleanor crouched and rubbed a hand along the cat's back.

'Hello, there. So, you're our only welcoming committee, are you?'

'Ah, made it, so you did!'

She jumped up and spun around in the direction the reedy voice had come from. On the doorstep was a short man carrying a lit oil lamp whose uneven-cut white whiskers, crinkle-lined eyes and high-domed bald forehead suggested he was in his early-to-late fifties. Despite the cold, he was dressed only in a wrinkled grey shirt over a thick green cardigan and dark wool trousers.

The man touched his forelock and grinned, the light from the lamp highlighting his stained, yellow teeth. 'You must be Lady Swift, m'lady. And a finer hour of whichever day it is now, you couldn't have chosen to arrive.'

He coughed wheezily, shaking the top button of his cardigan loose from its last strand of fraying thread. Clifford bent to retrieve it from the floor, his disapproving gaze never leaving the man's face.

'Corcoran, I presume?'

'It is that.' He turned back to Eleanor. 'Welcome, I'm sure, m'lady.'

Even though she found the man's manner endearing, it was very late, and she was exhausted, as well as emotionally drained after the evening's tragic events.

'Good evening, Corcoran. The rest of the staff are in bed, then?'

'Very likely. But I couldn't promise, so I couldn't.'

She shared a puzzled look with Clifford, who turned and frowned at the old retainer. 'A clear explanation, swiftly delivered, if you please.'

Corcoran laughed. 'Mr Clifford, you're every bit as I imagined from your letters. Especially the last one with the long list of instructions. Which is just grand. But there's no one here but me to carry them out and I surely can't...' He lowered his voice to a whisper, making them both lean forward, 'The staff have fled, you see. Because of old Eamon's antics.'

Eleanor shook her head, fearing they could be there all night. 'Who exactly is "old Eamon"?'

Corcoran's eyes widened. 'Why, the ghost of Hennelly Towers, of course!' The fear in his voice sounded genuine.

'Ghost?' She beckoned Clifford to one side. 'Tell me I'm dreaming. Or nightmaring, if that's a word.'

'Not that I've encountered in my humble voyage through the English language, my lady. And to answer your second, unspoken question, I do not recall his lordship mentioning a resident ghost.'

'I see.' She stepped back to the doorway, where the old retainer had remained rooted to the spot. 'Perhaps, Mr Corcoran, this "old Eamon" is a jovial, friendly sort of a ghost?'

'Well, that's precisely the thing,' he said earnestly. 'Of a normal day, he's harmless enough, the other staff always say. No more trouble than the furniture. But lately! Furious, he be, for the first time, in ever. They've been telling me of happenings that could turn the thickest head of dark curls white overnight.'

Clifford rolled his eyes. 'Well, still being here, Mr Corcoran, I assume you are made of sterner stuff. How have you found this apparent ghost to be?'

Corcoran gasped. 'Me! Why, I've never stepped further into the house than this very spot. Oh, dear me no. Never. Not since I started here as a boy.'

'And yet you've stayed in service all these years?' Eleanor said.

'Ah, truth be known, I've a scoundrel's reason for doing so.' He sighed. 'I mean, where's a bent old man who's seen fifty years and three like meself going to go? All the more at Christmas.' He shook himself. 'Anyways, I can tell you the kitchens be to the west side, if as you're hungrier than the wolves' heads hanging over the fireplace there. Fancy bedrooms are away up the main stairs and then back on yourself. Staff quarters is scattered along the top landing. And Tomkins'll see one of you proper for warming your bed.'

Seemingly oblivious to Clifford's reproving sniff, he passed him the oil lamp, touched his forelock again and left.

'Well, at least this fellow Tomkins must be around somewhere?' Eleanor said overenthusiastically, trying to find a positive in being stranded in an unknown, apparently haunted castle in the middle of the night in a country she'd never visited before.

Clifford pointed to the ginger cat, who was now rubbing itself on Gladstone's neck where he sat with one stiff back leg sticking out sideways, a soppy expression on his face. 'Tom. Kins. As in Tom Kitten, I would conjecture.'

'Ah!' She smiled fondly at her bulldog. 'Well, it seems at least Gladstone has a new friend. And—' She caught the telltale sign that all was far from right in her butler's world as he repeatedly tapped the palm of his hand. 'And, Clifford, it's alright. Fine, in fact. I know you're appalled by the lack of staff and anything being prepared, as you will have requested in impeccably clear detail. But it's Christmas, which is a very precious time for all of us. So,' she continued, pointing first out of the still open front door and then up the stairs, 'I leave the decision entirely to you. We can hightail it and speed straight back to England.'

He sniffed. 'And sanity!'

'Quite. Or, we can stay.' She perched on the edge of the nearest settee's thickly padded arm. 'And I shan't murmur so much as a word about whichever you choose.'

'Too gracious, my lady. As always. But I couldn't possibly.'

She mimed buttoning her lips, as he often did.

'Touché.' After taking a deep breath, he nodded. 'In the

inimitable words of the ferociously independent nine-year-old who used to plague my summers – albeit far too few of them – "what do consequences matter a scrap when there's the chance for—"'

    'An adventure?'

5

'Scrambled egg breakfast! Thank you, Clifford. Top-notch cheffing in unfamiliar surroundings. I'm famished.'

Eleanor helped herself enthusiastically from the first of the four lidded porcelain dishes on the tray he had placed on the red-clothed table. She was seated cross-legged in an alcove on a velvet-padded high-backed pew chair. Gladstone and his new ginger friend, Tomkins, sat expectantly beside her. Having not yet explored the castle, she and Clifford had agreed this room on the ground floor would admirably serve as the morning room. With its floor-to-ceiling latticed windows, it offered the most spectacular view over the now lightly snow-dusted countryside. Once, that is, she'd pulled aside the damask curtains intricately embroidered with Celtic animal designs and used her napkin to clear the condensation off the lead panes. With the brazier infusing her bottom half with comforting warmth, she couldn't have been any more cosy.

She lifted the lid of the next dish along. 'Ah! Poached eggs. A creative adaptation.' She took two and nodded to the third. 'And that contains...?'

'Devilled clutch.'

'Sounds exciting!' She peered inside. 'Oh! I see. Er, excellent adaptation again.'

He coughed. 'Regrettably, only a further strain on the egg motif, my lady, with the addition of some rather suspiciously pale mustard. I was significantly derailed by there being nothing else to work with. However, the eggs are definitely fresh. To the point I had to scrummage them from underneath the feathered ladies I discovered residing in the stables, a "clutch" being a collection of eggs in the nest.'

She hid a smile. 'Tsk, tsk! Scrummaging about with ladies first thing in the morning, Clifford. I know I suggested we drop a bit of formality, but I didn't mean you to hurl it at the wall altogether. Now, after we've breakfasted...' she paused, watching him avail himself of the teapot and nothing else, 'each in our own fashion, we'll go and ferret out the head of the village committee. And then we'll find somewhere to stock up on provisions, suitable for a feast that can match my appetite for a wonderful Christmas.'

'Hmm.' He stroked an imaginary beard. 'Tricky, perhaps.'

'Because we're in the middle of absolutely nowhere? Oh, no!' She dropped her fork with a clatter on the plate in dismay. 'Don't say we don't have enough fuel for the Rolls?'

'No, my lady. I was merely thinking that usually it takes the better part of all the tradesmen of Little Buckford to meet the demands of your rather, ahem, robust desire for tasty comestibles.'

'Nothing wrong with that during the festive season.'

'Nor year round, evidently. As I have been reminded repeatedly by a certain lady of the house.'

Before she could think of a suitably witty reply, Clifford tapped the lid of the fourth dish with his teaspoon.

'Actually,' she grimaced, 'I might save the last egg surprise for lunch. I'm rather egged-out. If it will reheat, that is?'

'Regrettably not.' He pushed it closer to her.

She lifted the lid. 'What the!' Her heart skipped as she recognised the familiar, efficient writing of her overworked policeman beau on the envelope. 'It's from Hugh! But how did he time it to arrive before us, since we left Buckinghamshire at such short notice?' Scooping it up, she pressed it to her chest, her shoulders lifting with glee. 'And what unearthly hour does the postman call around here, then?'

'I really couldn't say, my lady.'

She slapped her forehead with the envelope. 'Of course. Given the lack of address, clearly the postman is uncannily the precise same size, shape and devious demeanour of my own treasured butler. Thank you, Clifford.' She turned the envelope over. On the back was written 'To be opened on Christmas Day.'

She tucked the envelope carefully inside her skirt pocket and then turned her head back and forth as if posing for a photograph. 'Good job he's not here, though. I imagine I don't look my best at this moment? There's no mirror in the room you finally deemed acceptable for me to fall into last night. Or should I say "this morning" as it was probably only about four hours ago?'

'Three and three quarters, to be precise,' he said, not answering her opening question. 'But I hope the brandy snifters, in the plural, and raft of bed-warming accoutrements, aided you in securing some rejuvenating slumber?'

'Like Gladstone and his new chum, you mean?' She bent sideways to ruffle her bulldog's ears. He had given up hoping for sausages and had snuggled his bottom half under her lap blanket. The sight of the ginger tom standing on her bulldog, kneading the wrinkles of his neck with his front paws, lost in a trance of contented purring, made her smile. 'Actually, I did wake up several times. And not only on account of Gladstone's snoring. I imagined I heard strange noises. Not surprising after Corcoran's tales, though.'

'Indeed not, my lady.'

She peered at him. 'You too then? I didn't think he'd convinced you that there is a ghostly presence in the house?'

'He did not.' He busied himself aligning the handle of his cup with the pattern of the saucer.

'Really? Come on, spill the beans. What did you get up to while I was fitfully sleeping then?'

He permitted himself the luxury of a small sigh. 'Rising several times to investigate certain recurring noises.'

'Gracious! And every time you got to where you thought they were coming from?'

'The noises stopped abruptly. And recommenced as I returned to my room.'

She frowned. 'Gosh, that's quite spooky to my mind. Definitely something to check out later. For the moment, we'd better drive back into the village to find Miss... whatever her name is, the head of the committee. I think I ought to let her know I am here as soon as possible.'

His eyes twinkled. 'If only to give her sufficient notice for the catering arrangements.'

Driving back into Derrydee in the light gave Eleanor her first glimpse of the area. The track was worse than the main road, so she had plenty of time as Clifford navigated the Rolls around as many potholes as he could. Either side of the endlessly twisting road, scrub consisting mostly of rough grass and straggling brambles petered out into the burnt umber of an endless ocean of snow-sprinkled peat. Only a distant ring of bluish slate peaks hinted to an end of the bog.

After the long ribbon of unevenly surfaced track narrowed even further, the first huddles of low stone houses appeared, ringed by walled enclosures housing a few scratching chickens, squabbling pigs or vacant squat brown sheep. Around them, the last of the year's vegetables hung on in neat, bare beds.

Finally, they emerged into what could pass as a main street, given that it opened out into a tiny square bearing a precariously leaning monument of a man carrying a donkey across his shoulders. Gladstone's wet nose left a smear on the windscreen as he eagerly scanned the area for possibilities of mischief or food. Eleanor and Clifford shared a look.

'It is curiously quiet, my lady.' He braked to let a floppy-eared pink-brown pig continue its languid rutting of the dirt street in front of them.

She smiled as the pig slumped down in the road and began to roll contentedly in a muddy puddle. 'I think you're going to have to get out and shoo Mr Snouty there out of the way, Clifford. He's set until New Year, I'd say.'

He eyed her sideways. 'I learned long ago, my lady, never to wrestle with a pig. You get dirty. And besides, the pig likes it.'

She laughed. 'How I wish I'd been there to see that!'

'It is a quote, my lady. Attributed to the eminent Irish playwright, George Bernard Shaw. However, we were saying it is really rather early, even for rural folk.'

She snorted. 'Not if they'd been kept awake most of the night by old Eamon, it isn't! Still, just look at those darling shop fronts. They're little more than one tiny central window of someone's front room with a miniature display of goods on offer underneath.'

'Or a serving hatch.' He pointed to a low thatched dwelling. Within the curved front door, a neat rectangular hole had been cut and a stout plank fixed beneath it.

'For the customers to count their coins out on for the goods bought, do you suppose, Clifford?'

'I should think, my lady, more to offer a comfortable ledge to lean on while swapping local news, which makes up so much of rural life. That particular establishment being the baker and cobbler, I would conjecture from the amusing painted sign of shoes made from loaves.'

'An unusual combination of trades.' She peered up and down the high street. 'Perhaps we'd have more luck finding someone on foot, since this pig evidently isn't for moving? And driving up and down in the Rolls does feel a tad ostentatious. We haven't seen another car since yesterday afternoon.'

Progress without the Rolls, however, was slow. They had to skirt around large puddles left from the night before and Gladstone had to painstakingly sniff every inch of this strange-smelling place.

Back where they'd started, Eleanor shook her head. 'I was expecting us to at least be a point of interest worth twitching the curtains for.' An idea struck. 'You said the head of the village committee, Miss... umm, what was her name again?'

'Miss Breen.'

'That's it. She's also the headmistress, yes?'

'Indeed. But I imagine the local school is closed for Christmas, my lady.'

'Well then, where else can we look to find anyone who might know where she is?'

'The church, perchance, my lady?' He pointed behind her at the spire visible beyond two winding streets of more thatched roofs.

'Or...' She gestured to an ancient motorcycle propped against the wall of the only double-fronted building in the street, a policeman's helmet balanced on the saddle. It actually looked more like a turn-of-the-century bicycle converted to a motorcycle by the simple means of bolting a minute engine and equally minute fuel tank to the frame. Before Clifford could speak, she shook her head. 'We haven't got time for your fascination with all things mechanical, Clifford. Come on.' She headed for the door.

His brow flinched. 'If I might suggest you stick only to asking about the commi—'

But she flapped a hand behind her as she strode ahead. 'Honestly, Clifford, what kind of undiplomatic rhinoceros do you think I am!'

'Constable Doyle?' she called brightly, ducking under the low, timbered door frame. 'Oh!' Far from there being just the long wooden counter of a dour police station she'd expected, a comfortable-looking bench seat with a few homespun cushions occupied the right-hand wall. In front of it, a narrow table bore a typewriter and four neat piles of paper. Two wicker baskets, one filled with newspapers, the other clothing and footwear, stood next to a dark-wood bookcase, which held a section dedicated, surprisingly, to poetry.

'In English and Gaelic,' she whispered to Clifford. 'How peculiar. Is this actually the police station?'

'No, it's a bathing house for three-legged sheep!' came the sharp reply.

Gladstone let out a low grumble and heaved himself up from where he'd plopped on the floor.

Eleanor and Clifford looked over to the stable door in the far wall, the top half of which was now open and filled with the frowning, beetroot-cheeked face of Constable Doyle. He ran one hand over his thinning ginger hair, the other being rather encumbered by the doorstep sandwich he was halfway through eating.

She stepped over. 'Good morning, Constable. Well, bathing house or otherwise, I'm hoping you'll be kind enough to help with a little information. With apologies for disturbing your breakfast, of course.'

'Lunch!' He eyed Gladstone darkly. 'And maybe supper too if I'm expected to waste as much time now as I did last eve up at the abbey.'

She genuinely hadn't intended to probe him on the death of

the stranger. At least not now, but since he'd started the conversation, she felt compelled to continue it. Her remorse at not having reached the poor man earlier was genuine and something just hadn't seemed right.

'Indeed not. And I have no wish to tear you away from your investigation of how the tragic incident occurred. But I did wonder—'

He held up an authoritative hand. 'Investigation? There's no investigation. I know how it happened, like. I received a summons from the Reverend Mother.' He waved his sandwich haughtily. 'You see, it's all fine and dandy for the sisters to refuse to let us menfolk set foot in the place. But then, blow me, if suddenly they can't do without us at the mere whiff of something they think too messy to tackle in their starched nuns' habits. Not that I'm intending any blasphemy in that, of course,' he added hurriedly.

She smiled soothingly. 'Of course. But actually, I meant investigation into how the poor fellow died?'

Constable Doyle took a bite of his sandwich and swallowed. 'He died in the presence of a priest, as you know.'

Unsure if he was trying to be obstructive, or she was just phrasing her questions in too English a fashion for his Irish ears, she tried again. 'Constable Doyle, at the risk of sounding insensitive, I mean, what killed the poor fellow exactly?'

He sighed in exasperation. 'As you were told – and by none other than the doctor himself – it were on account of his having a traitorous heart. Betrayal is a wicked thing, especially when it's part of you, so to speak.'

'Strange then, that he should have looked more like he simply slipped into a deep sleep? No hand clutched to his heart? No sign he'd been clawing to loosen his collar?'

Doyle's lips creased into a knowing smile. 'And isn't that a lesson about the dangers of over-enjoying the drink? Some men'll never heed the warning, and that's that.'

She shared a glance with Clifford. 'You're saying he was drunk, Constable?'

'Drunk enough to not see the vehicle that knocked him down before you arrived. Assuming there was one and it wasn't yourselves. Either way, the shock caused him to have a heart attack. And at the abbey, well, it was all over for him by then.'

Eleanor shook her head in confusion. 'But there was no blood. Or sign of an injury.'

'A glancing blow,' Doyle said quickly. 'By Sullivan's account. Doctor O'Sullivan to those not local, mind.'

She tried another approach. 'Talking of not local, Constable. What have you deduced a complete stranger to the area was doing out there all by himself at gone midnight? Not staggering from a public house, I'm sure. There's not even so much as a cowshed along that route.'

Constable Doyle let out a patronising whistle. 'He'd a been passing through then.'

Clifford took a step forward. 'Given the state of the road, it would have been unlikely that any vehicle would have been travelling at more than ten to fifteen miles an hour. Surely, therefore—'

The beetroot of Doyle's cheeks was now nothing compared to the irate scarlet flash that ran up his neck. 'Don't be thinking I've time, or the patience, mind, for any more of your sort of nonsense.' He pointed the remains of his sandwich at them both. 'Stop stirring up trouble! You English have done enough of that! I'll be keeping an eye on you both.'

He stuffed the rest of the sandwich in his mouth and slammed the top half of the door shut.

6

As they left the police station, Clifford pointed down the road. A man with his back to them was standing in the middle of the street.

'Excuse me,' Clifford called. The man jerked to attention and gazed heavenwards. This caused his untamed dark locks to fan out over his collarless shirt.

'I say!' Clifford called again as he and Eleanor stepped closer.

The man spun around. He wore a leather tunic and in his left hand he held a large hammer. He stared at Clifford for a moment and then gave a hearty sigh of relief.

'Oh, 'tis not Himself!' He gave Clifford a meaty clap on the shoulder. 'You want to be careful having a voice that regal and commanding. You'll be giving all manner of folk a shock fit to send them to the afterlife early.' His tongue clucked against the roof of his mouth. 'Is it fair to say I'm relieved and disappointed in the same measure? Yes, so it is, I am.'

Eleanor laughed. 'Well, whichever it is, perhaps you could direct us to somewhere we could get something to eat and drink?'

The man cocked his head. 'At this hour you'll be asking Murphy to swap his sleeping bones for opening the taps, would you?'

She looked at Clifford, hopeful he could translate. 'The landlord of the local public house is still asleep, I conjecture, my lady.'

She peered up the length of the main street. 'But we haven't passed any pubs.'

'Amid Aubin's Fields,' the man said, as if that made it perfectly obvious.

'Forgive a silly question,' she said tentatively. 'But why would Mr Murphy have opened his pub in the middle of a field?'

Her stomach let out an unhelpful, unladylike grumble at that very moment, drawing a disapproving sniff from her butler. The man laughed again.

'Why indeed? Now, sounds as though you should go bang on Murphy's door and call for traveller's dodge.' She stared at him blankly. He chuckled and shook his head. 'See, isn't that the trouble with a special law for strangers?'

'Law?'

'Sure. But it's never known by those who need it most. You see, the law of the land states that if you're bona fide travellers...' He looked them over and nodded. 'Fancy threads, fancy inbred-looking hound, fancy English accent – you can demand food and drink from the likes of Murphy or any other landlord.'

Clifford glanced up from consulting his pocket watch. 'At only five and ten to nine in the morning?'

'For sure. Law says if you're a stranger, more than three miles from home, you can sup and dine at any hour. And a splendid law it is. If you can wake the landlord, that is. But if you can, Murphy'll leap at the chance for your business.' The man laughed again. 'And if you're still supping at midday, save me a seat.' He spun Clifford by the shoulders and pointed to the small thatched building at the top of the high street. It was painted the colour of an overripe gherkin. With a cheery wave, he went off, swinging his hammer.

She stared after the man, frowning. *Aren't the Irish supposed to be one of the most inquisitive nations on earth, Ellie? And yet this man seems to have little interest in what exactly a pair of 'fancy threads with fancy English accents' are doing in this far-flung part of Ireland.*

As they approached the establishment, Clifford hesitated.

'My lady, are you sure you wish to run the untested culinary gauntlet of a country landlord you have dragged from his slumbers?' He shortened his stride to stay his customary respectful two paces behind her.

She nodded vehemently. 'Absolutely! But not because, despite devouring all your wonderful egg-based efforts first thing this morning, I'm hungry again.' She paused. 'Well, partly that.' She waved him to step to her side. In a low voice, she added, 'But also because I'm desperate to talk through the unsettling conversation we just had with Constable Doyle.'

'Unsettling?' The edge of caution in his tone didn't miss her.

'Yes, Clifford. Unsettling. And before you launch into an admittedly perfectly valid diatribe about this supposedly being a holiday.' She nodded at the shudder he gave at the 'H' word, just as he had done during their drive the night before. 'Come on, confess. You felt something was very off about it all too, didn't you?'

'Only as much as the milk I discovered in the pantry this morning.'

She wrinkled her nose as they set off again. 'Curdled, was it?'

'Once upon a time, yes, I imagine. Today it had reached the dubious accolade of being inseparable from the bottle itself.'

They shared a wince.

A few moments later she pointed to a hand-painted sign above the weathered wood door. 'Look! Amid Aubin's Fields. That's the name of the establishment, not a description of where it is. And just when I thought Irish ways couldn't get any more confusing.'

'Actually, my lady.' He gave the door a rousing round of thumps with his gloved fist. 'One thing I do know about public houses in Ireland is that the sign must include the family name of the proprietor.'

'But he's supposed to be called Murphy? Not Aubin? I—'

She stopped speaking at the sound of a bolt being drawn back.

'It had better be good this time!' came a disgruntled voice that sounded long-gravelled by smoke. The door opened to reveal a middle-aged man more athletically built than she expected for someone who surely spent most of his day standing behind a bar. The frayed sky-blue shirt cuffs poking from his grey dressing gown matched the bright eyes beneath his unruly near-black fringe perfectly. They also made his already healthy complexion seem all the more inexplicable. 'Ah.' He broke into a smile. 'Travellers, you be! Welcome then, you are!'

'Good morning. And thank you for opening up for us at this early hour, Mr...?' She went to step inside, but he held up a hand and shook his head.

'There's no "mister" ever worn my shoes. Only Murphy. The name's supposed to be awash with the romance of the sea, meaning as it does "sea-warrior", you know. Only none of my relatives as far as I can glean have ever set foot on anything more seafaring than a coracle.' At her puzzled look, he smiled genially. 'Irish names all have meanings. And I'm sorry, but you can't come in here, miss. Only your man there and the dog can.'

She bit her tongue. *Not the time or place to make a fuss about women's rights, Ellie.* She smiled sweetly. 'Ah, of course.'

The landlord leaned around the doorframe and waved to

the right. 'You can go into the snug. It's reserved for the ladies. Blue door under the porch. Install yourselves and give the fire a shake. I'll be right with you.'

The small bar reserved for women accompanying their menfolk was furnished with five light-oak tables and a mismatched collection of cushioned stools and patterned cotton-covered chairs. The higgledy-piggledy lines of earthenware beer tankards and jugs hung from the low black beams forced Clifford to continually duck. A generous sprinkling of berried holly and a bevy of tiny brass bells offered them a genial Christmassy welcome. The lantern-style oil lamps in each of the loosely arched recesses bathed the diminutive space in a warming orange blush matching the glow from the low-burning fire. In one wall was a hatch that gave onto the back of the bar so men could order drinks without their female companions being seen. Halfway over the threshold Gladstone dug his front feet in, his fur standing up on end. He let out a low growl. Clifford rolled his eyes.

'Master Gladstone, the animal is quite dead.' He walked up to the enormous stuffed bear staring glassy-eyed at the bulldog and rapped it. Gladstone shrank back at the noise. But seeing no response from the terrifying creature, he edged around it, hurriedly skipping the last few steps to the safety of the table Eleanor now sat at. Clifford joined her after rousing the fire and dropped the bulldog's lead as Gladstone settled down, still with one wary eye on the bear.

The hatch slid open and Murphy's head appeared.

'What's your persuasion, good people?' He'd swapped his dressing gown for a smart blue-and-grey striped waistcoat and a matching neckerchief tied flamboyantly at his throat.

'Well, whatever you suggest.' She ignored Clifford's flinch of horror.

'Right you be. You'll be wanting to temper your hunger too, no doubt?'

'Absolutely, if it isn't too much trouble? But maybe you run this wonderful public house alone, in which case—'

'Not to worry, I don't. My daughter Kathleen's a grand help and no stranger to rustling up something hearty. Though you're an unlikely pair to have stumbled over my rear step this morning. We don't get many strangers the likes of you.'

Again, she waited for the inevitable enquiries as to what they were doing there, but none came. *Perhaps you've been misinformed, Ellie, and the Irish keep themselves to themselves?*

'Actually, we're here by invitation. I'm the niece of Lord Byron Henley, who you won't have met, sadly. But he generously left me Hennelly Towers. Perhaps you've heard of the house?'

Murphy's eyes shot up. 'There's no soul from here to Tipperary that hasn't, I'm sure.' He grimaced. 'Fair play to you taking it on.' He smiled weakly, saying quickly, 'Er, pretty a pile of stones it is, though.'

Trying to brush off the disconcerting feeling his words had generated, she glanced at Clifford who merely raised an eyebrow and turned to the landlord. 'Perhaps, Murphy, you might be able to help her ladyship? You see, the Head of the Derrydee Village Committee, a Miss Breen, sent her an invitation to be guest of honour at this year's Christmas festivities. Where might we find the lady this morning?'

The landlord's bushy eyebrows met. 'Is that right now?' He shook his head. 'Sure, I've no idea where she'll be out of school days. Especially when we've no committee come-together booked.'

'We?' Eleanor said.

He nodded. 'I'm one of the seven members of the committee. Makes sense, this place being the heart of the village. But,' he said, scratching his forehead, 'I've no recollection about sending any invitations to titled ladies. Especially one who now owns the House of Towers, as it's known around here.'

'Oh.'

She felt at a loss to know what to say. Even Clifford seemed nonplussed. Murphy rapped on the bar.

'Anyways, I've work to do. I'll be back laters.'

Left alone, she raised a questioning eyebrow at Clifford.

He held out his hands. 'It seems nothing is going to go according to plan on this trip. And, in fact' – his expression darkened – 'nothing seems to be quite as it appears.'

She nodded thoughtfully, then shrugged. 'Well, we decided to stay last night, so we're going to see it through. Now, to distract ourselves while waiting for food, let's discuss our recent conversation.'

'With Constable Doyle?'

'One and the same. Nothing he said added up, to my mind. Just as nothing the doctor or the priest said last night tallied up either. But do you know what really bothers me most is—'

'That the gentleman we found in the road passed away with neither of us present?'

She nodded. 'Rather conveniently, one might say. And everyone involved has brushed his death off as some form of misadventure. Yet you were sure there was no sign of alcohol on his breath?'

'Most assuredly, there was not.' He frowned. 'And I confess to being perturbed by the constable's airy assertion that a vehicle had struck the gentleman, ours or another before us.'

'Me too. I saw no blood or injury, as I told him, and I am, or was, a trained nurse.'

'Indeed, my lady. And my perturbation is even deeper if Constable Doyle truly believed the gentleman had been struck by a passing car because—'

'He didn't seem in the least bit troubled that a driver had knocked the man down in the road and simply driven off! Nor did he seem intent on finding the person responsible. Mind you, he made it clear he suspects it was probably us. And another thing. When Doctor Sullivan—'

'O'Sullivan.'

'Yes. Him. When he delivered his diagnosis of cause of death, you had that exact same look as when we first examined the man where he lay in the drizzle.'

'Indeed. The night was wet, but only due to the drizzle you just mentioned, which suggests damp hair and clothing on the gentleman would have been understandable. However...' He held out an expectant hand.

'He wasn't damp. He was soaked through.'

'Exactly.'

'You think he'd been there for hours then?'

'Unfortunately, or fortunately for the gentleman, no, my lady, since you observed at the time a puddle was only just beginning to form around his head.'

'But what other possible explanation could there be then for him being so sodden through?'

He let out a long breath. 'I believe, my lady, the gentleman did not, in fact, die from a heart attack. He was drowned.'

7

Eleanor was still reeling from Clifford's revelation as the hatch slid open and he rose to accept a wooden tray bearing two steaming bowls. This was followed by a lidded oval dish and a shallow wicker basket covered with a blue-and-yellow flower-print cloth.

'Thank you, Kathleen,' he said.

A striking dark-haired girl Eleanor put to be about seventeen nodded back. 'Ah, it's our pleasure. Knucklecoddle, golden clover and fresh farls. The best supper to have at breakfast.' She laughed brightly. 'And if as you fancy some more, just holler. First drinks too, here you go.'

Clifford set the two pewter mugs down next to the tray on the table. Gladstone lumbered up on his stiff back legs, front paws in her lap, sniffing excitedly.

'You're right, old chum. It smells nice,' Eleanor said.

'Oh dear.' Clifford shook his head. '"Nice", my lady, is not a word my ears have ever heard you utter regarding a hot meal. I fear this regrettable business is affecting you more deeply than I can countenance.'

She flapped him down into his seat. 'My nurse's training

told me something was wrong when I examined the poor man, but as I was only ever a nurse in the war, of all the terrible things I came across on a daily basis, drowning wasn't one of them! But now you point it out, it was obvious. His eyes were glassy and empty, unable to focus. And his skin was blue. I thought from the cold but now I think of it, it was bluest in the beds of his fingernails and around his lips.'

'Exactly, my lady. I also observed that he was frothing at the mouth somewhat and his whole body was rigid.'

She thumped the table. 'All sure signs of drowning, or near drowning!'

'In hindsight, my lady, perhaps. But on a deserted road miles from any source of water, easily misinterpreted.'

She sighed. 'Honestly, this is eating me up. I can't let go of needing to know the truth about what happened to that poor man. I realise it stems from never finding out what happened to my parents the night they disappeared, but if he was deliberately drowned, then someone needs to be brought to account. Just as someone needed to be brought to account for my parents' disappearance. However,' she swallowed hard, 'there was no one to do so, and I was too young.'

He held up a placating hand. 'My lady, please do not upset yourself by running over the past. I agree entirely with your sentiments.'

She paused while he placed what looked like a hearty stew in front of her.

'Thank you, Clifford. I just wish I'd packed my notebook.'

'The one you have used before when working through the numerous regrettable incidents one is disconcerted to refer to as "murders", my lady?'

'Well, of course that one. And it was "we" worked through, remember? We've been a team on every one of them.'

'That is kind of you to say so.' Reaching inside his jacket pocket, he pulled out a slim, black notebook.

She stared at it in surprise. 'Clifford! My notebook. Why on earth did you bring that along?'

'Sombre experience, my lady.'

She took it and opened it on a clean page. He offered her his favourite fountain pen, the one bearing a fond inscription which she had given him several Christmases previously.

'Thank you. Now, everyone's response so far is eating at my thoughts like a starved rat gnawing on the bars of its cage. Half of them seemed defensive, the others more... *scared*, I feel. However, I'm also as hungry as that starved rat and it would be criminal to let this lovely food spoil. Which, by the way, genuinely smells delicious. So, you'll help me order my thoughts while we eat? Because you know I'm lost without your exasperating logic and infuriating methodicalness.'

He bowed. 'Is there another fork, perchance, my lady?' She frowned, confused, since he already had one. 'To allow me to dig out the compliment so deeply interred in your request. Assuming that is what it was, of course?'

She laughed. 'Sorry, I could have put it more diplomatically.'

'Apology accepted. A serving of golden clover.' He lifted the lid of the oval dish. They both leaned forward to inspect it. 'Or a masterful variation on buttered cabbage, as we might better recognise it.'

'Looks and smells delicious, whatever. And what's in the basket again? "Furls", did Murphy's daughter say?'

'"Farls", my lady. Or griddle cakes. A blend of potato flour and seasoning, I would venture.'

She took a spoonful of the last dish.

'And this stew! It's divine. Tastes like Mrs Trotman's secret cooked ham recipe at the base with all manner of extras. Must be from a local town or village, I'm guessing from the name. I love how quaint it sounds.'

Clifford stirred his bowl, peering at the contents. '"Knucklecoddle", my lady, may be a place, but in this instance, I feel it is more likely a description of the main ingredient, pigs' knuckles. Hence the "knuckle" in the name. 'And the "coddle" being, I imagine, the method of cooking. Many hours of gently simmering the knuckles with what appears to be more cabbage, potatoes... onions, bacon, pearl barley... parsnips and...' he took a dainty sip from his spoon, 'thyme.'

'Pigs' knuckles?' She looked down at her bowl and shrugged. 'I've eaten a lot more unexpected items in my travels. And it tastes good.' She savoured another mouthful and then risked his disapproval over an unladylike dunk of her farl in the gravy. 'As do the farls.'

He nodded and pushed a mug of black liquid topped off with an inch of cream-coloured foam across the table to her. She eyed it suspiciously.

'Why am I minded of the brutish hangover penance you usually inflict upon me under the guise of it being some sort of stomach salve for a minor overindulgence?'

'I really couldn't say.' He raised his glass.

She did the same. 'To?'

'Finding out the truth, that the mistress might then be at peace in one regard.'

'Thank you, Clifford.' She took a sip. 'Mmm. It's quite malty. And sweet and bitter at the same time.' She tried it again, smacking her lips. 'I love how dense it is.'

'But velvety smooth. Just as Guinness should be. It is the perfect porter.'

'Ah! Your favourite tipple. On the very rare occasion you allow yourself to indulge.' She imitated his bow from the shoulders. 'It is an honour, sir, to share a drink in such good company.'

His eyes registered that he was touched by her words. 'To business then.'

'Right.' She held the pen poised over a fresh page. 'If you're right and our poor friend did drown, he must have only partially done so and then staggered onto the road. Maybe he fell – or was pushed – out of a boat?'

'A coracle, perhaps?'

'I know Murphy mentioned it, but I've no idea what it is.'

'An Irish one-man, sometimes square-ended bowl-shaped craft woven from reeds, or the slenderest of saplings.'

'Gracious! I've been in various small boats in my travels, but that sounds quite unstable. Maybe he did just fall out, then?'

'Only if he was a total novice. If you will forgive the correction, coracles are considerably more stable than they look. Which would suggest the worst.' He stared at the table. 'That someone tried to drown him.'

'But failed. At least partly to start with.' She added a hasty scribble in her notebook. 'That might explain the reaction of the doctor. And Constable Doyle. If they'd had a hand in the dark deed and believed the man had drowned, imagine their consternation to find him still alive?'

'Indeed. Following a different avenue of conjecture, what if the perpetrator – or perpetrators – dumped the gentleman most unceremoniously in the road?'

'Possible.' She added another piece of farl to her stew and watched it become saturated before sinking out of sight. 'But why would you drown someone and then leave the body somewhere so public? Why not leave it at the bottom of the lake or river, the perfect hiding place? Unless—'

'Unless one wanted the body to be found. Even if that would be the following day, given the remoteness of that stretch of road.'

She shook her head slowly. 'But again, why?'

'As a warning to others? There seems to be a palpable air of fear in the area. Due, perhaps, to the recent fighting between the British and the Irish over independence. And then between the two opposing Irish factions, one of whom wishes to see all of Ireland independent, and one of whom wishes to keep the recently agreed divide between North and South?'

She tried to hide the shiver that threatened by busying herself with her hot stew. 'Either way, given our belief that the man drowned, the doctor's diagnosis feels even more odd now. All that about his heart giving out. And then the "glancing blow" from the car that subsequently passed.'

'Although, that was reported to us second-hand by,' he lowered his voice, 'Constable Doyle.'

'Who is far from my number one fan.' She ruffled her bull-dog's ears as he'd let out a low grumble at the mention of the policeman's name. 'Or yours, my friend.'

'However, the wider troubles, as I just mentioned, might have initially been responsible for the constable's lack of enthu-siasm to deal with us.'

'Eminently diplomatic of you because I know you mean until I actually started asking him about the dead man.' She dropped her spoon, shaking her head. 'It's no use, Clifford. There seems little doubt in my mind that our hypothesis is correct: the poor man was half-drowned somewhere other than where we found him and then transported to that stretch of road and dumped. On top of that, we took the man to the abbey where he died – out of our sight, conveniently! And the diag-nosis we were given by O'Sullivan, who is apparently a trained doctor, was that his heart gave out from being hit by a car, even though there were no visible signs when we examined him.' She lowered her voice. 'And if you add in everyone else's manner up at the abbey – and Doyle's down here in the village – there's only one conclusion. It was—'

'Murder!'

She nodded slowly. 'And someone is trying to cover it up!'

For a moment they sat in silence, then she sighed and picked up his pen again. 'So, let's assemble a list of people we need to visit at some point and drop a few innocent questions into the conversation.'

'As you wish, my lady. Starting with?'

'The Mother Superior.' She wrote the name at the top of the page.

'Because?'

'Because she insisted you were the only man in the abbey even though I saw another quite clearly.' She seesawed her head. 'Actually, not clearly at all. He was the other side of that stained-glass window. Obviously, that was before Father Quinn, Doctor O'Sullivan and Constable Doyle attended.'

'Then whoever he was, he needs to be on your list too, would you say?'

'I would, although I suppose it could have been the priest, or the doctor? Or even Constable Doyle? Perhaps one of them was already there and the Mother Superior didn't know or didn't want to say.'

She wrote their observations about the Mother Superior under her name and then 'Man in Abbey' a random number of lines down. 'We've nothing on this man yet, so Constable Doyle next because I was unconvinced when he said he didn't recognise the dead man. And he seemed peculiarly keen to dismiss his death as one of natural causes.'

'And all the more so for us to keep our noses out of it.'

'Mostly mine, I'm sure. But, yes, that too. All very odd.'

'Indeed. Furthermore, there is another matter I have yet to mention. If you remember, when we found the gentleman in the road and manhandled him into the Rolls, I noticed a patch of what looked like oil under the car?'

She nodded. 'Yes, and I do appreciate that you keep the Rolls in perfect running order, Clifford, but it hardly seemed the most pressing matter.'

'A sentiment I concurred with at the time. But this morning before we left, I checked where the Rolls was parked and there was no sign of any leak. However, where Constable Doyle had parked his motorcycle outside the police station, I noticed considerable leakage.'

She gasped. 'Top observation, Clifford!'

'Thank you, my lady. Also, given the conditions under which we found the gentleman yesterday evening, the persistent drizzle would have diluted any oil fairly quickly, which suggests the constable's motorcycle had been there recently.'

'Then he's definitely going on our list.' She plucked a line further down and added Constable Doyle's name and their observations. The tip of Clifford's finger hovered down the lines as if counting the number she'd left between.

She looked up. 'Space to add anything we uncover in the future.'

A pained expression flashed across his face. 'So unevenly selected? However, next person? Doctor O'Sullivan, perchance?'

'Right! Because, did you see that look he exchanged with Constable Doyle when I asked if either of them knew who our friend was?'

'I did observe such, my lady. He was also the one who examined the gentleman.' He arched one brow. 'Possibly alone?'

'If Father Quinn had left him to it, then yes.' She dropped her voice to a whisper as he gestured towards the closed hatch and then tapped his ear. 'The doctor could have slipped our friend something to hasten him off, Clifford, as we mentioned before. But to prove that would mean finding a way to get a post-mortem done.'

'I can only envisage a royal battle in that instance, my lady.'

'Me too. And it might prove nothing anyway. Whatever the doctor might have given him could be all but undetectable. Or could simulate a natural condition. Or all traces of whatever it was could have left the dead man's system by the time of an autopsy.' She slapped the table. At Clifford's raised brow, she grimaced. 'Sorry, but I just remembered something I observed but at the time couldn't work out the significance of.'

He leaned forward. 'I'm all ears, my lady.'

'Well, when I snuck over and looked into the doctor's car, I noticed that the rear seat was soaking wet.'

'Mmm.' He steepled his fingers.

She nodded. 'Exactly. Was it wet from his coat and bag because our good doctor had been visiting patients in the constant drizzle of that night? Or...'

'Was it wet from transporting a nearly drowned man?'

She nodded again and added the doctor's name and their thoughts and then immediately Father Quinn's further below it.

'Father Quinn was the last person to see our nearly drowned man alive. As far as we know, anyway. And he definitely deflected when I asked if the man had regained consciousness and said anything.'

'Although that might merely be him upholding the sanctity of confession. Words spoken in confidence cannot be repeated.'

'Good point.' She scanned the list. 'Which would just leave anyone else in the vicinity at the time to talk to.'

'Aside from any number of other resident nuns, the only persons present—'

'Were you and I.' She tapped her chin thoughtfully. 'I would like to ask Corcoran a few carefully worded questions. As the retainer at Hennelly Towers, he must know everyone. As he said he's been here since he was a boy.'

Clifford's hand strayed to his perfectly aligned tie. 'If we might consider composing the aforementioned questions together, my lady?'

'Of course. Officially, you are his superior in rank while you are here. And please know, I am acutely aware of the difficulty of your position with him. They clearly don't have the sort of staff hierarchy you're used to and manage so admirably at Henley Hall.'

'Most gracious, thank you.'

She wrote a few lines under Father Quinn's name and shook her head. 'We haven't even really started to investigate this sorry affair yet, Clifford, and yet our list consists mostly of men or women of the cloth, policemen and doctors!'

'True. The very people you would hope are champions of morality, law and life. However, they are, at this stage, merely individuals we wish to ask a few questions of.'

'Absolutely. "Persons of Interest," as Hugh would call them if he were here. Not necessarily suspects.' Her hand shot to her mouth. 'Dash it! Maybe I could just not mention this to Hugh when we get back? Or ever.'

He nodded. 'A wise decision, I feel, given the chief inspector's previous feelings about you investigating matters of this nature.'

She winced. 'Mmm. Anyway, for now, who shall we talk to first?'

He ran his eyes down the list. 'I would propose Father Quinn be our first port of call since the church is not far off.' At her nod, he rose and slid open the hatch. 'Ah, Murphy, a question, if I may? Father Quinn, would he likely be in church at this hour?'

'Where are we now?'

'Twenty past ten.'

'Ah, then sit tight, if as you want his ear. He'll be along straight after finishing Mass in ten minutes. A medicinal Guinness each morning is his persuasion.'

'Very wise of the gentleman.' Pulling his wallet from his pocket, Clifford dropped some change on the counter. 'If I might purchase such a medicinal for him to enjoy here in the snug?'

'Right you be.'

Eleanor rose and joined Clifford at the hatch. 'With as much propriety as I can muster to spare your blushes—'

'Through that door, down a flight of steps at the end and then left,' Murphy said hurriedly.

She hid a smile and set off along a whitewashed corridor lit only by two flickering oil lamps. A few minutes later, however, the smile had faded.

Did he say left or right at the bottom of the steps, Ellie?

She shrugged and chose one at random. Turning the corner, she froze. Ahead of her, there was an open door. And inside...

Her scream echoed down the corridor.

8

The pounding of shoes clearing the stairs in three long strides, then running down the corridor echoed along to her.

'My lady! Where are you?'

'In here,' she called back weakly.

Another set of heavier feet joined Clifford's.

'What's she doing in there?' Murphy's voice echoed down the corridor.

Clifford swung round the corner, his coat-tails flying out behind him, his face filled with concern, the landlord on his heels.

'Are you injured, my lady?'

'No. And apologies for the drama, but... well...' She moved aside so Clifford could see into the room.

Against the nearest wall, a washstand held an enamel bowl, a cracked bar of soap and a jar of yellow oil. A worn leather shaving case holding a selection of wood-handled brushes and razors lay nearby. Above the washstand, on a line stretched between two hooks, a row of off-white cloths hung by a loose knot in each corner. And below that was a shelf full of coloured glass bottles of different size and shape. Beside the washstand was an oak barrel filled to the brim with water, a ladle languishing by its handle on the outside.

And lying on the marble-topped table, the body of a man.

Murphy, who was leaning against the doorframe, nodded. 'Fair play to you. You're made of sturdier stuff than any fancy ladies I've met, seeing as you're still more upright than he is. It's not every day you come across a corpse, is it now?'

She caught Clifford's eye. 'Don't answer that!' To the landlord, she said, 'Forgive my initial histrionics, but why exactly is there a body laid out in what appears to be your cellar?' *And why this body, Ellie? The man we found last night in the road!*

Murphy shrugged. 'Sure, he's just waiting for me to tidy him up, that's all. I would have started first thing only I got called upon to show two travellers what Irish hospitality is all about.'

Eleanor's brows met in confusion. 'And it has been second to none in every regard. But... but that doesn't explain what he is doing *here*. And waiting for what? The poor fellow is... dead, after all.'

Murphy cocked his head, looking equally confused. 'I'm not just the landlord of this fine establishment, you know. I'm the village undertaker into the bargain, as usual.'

'Undertaker?' Eleanor echoed in disbelief, her eyes flicking back to Clifford. 'And you undertake, as it were, in... *here*?'

Murphy scratched his forehead. 'And where else would it be making sense for me to? In the street, perhaps?'

How about anywhere except in a public house I've just eaten and drunk in!

Understanding dawned in the landlord's eyes. 'Are you telling me it's not the same in England?'

She shook her head. 'I can categorically tell you it is not the same. No landlord pours a pint one minute and' – she waved at the table – 'and the next messes with dead bodies in the same establishment. You'd have the police around before you could blow the froth off your Guinness.'

Murphy shrugged. 'A pub's cellar's the fittest place for a body to be stored in. In out-of-the-way villages like Derrydee, that is. No folk have got a room this cold to slow a body from decomposing. So, us landlords not only store the dead'uns but also get the job of undertaker to earn a little in compensation for the inconvenience, as it were.'

'Da!' Murphy's daughter's voice hollered down to them. 'Delivery's just pulling in.'

'Ah, that's me.' Murphy rolled his sleeves up, revealing fore-arms sculpted by years of manual labour. 'Go install your battered sensibilities back by the fire, woman, and I'll stand you both a whiskey when I'm done.'

His merry whistling receded with his boot steps until they were left in silence.

'Clifford?' she whispered. 'Don't you find it rather odd that—'

'The landlord didn't explain where the body came from?'

'Which suggests—'

'That he already knows that we know where it came from, as it were, my lady.'

She nodded. 'But, once again, seems entirely uninterested in knowing anything further. Which is just a tad... odd.' A thought struck her. 'You know, we could just—'

'Return to the bar and await the arrival of Father Quinn as planned?'

'Y-e-s. Or we could...' she nodded towards the table, 'seeing as someone has considerately dried and redressed him in the clothes you changed him out of at the abbey.'

After a pained silence, Clifford sighed. 'If you insist, my lady.'

In a trice, he lit the three oil lamps that sat along the brick ledge of one wall. He carried two over and set them down on the table either side of the dead man's head. From his inner pocket, he pulled out his pince-nez and miniature magnifying glass.

She looked sadly over the man's near-alabaster face, her heart aching at the limp cheeks and lifeless green-blue eyes. She couldn't tear her gaze from scrutinising the man's features framed by the tight waves of his russet-brown hair.

'My lady,' Clifford said in a low tone, 'Murphy will be back all too soon if we hesitate. However,' he continued, his brow furrowed, 'now I see this man's face clearly for the first time, I have the oddest feeling of déjà vu.'

She started. 'Really?'

'Fleetingly, but, yes. However, since I have never visited this area before, it must be that the gentleman has one of those faces.' He bowed from the shoulders at the corpse. 'With no slight or disrespect intended.'

'But, Clifford, he's no more from this area than you or I. If we can believe anything Constable Doyle or Doctor O'Sullivan said, that is.'

He pulled back the man's shirtless collar to examine his neck. She frowned and opened her mouth, but then closed it. *Something's wrong, Ellie. No, not wrong. Different.* Moving round to the other side of the table, Clifford gestured for her to come to his side. She shook the thought out of her head. They only had a short time.

'Running the discomforting risk of requesting your assistance, ahem, in touching the gentleman again, my lady.' He slid his hands under the man's shoulders and heaved him upwards. 'While I lift the gentleman's top half, will it distress you too much to reassess for the signs of a blow to the head? We might have missed it in the dark and the rain.'

'Not if it helps us find out the truth for this poor fellow.' She took a deep breath and parted each section of the man's hair, scouring for any sign of injury. Pressing her fingers over his scalp, she felt for the telltale dip of a minor fracture to his skull. 'Absolutely nothing.' She stepped away to let Clifford ease the body back down onto the marble slab. 'But what about the rest of him?' She flapped a hand at Clifford's horror. 'Oh, I wouldn't look, for goodness' sake.'

'Fortunately, not necessary anyway, my lady, since I was privy to such scrutiny when I changed the gentleman into the dry cotton shifts the Mother Superior provided.'

'Then I'll rummage through his shirt and jerkin pockets. You'd better do his trouser ones. For decorum's sake.'

'Thank you for alerting me that any still remains,' he said drily.

She let that go, trying to focus on stopping her fingers shaking from the cold of the cellar and the fact she was searching through a dead man's pockets. But on finally succeeding, she was disappointed to find nothing more than half a palm's worth of matted white and blue lint.

'Anything your way?' she asked hopefully as Clifford straightened back up.

'Regrettably not. However, perhaps unsurprising. Undertakers rarely send the deceased on their journey to the afterlife encumbered by the raft of earthly oddments generally carried by the majority of people about their persons.'

She turned to the washstand and shifted through the items on top. 'But if Murphy cleared out any possessions our friend was carrying, they'd be here, surely? But there's nothing. I'll have to find a subtle way to ask him.'

'Do, ahem, let me know if I can assist in that regard, my lady.'

As she stepped back over to remind him this was hardly the time for teasing, she noticed he was staring pensively at the underside of the dead man's boots.

'Hmm. As I suspected.'

'What is it?' she hissed.

'An anomaly in one heel, my lady.'

'Clifford, I know how dearly you value craftsmanship, but this poor chap probably had a knock-knee and didn't have the funds to purchase the best quality footwear.'

'With sincere apologies, my lady, if I might disagree.' He traced around the outer edge of each heel. 'Minimal but equal wearing on both, indicating a consistent supination. Or a reduced inward rolling in the gentleman's gait, which would have gone unnoticed by all but a man of extensive medical practice. But here' – he tapped the right-hand heel – 'a subtle deviation from the spacing of tacks when compared to the other.'

She shrugged. 'Marvellous observation, I'm sure, but that means what? That he went to a different cobbler to get the right-hand one repaired?'

Clifford's eyes glinted in the lamplight. 'No, my lady. I believe this a home repair. Or rather a home...' he whipped out his pocket knife and adroitly winkled the heel loose, 'adaptation.'

Pulling it away from the shoe, he turned it to face her.

'It's hollowed out!' she breathed. 'Clifford, you clever, eagle-eyed bean!' She prised the item hidden in the heel free, then gasped as her sharp hearing caught the approach of footsteps. 'Hurry!' she urged as Clifford set to in pressing the heel back in place.

'What an unexpected plenitude of persons in this supposed haven of rest.'

Eleanor turned at the rich-timbred voice behind her. 'Good morning, Father Quinn.' She smiled at the white-haired priest, despite his stare boring into her skull. 'I didn't expect to meet you here.'

'Nor I you.' His black cassock folds swished against each other as he stepped further into the room. 'Most especially here.' He looked between her and Clifford. 'May I ask what is the purpose of your presence?'

Clifford nodded. 'Of course, Father. Her ladyship has been deeply troubled by this gentleman's passing. We were hopeful for a modicum of closure from the opportunity to bid a respectful farewell.'

'Troubled?' His eyes darted to Eleanor. 'For why?'

'Because we tried to save him. And failed.' She felt the familiar wash of sadness.

He tutted. 'Salvation is not the duty of those who walk this earth.' He moved closer to run a finger along the tabletop. 'Whatever part you played in this man's life was but fleeting and thus warrants no self-remonstrations.'

'Maybe. But that doesn't stop me wishing he was still alive.' She tilted her head. 'As I'm sure everyone would wish for him. Wouldn't you?'

'It is my life's work to do the bidding of the Lord, never to question it. Thus, no, it is not a wish I would insult his maker by considering.'

'Still, I'm troubled that no one can have imparted the sad news to his family. Unless, of course, someone has been able to identify him now?'

'Names are given, souls are created, my daughter.' As she held his gaze, his lips twitched. 'You might choose to take solace that he will be buried tomorrow and thus move on in your thoughts.'

Tomorrow, Ellie? That's rather quick. Especially as, if he was a stranger in the area as everyone insists, it seems no effort is being made to trace any relatives. She chose her next words carefully.

'In truth, Father, what made his last hours seem so tragic is that he was so alone. Oh, except for your gracious administering of his last rites, silly me. And I suppose Doctor O'Sullivan must have been there at the end, too?'

'How could that be of import?'

'Since you were both strangers to him' – she caught his

minute flinch at this – 'you're right. However, you said he is to be buried tomorrow? Here in Derrydee?'

'That he is. By myself.'

'Then we shall leave you to ponder your tribute to an anonymous man who died as a result of... of... what was it again?'

Father Quinn swept her towards the door. 'God's will. Naturally.'

As she walked back up the stairs to the snug, she shook her head to herself. *Well, he certainly died by someone's will, Ellie. But I'm sure it wasn't God's!*

9

Eleanor patted Gladstone's wrinkled forehead. 'I think you're in for a telling-off, boy,' she whispered.

While still negotiating the Rolls carefully around the many donkey carts and bicycles now straggling along both sides of Derrydee's dirt high street, Clifford waved a stern finger at the sheepish bulldog.

'Master Gladstone, not dashing to your mistress' aid at her distressed cry was unforgivable.' He tutted sharply. 'But to compound your disgrace by stealing the remainder of the potato farls instead was beyond reprehensible!'

The bulldog gave a soft whine and licked Clifford's sleeve, drawing an even louder tut.

'It *is* Christmas,' she said, coming to Gladstone's aid, 'and we were hungry, so think how famished he was! And before poor Gladstone receives any more tellings-off, are you going to tell me now what's really bothering you?'

'If you insist.' Whipping out his slim leather pocketbook, Clifford held it out to her. 'If you would be so gracious, my lady. The double page marked with the black silk ribbon.'

Balancing the book on Gladstone's head, she reverently

opened his bible of schedules and lists. 'Yuletide in Ireland. Arrangements and plans.' A full minute of silent reading later, she smiled up at him. 'Comprehensive doesn't begin to cover it. Thank you, Clifford.'

However, even her genuine appreciation didn't seem to have mollified him as he reached over and tapped the page. 'My apologies for the series of omissions on my part.'

She read it again. 'You can't possibly have missed anything? Just look at this endless, beautifully written out list.'

His eyes flicked over the pages, then back to the road. 'I cannot see an entry to remember to spend Christmas finding bodies in the middle of nowhere. Nor to spend Christmas in a remote Irish village where no one apparently remembers inviting us. Nor to spend it in a castle without staff! His lordship would turn in his grave, God rest his soul.'

'Clifford?' she said gently. 'It's probably hitting home harder than I realised since we are staying at Hennelly Towers. We both wish with all our hearts Uncle Byron could be here with us. And for you, it's dredging up memories of your many wonderful years together with him, isn't it?'

He sighed and held his fountain pen out to her. 'True. Therefore, perhaps you would be so kind as to jot a reminder for me to check more thoroughly that no whispers of sentimentality slide into my travelling bag? Should we, that is, not spend next Christmas at Henley Hall.'

She batted his hand away with mock disapproval. 'And listen to you groaning every time you open your notebook on that page and see my untidy, spidery writing?'

He momentarily closed his eyes. 'Perhaps not, my lady.'

'Last word on the subject, then?' she said tentatively.

'Would that be a Lady Swift's last word?' His lips twitched. 'That is, anything but?'

She laughed. 'Probably. It's just that, I can't help thinking that Uncle Byron would never have let this matter rest if it had been him that found... you know.'

He eyed her sideways. 'And?'

'And as you were embroiled in almost every adventure he threw himself into—'

'Except for the few which arose in the school holidays, as I had to remain at Henley Hall and fend off the wily tactics of his young niece. The wiliest of which are rushing back to me now with alacrity. So, to save a protracted entreaty on your part, yes, my lady, we shall continue seeking the truth about the deceased gentleman as his lordship would have done.'

She hugged her bulldog, wishing it could be her butler, just for once. 'That means the world. It also reminds me you promised to spend our evenings while here with our favourite port tipple and tales of those adventures. Well, the ones you are at liberty to tell me about. Until then,' she said as she pulled out the item they had retrieved from the dead man's heel and stared at it, 'we'll need to work out what this is for.'

It was a small brass key. But to what, she had no idea. Before she could examine it properly, the Rolls slowed. She looked up to see the street ahead blocked.

'Oh no, not another donkey hold-up.'

Two carts had stopped opposite each other to chat. Clifford turned off the engine and folded his gloved hands in his lap. 'When in Rome, my lady.'

'Knowing the Italians, one would be charging about at breakneck speed. Not taking every day as if it will last a life-time. Though it is very refreshing, just not when we have a suspicious death to investigate.'

Ahead of them, the owners of the two carts were being most unsubtle, pointing repeatedly at the Rolls and then her. Offering a cheery wave, she smiled as the one facing in their direction finally coaxed his donkey forward, only to stop when he reached Clifford's side window. Winding it down, her butler nodded.

'Good morning.'

'Ah, and isn't she a beauty,' came the reply, delivered on a wheezy breath in a grizzled face. Despite the chilly morning, he seemed comfortable in just a thick cable blue jumper under a grey waistcoat with what looked like a sprig of green cress in his top buttonhole.

Clifford leaned out of the window. 'The morning? Or the car? Or both?'

'Tsk, and why leave the lady out of your list, when a fairer face and head of flaming curls you'll never see? From the House of Towers, you be?'

'Indeed we are. Her ladyship has inherited the castle from her late uncle, Lord Byron Henley.'

The man's donkey took that moment to turn and poke its soft black velvet nose in to nuzzle Clifford's cheek. Gladstone lumbered onto Clifford's lap, venturing a wide-eyed sniff of the slow-blinking creature. Eleanor would have laughed but for the sombre tone of the man's parting words as he leaned over and pressed his sprig into her butler's hand. 'For the lady, since she'll be needing luck in more bucket loads than'd fit in me cart, for sure. Good day to you now.'

They drove on, Eleanor turning the sprig between her fingers, a frown on her face.

'What do you think he meant by that?'

Clifford shook his head. 'I do not know, my lady. That is wood sorrel to you and I. "Shamrock" to the locals. And a powerful symbol of good fortune.'

'But why would I, particularly, need good fortune? And anyway, I thought it was a four-leaf clover that was supposed to bring good luck?'

'Correct, also. However, the name "shamrock" is applied to several plants with leaves divided into three leaflets. And Irish legend holds that St Patrick heralded the three-leaf clover as a symbol of the Holy Trinity, so it is still worth having.'

She sighed. 'I wonder if the same can be said of this key.' She held it up again. 'Without knowing what lock it fits, it's useless to us. Dash it, Clifford! If only we'd found something more obvious.'

'Actually, my lady, it is revealing in itself.'

She frowned. 'What is?'

'The fact that the deceased gentleman had no personal effects about his person except this key. Do you concur when we asked him later that Murphy seemed genuine when he told us he had removed nothing from the man's pockets?'

'As far as I could tell, yes.'

'Exactly.'

She seesawed her head, processing his words slowly. 'You mean the man clearly wanted to remain incognito?'

'Quite.' His brow flinched. 'Although his attacker – or attackers – could have taken his personal effects.'

She nodded. 'Nevertheless, that still points to the man's identity being at the root of his sad demise. Either he didn't want anyone to know who he was or his attacker didn't want anyone to know whose body it was.'

Clifford stroked his chin. 'Which would only be effective if the man was indeed a stranger in these parts. Otherwise, he would be recognised, anyway. Unless, of course, his physical appearance had changed considerably since he had last been seen in the area? And if we assume the latter, it also suggests that the man knew he might be searched by those he wanted to keep his identity hidden from.'

She nodded eagerly. 'And also that he wanted to keep whatever this key opens – or the contents – equally secret from them.'

She stared at the key again and then held it up so he could study it. 'You're good at these things, Clifford. And not just because of your unbutlery skills of being able to pick any lock we've ever found standing in our way. What might this fit? A padlock? A money box? A door?'

He glanced at it, and then back at the road. 'Regrettably, it being entirely unmarked, I would need to scrutinise it under magnification. And even then, I am not sure I could conclusively answer that question.'

She put the key back in her safest pocket and stared around at the less than hospitable landscape. An endless peat bog adorned with scattered clumps of wind-battered, snow-laden bushes stretched to the horizon. On one side, a thick copse of trees ran in a higgledy line off into the near distance.

Clifford's voice cut through her reverie as he pulled up by the trees. 'We have arrived, my lady. This is where we found the gentleman and then set off to Ballykieran Abbey.' He pointed through her side window to a set of deep tyre marks on the soft ground.

'Well spotted. Let's drive around first and see if we can spot a river or lake where he could have drowned.'

'First, my lady?' he said with a wary edge to his tone.

'Yes, first. Because then I am going to splosh through the peat to see if I can find anything else. You will be very welcome to remain mud-free and watch from the safety of the Rolls.'

In reply, he tapped the map, which was still folded neatly in the holder mounted on the walnut dashboard. 'This is of a particularly large-scale, which conversely to the image that conjures up, covers only a small area but in great detail. I have noted it is of exemplary accuracy, yet not even a minor body of water or river is recorded within three or more miles of here.'

'Really? Well, he can't have staggered that far, not in his state. So how did he end up drowned in the middle of the road? It seems equally unlikely he was transported a long distance after he was drowned. What would be the point? And if he was deliberately dumped here, why this particular spot?' She took a deep breath. 'Either way, for my own peace of mind, let's search the immediate area.'

Clifford strode to the rear of the Rolls, reappearing a moment later with a tall buckled case, which he placed at her feet.

Her eyes lit up. 'Excellent! A picnic!' Gladstone pulled his head out of a rabbit hole and woofed at the 'P' word. She nodded. 'I know, our most favourite thing ever.' She turned back to Clifford. 'But how did you have time—'

'Wellingtons, my lady.'

She stared at him. 'Beef Wellington? Not the usual type of picnic fare. Better save that for enjoying in style back at Hennelly Towers, surely?'

He rolled his eyes. 'Not Wellington. *Wellingtons,* my lady. Wellington boots. Yours.'

'Ah! I see. No picnic.' She and Gladstone shared a disappointed look. 'Still, excellent preparation having them to hand. I didn't even know they'd been packed.' She bit back a smile on noting that he'd swapped his own immaculate shoes for a long pair of bottle-green rubberised boots. 'Not quite what we were expecting to be doing at Christmas, but there you go. Come on, let's get this over and done with. All that talk of a picnic has made me strangely hungry.'

'Anything in the bushes on your side?' she called a while later in a tone laced with frustration. All she'd managed to do so far was tear her dress and scratch her face.

Even though they hadn't passed a soul since leaving the village, Clifford held a finger to his lips as he crossed the road with her overexcited bulldog. The amount of dirt and snow on Gladstone's nose confirmed that he had been 'helping' by digging up most of the surrounding area.

'Not so much as a footprint, my lady.' He jerked to a stop in horror at her appearance.

'Oh, it's just a bit of the local countryside on my stockings.'

She hopped on one foot as she bent to try to retrieve her boot from where it had got stuck in a particularly cloying stretch of peat bog. Clifford hastily turned away as she wrestled her tweed skirt up to brush off some of the thick mud. Gladstone squelched over, clearly delighted with his efforts so far. She couldn't help laughing despite Clifford staring at the bulldog with even more horror than he had at her.

'He looks like he's wearing long black socks, Clifford!'

He sighed resignedly. 'Perhaps we should continue searching?'

Twenty minutes later, the only result was more peat on her dress and Gladstone now looking as if he was wearing black waders, not socks. Clifford joined her, shaking his head.

'I feel we may have exhausted this line of the investigation, my lady?'

She straightened up and groaned. 'Agreed. To the Rolls!'

They tramped back through the undergrowth until the car hove into view. And then they saw them.

'You there! Halt!' Clifford pulled his ex-army revolver from his pocket. 'I'm armed!' The heads of the two men they'd spotted fiddling underneath the open bonnet of the Rolls shot up. Just as quickly, they ducked down the other side of the car.

Clifford's long legs reached the Rolls a second before hers. Aiming the gun at the spot the men's heads had been, he called again. 'Come out now with your hands up!'

After waiting a few seconds, he edged around the bonnet while she stood back. Once on the other side, he lowered the gun and stared into the bushes, shaking his head.

'They have gone, my lady.'

She hurried up. 'What were they doing? Trying to steal the Rolls?'

He stared at the bonnet. It had been jimmied open, a deep scratch on the front edge. Then he peered inside. A moment later, he pointed to one of the few parts of the engine that she recognised.

Her brow furrowed. 'I say, shouldn't there be some cable things attached to each of those coil-ended fellows?'

'Indeed. Spark plug or ignition cables, to be precise.'

Her brows knitted even more. 'So those two men... removed the cables. But why? They'd hardly be worth that much around here, would they? I haven't seen another car since we arrived, certainly not a Rolls. So what...' She tailed off as she caught the look on Clifford's face. 'It's not vandalism or robbery, is it?'

He shook his head. 'No, my lady. It's a calculated attack to put the Rolls out of commission.'

She rubbed her face with her hands. 'But why? And, actually, more pressingly, can it be fixed?'

He nodded. 'Indeed. A new set of cables could be reattached without too much trouble. However,' he patted his pockets, 'I seem to have been remiss in carrying a spare set on me.'

She bit back a smile. 'Well' – she looked up and down the deserted road – 'in that case, I suppose we'd better lock up the Rolls as best we can and start walking...'

10

An icy blanket of grey snow clouds hung above them as they trudged along the ribbon of rutted road. Eleanor rubbed her mittens together, trying to stop the numbness in her fingers from spreading any further. She then yanked her hat harder down over her ears, equally grateful for her thick woollen coat and socks.

'How far is Hennelly Towers, would you say, Clifford?'

'Seven and three-quarter miles, my lady. However, there is a possible shortcut back to the village through the undergrowth and then the bog. Nevertheless, I would not advise it.'

She nodded in agreement. The undergrowth had proved hard enough to struggle through before, but the endless bog on the other side looked worse. Ankle-turning tussocks vied with patches of boot-sucking mire. She pointed to Gladstone.

'Poor chap. Seven miles is far too far for his stiff joints. Especially on this rough road. We'll have to take turns at carrying him.' She ran her eyes over the dog's portly frame as he trotted between them and grimaced at the near-black mud cloaking the dog's entire underside and legs.

'Hence the blanket, my lady.' He swung the brown canvas

bag with sturdy leather straps off his back and showed her the tartan picnic rug he had retrieved from the boot of the Rolls. 'To act as a mud guard.'

'Ah. Not, as I thought then, for us to take turns with when the cold penetrates our poor bones.' She gave a mock scoff. 'Really, there's no end to how much we spoil Mr Wilful, is there?'

'Hopefully not,' he said softly, bending to ruffle the bull-dog's ears.

Her heart swelled with affection for both of her companions. He straightened up and produced a silver hip flask and a striped paper bag from his pockets. 'Whereas, regrettably, the mistress will have to manage on nothing more than these.'

'Brandy and mint humbugs. Perfect! If only you'd been on hand when I cycled over the Himalayas. All I had for three days on the remotest section was a pouch of yak fat and a strip of dried meat of some sort. Probably more yak. It nearly broke my jaw trying to chew it.'

'Beyond commendably intrepid, my lady.' He shuddered. 'And equally revolting.'

She shrugged. 'Mind you, some days I had nothing at all.'

They continued in silence for a few moments.

'Clifford?' she said tentatively as she finished her first sweet. 'I was hoping to slide along to the burial tomorrow of the poor man we found. I don't suppose you'll countenance my going alone? We've been to too many of late. And every time, I feel terrible for you.'

'For me, my lady?'

'Yes, because,' she hesitated, 'well, to my eyes only, it takes you back to Uncle Byron's funeral. Which I'm still so sorry you had to organise and deal with all on your own.'

'No apology needed. You were uncontactable, somewhere in the deepest part of the South African Bush.' He offered her another humbug. 'You came the moment you received my letter, I know. And you were instrumental in catching his killer.'

'Almost.' The word flew from her lips before she could stop it.

He nodded. 'We brought the person to justice who switched his lordship's heart pills for those that... killed him. I am painfully aware, however, as you are, that she was merely paid to make the switch by someone else. The real culprit is still out there. Someone whom we have yet to bring to justice. But we will. One day.'

She nodded back fiercely. 'Without a doubt!'

'Indeed. So, tomorrow, we will both attend the funeral.'

'Thank you.' She rubbed her mittens together again. 'To distract ourselves from the cold, how about you explain what you meant about the hollowed-out heel where we found that key having been a "home adaptation"?'

'Ah! That would require me to relate one of his lordship's adventures.'

'You mean *your* adventures. I know you played an equal role, especially after you both left the army. And don't pretend you haven't time for details since we've got hundreds of miles left to walk yet.'

'Actually, only seven, I estimate. But,' he continued, his lips quirking as he pointed over his shoulder, 'salvation arrives, perchance.'

Spinning around, she saw what her sharp hearing would have caught, but for her woollen hat hugging her ears. Behind them was a cart pulled by two donkeys and commanded by the stiffest-looking middle-aged woman she'd seen. In the back, a huddle of ragged, dark-haired and blue-eyed children perched high on heaps of what looked like rectangles of black turf.

Thinking that even with the custom of Irish families being larger than English ones, this woman had produced a remarkable brood, Eleanor gave her a cheery wave. 'Good morning.'

The woman pulled sharply on the reins, bringing the cart to a stop. Adjusting her wire-rimmed spectacles, she looked down at them.

'You're treating your boots to a goodly jaunt, being this far out.'

Eleanor didn't miss the shroud of suspicion wrapping the woman's words, thicker than the worsted brown jacket she wore. Eleanor estimated she was maybe forty, given the slight lines across her brow and running down her thin top lip.

Clifford doffed his bowler hat. 'Sadly, not an intended constitutional, madam.'

This drew a round of whispered giggles from the children who Eleanor hazarded ranged from five to eleven or so.

'Manners!' the woman said, swinging around to the children, her glare silencing them instantly.

Eleanor pointed back the way they, and the cart, had come. 'You probably passed our car. We had a... a problem.'

The woman kept her eyes on Eleanor. 'Well, as we are returning to the village, I suppose you'll be wanting a lift?'

Again, Eleanor got the impression that either everyone knew her and her business before they'd even met, or they simply weren't interested in finding out.

Before she could reply, the lady held up a finger. 'But a lesson is to be learned first.' She turned to the children, her hands raised as if to conduct an orchestra. 'Children! Our maximum load is equivalent to fifty-five bushels and we are at fifty-one. With one adult representing one and three-quarter bushels, how many extra passengers can we ask our donkeys to pull?'

After lots of counting on mud-caked fingers, a flurry of hands shot up from the older children. The woman pointed at a hollow-cheeked boy of about nine, enveloped in a threadbare brown jacket several sizes too large.

'Connor?'

He jumped up, causing those either side of him to topple into each other. 'Two. And an almost dog, miss.'

Eleanor couldn't stop the laugh that erupted at his description of Gladstone. She stepped round to the rear of the cart and leaned on the wooden rail.

'How big is a proper Irish dog, then?'

Wide-eyed, the ring of young faces gaped back at her until she whispered loudly, gesturing between herself and Clifford. 'It's alright, we might sound a little different but we don't bite.' In unison, every child gestured up in the air, which, given their varying heights, suggested everything from an Irish wolfhound to a giraffe, which made her laugh again.

'How fortunate then, that my dog is so much smaller than the ones any of you have.' She beamed round the silent group, who seemed spellbound by something about her. Their clear blue eyes seeming to swim with questions, or wonder, or both. She looked down to see a mesmerised doll of barely five slowly running her finger along the sage-green velvet piping of her coat's cuff. 'Princess pretty,' the little one mumbled. Catching Eleanor's gaze, she pulled her hand back with a shy smile and snuggled into the older girl beside her.

Eleanor smiled back at them and then at the rest of the children in the cart.

'We would be very grateful for a lift. Thank you.'

Two awe-struck boys who had to be twins, given the identical pattern of freckles covering their frost-nipped cheeks, offered a hesitant and grubby hand to her.

'Ahem.' Clifford gestured to the plank of wood up front beside the woman.

Disappointed not to slide in among the children, Eleanor was soon installed in what was still a far cry from the ladylike manner her butler would normally accept. All the more so given that the mud-strewn Gladstone was sprawled inelegantly across the tartan rug on her lap. Clifford perched stiffly beside her, his canvas bag next to him. Craning his head, he addressed their conductress as the cart jerked off.

'Most kind of you, Miss Breen.'

'You're welcome,' came the short reply. Her eyes slid over him quizzically, then Eleanor. 'And you're the people from the House of Towers, evidently. Though I've no label stitched to my hat last time I looked, so how you should know my name is a mystery.'

'Oh gracious!' Eleanor slapped her forehead. 'Of course, you're the headmistress in Derrydee.' She glanced at the cartload of eager faces. 'And these, they're... ah, your pupils?'

'Naturally. For sure, why else would I be carting them around the countryside when the school is shut?'

Eleanor shrugged, which proved too much for Gladstone as he huffed and wriggled under her arm to the coaxing outstretched hands of the children behind.

'Maybe English schools are different. I certainly never had the chance to go on such a jolly when I was their age.'

'Jolly!' Miss Breen scoffed. 'What a notion!'

Clifford coughed. 'I believe Miss Breen and her pupils have been collecting peat to heat the schoolroom, my lady.'

Miss Breen nodded at him, a hint of appreciation in her gaze. 'The government's edict that each child needs bring a brick of peat a day to school in winter is quite simply illfounded! It would mean that many' – she jerked her head at the children behind her – 'would go without heating at home.' She lowered her voice. 'If they have any heating at all, which too many don't. Hence, I take them out at the end of each term and one Saturday in each of the winter months and we cut our own. That way we can bring enough back to the school so at least they have a modicum of warmth when learning and they don't have to do without at home.'

'Oh my!' Eleanor muttered, making a mental note to find a way to aid some of the needier families in the village before they returned to England. Peeping over her shoulder, she watched the children running fingers along Gladstone's wrinkled jowls and stiff pig-like ears while he sat there with a soppy grin on his face.

Clifford leaned forward again. 'As I said, her ladyship and I are most grateful for the lift.'

'*Ladyship?*' the children whispered.

He turned to them. 'Children. This is Lady Swift of Henley Hall, England. Also, Baroneteess Derry of Ross. And' – he indicated the bulldog – 'that is Master Gladstone.'

At his name, the bulldog let out an excited woof and sprawled across the laps of two delighted girls who scooped their arms around him.

'Swift?' Miss Breen repeated, eyeing Eleanor askance. 'Not Hennelly? Tsk, I always said there's no merit in bakery gossip.'

Eleanor laughed. 'Forgive me, but when you said that we must be from the "House of Towers", I thought you had realised who I was. It was remiss of me not to introduce myself then. But more so, not to start with a heartfelt thank you for your invitation on behalf of the Derrydee Committee to join the village in celebrating Christmas. It was so thought—'

Miss Breen brought the cart to an abrupt halt. Had it not been for Clifford's restraining arm thrown across her path, Eleanor would have flown from her seat.

'Is something wrong?' she said, having pulled herself upright. 'Didn't you receive my reply?'

Miss Breen shook her head curtly and took up the reins again, urging the donkeys forward.

Eleanor waved her hand. 'Well, no matter, please don't worry. I had hoped there wouldn't be too much fuss. It's just a treat to meet you all, and see this wonderful part of my family's heritage, really.'

'Lady Swift,' Miss Breen said, her voice rising shrilly, 'I

don't recall receiving your reply any more than I remember sending you an invitation!'

Eleanor sensed Clifford stiffen beside her.

'Forgive the question, Miss Breen,' he said, 'we understood you are the chair of the Derrydee Committee?'

'And you understood just fine, too.'

'Yet you didn't send the invitation her ladyship received?'

The headmistress glared at him. 'I never sent any invitation, I tell you!'

'Golly.' Eleanor frowned. 'Strange. And not a little awkward.'

'Maybe. And maybe not.' Miss Breen appeared deep in thought for a moment. Then she shrugged. 'We Irish aren't known for our hospitality without good reason. Strangers you are. Welcome to Derrydee, you needs be. So, a verbal invitation will have to suffice. Lady Swift – I can't remember the other things your man here addressed you as – you, and your man, are officially invited to an Irish Christmas with the folk of Derrydee.'

Eleanor gasped. 'That is so kind of you, Miss Breen. I—'

The lady held up a hand. 'Yes, I'm sure you are. Now, we've a host of events. Like... yes, well,' tilting her head, she called behind her, 'Samuel, Patrick, Cornelius, tell Lady Swift...'

Eleanor and Clifford spun round to see three of the taller boys crawling to the front of the huddle around Gladstone on their already mud-covered knees. Tongue-tied, however, they fell into elbowing each other in the ribs, none of them speaking up.

'We're very excited,' Eleanor coaxed. 'Neither of us has ever experienced an Irish Christmas.'

'I'm Cornelius,' the brightest-eyed of them blurted out in the strongest lilt she'd yet heard. He wore a blue and pink jumper, the bottom half of which had clearly been unpicked and re-knitted from a lady's cardigan, given the silver threads running through it. 'There's Midnight Mass on the Eve of Christmas night. You should come hear us sing, miss.'

'But the morrow after is the bestest, because it's Christmas Day itself and there's lunch in the crinkly tin hall!' the middle boy cheered.

'Best!' Miss Breen corrected. 'Samuel, concentrate!'

One twin pushed his way to the front. 'Dancin' and singin' and playin' there'll be, miss. Until after sun-up.'

This brought a cheer from the rest of the children.

The last of the three summoned boys put his hand up. That he was the only one with a robust physique and rosy cheeks made his timidity seem all the more charming.

Eleanor smiled. 'Yes, err, Patrick, is it?'

'That's me, miss. Would you be after joining us all on St Stephen's Day, too? There's the parade of the Wren Boys and then the hurling match against Mullakerney.'

'Boys and girls,' she tried to hide the wobble in her voice as she looked around the ring of hopeful faces, 'I would be beyond delighted. As would Mr Clifford.' Like her butler, she clapped her hands over her ears as the unanimous cry went up.

'Hurrah! And bring Master Gladstone too!'

11

In the village, Clifford offered Eleanor a respectful hand down from the donkey cart. Stepping round to the tailgate, he stood, tartan picnic rug at the ready, waiting patiently until Gladstone was finally relinquished from the reluctant arms of the last child.

'Until Christmas Eve, then,' Miss Breen called behind her as the cart lunged on to the school, a sea of swaying mud-caked palms mirroring Eleanor's enthusiastic waving.

'Well, that was delightful,' she said, with a wistful edge.

Clifford eyed her sideways. 'And perplexing.'

She nodded as they set off to the path that led to Hennelly Towers. It had started to snow, the tiny flakes darting around like white fireflies. 'All I wanted to do was keep questioning Miss Breen about the invitation, but I couldn't work out how to without, well, suggesting she didn't have all her faculties.'

'I must confess, I was in the same quandary. And as the lady had rescued us from an arduous walk, I hardly felt it would have been polite to do so.' He offered her the brandy flask as she turned her collar up against the mesmerisingly pretty, but chilly, snowflakes. 'Shall we hasten the last mile before there is any chance you might catch a chill, my lady?' He gestured down the gorse-flanked path, which was less distance to Hennelly Towers than taking the main track. 'How fortunate that two people also shorten the road, as the Irish expression goes. Though strangely, it omits mention of a lumbering and grimy bulldog.'

She laughed as she took the flask and set off. 'Their mistake, I'd say. He's the second best company I've ever found. Especially when things have gone a little awry. Like now.' He acknowledged her heartfelt compliment with a bow. 'What do you make of Miss Breen's denial that she hadn't sent the invitation though, Clifford?'

'Truthfully, I am at a loss. The lady seemed genuine.'

'But, like me, you're hesitating about something in her words or manner?'

He nodded. 'She had the air of one who is...'

'Scatterbrained?'

'Possibly, yes.'

'Well, she's invited us now! And it is almost Christmas, and it's beautiful here. The colour of those hills over there is exquisite. That patch of woods at the top of this rise is filled with trees I can't begin to name. Even the endless miles of peat bog are captivating in their own way with their patches of emerald moss poking out from the snow. And the majority of people we have met are the epitome of the fabled Irish charm.' She frowned. 'With the exception, perhaps, of Constable Doyle.'

'And, perhaps, Doctor O'Sullivan?'

'Y-e-s. Oh, and Father Quinn.'

'And the Mother Superior?'

She waved a dismissive hand. 'True. Anyway, even though some of the locals may have been wary of us, they've still welcomed us. Like Murphy with his endearing gift of the gab. No wonder he's the local publican.'

'And undertaker,' he muttered.

'Mmm.' They lapsed into silence as they pushed on, heads down, into the now whirling snow.

A short while later, Hennelly Towers' gatehouse hove into view. Clifford blinked the sleet from his eyes.

'Might an afternoon exploring your ancestral home appeal, my lady? After a warming bath, and drink and' – he eyed her crumpled, mud-streaked clothing – 'a much-needed change of attire, naturally.'

She shook her head, laughing. 'One day I will be too old for you to hide a telling-off in a seemingly harmless sentence!'

His eyes twinkled. 'Do remind me what age that is at some point.'

'Ah, a grand time you've had, I see, m'lady.' Corcoran's reedy voice pulled them up short in the hallway. Gladstone scampered back to scrabble a muddy greeting up the old retainer's worn brown corduroy trousers as he stood on the doorstep.

She turned with a smile, taking in his mis-buttoned and green-streaked cardigan over a shirt that had possibly never seen an iron in its lifetime. 'It's been interesting for sure. And not a little unexpected.'

Corcoran tugged a remaining forelock on his balding, domed pate. 'Well, what a waste of travelling time it would be if everything were like home.' The crinkles at the corner of his eyes deepened as he ran a hand over his uneven-cut white whiskers. 'Although, of course, in some regards it's fair the opposite. Seeing as, really, you've come home, so to speak, m'lady. And welcome again, if I may say.'

Her hand strayed to the buttons of her jacket. 'Gracious, I hadn't thought of it quite like that.'

Clifford cleared his throat. 'Corcoran, I trust you found the note I left for you?'

The old retainer saluted. 'I did, I did, Mr Clifford. However, there's only the one of me, but I did my fiercest.'

Unmoved, Clifford eyed him firmly. 'Christmas is a particularly special time for her ladyship, hence my detailed list.'

Corcoran nodded. 'Which is why I added a little something in place of the bits I couldn't manage.'

Clifford pursed his lips but said nothing. Aware that Corcoran was staring at the mud covering her skirt and the lap of her jacket, she shrugged.

'We had a spot of bother with the Rolls. But the upside was we enjoyed a wonderful ride with the children of Derrydee School. And had the chance to meet Miss Breen, the headmistress. She's an... an interesting lady. Perhaps you know her?'

Corcoran rolled his eyes. 'In a small village like this, how could I not?'

'Of course, silly me. It was, er, odd, actually.' She searched for the right words. 'You see, Miss Breen invited us to come to Derrydee for Christmas, yet she told us both just now that she hadn't.'

'Ah!' Corcoran tapped his nose. 'Miss Breen, well, not wanting to say anything of a maligning nature, but she is known for being one to go jigging abroad with the leprechauns, as it were.'

'Lapses of memory and or lucidity, I imagine,' Clifford translated at her questioning look.

Corcoran nodded. 'Oh, for the silver tongue Mr Clifford has, m'lady, just as I'd imagined from his letters. Maybe as it'll soothe you to know, though, you aren't the first personage of standing she has invited and then forgotten about.'

'But she's the headmistress! And I'm guessing the only teacher?'

'Both, she be. And a finer one of either you couldn't ask for. The way she cares for those curious little minds is worth all the gold one could ever hope to dig up.' He cocked his head, then looked behind him down the empty drive. 'But trouble with your beautiful vehicle, you said?'

Beside her, a sigh escaped Clifford. 'Yes, Corcoran. Regrettably, we were forced to abandon the Rolls and thus I need assistance in securing someone to tow it back this afternoon.'

Corcoran grimaced. 'Sheeply Walsh will do it alright with his tractor, but he's away until tomorrow. And if it's spare parts, you're needing?' At Clifford's nod, Corcoran held his hands out. 'In all my years, I've never seen anything as fancy as even the silver lady on that bonnet of yours. There's no way you'll be getting any spares for that around here. Sure, no one even has a car except Sullivan, the doctor. Your best chance is to try the garage in Kiltyross, the only town near here. Transport'll be along day after tomorrow up on the main road. But make sure you don't miss it. It only goes once a day.'

'A bus?' Eleanor said.

'If as you'll consider two long slings of wood either side of the back of a passing lorry as a bus, then you're right on the shilling there. A few coins and your man will take Mr Clifford in with any other waiting passengers.' He grinned. 'And for a few more, he'll even bring him back later that afternoon when he passes through again.'

'And me, naturally!' She turned to Clifford. 'I know we'll be on a mission to fix the Rolls and find out about—' She stopped at Clifford's warning look. 'About that other matter, but if we're going all that way, it would be churlish not to bring a few things back to Hennelly Towers to enjoy over the festive season.'

He nodded. 'I believe a modicum of shopping can be accommodated, my lady.'

Corcoran laughed. 'I hope as you don't mind me saying, m'lady, but tongues'll be flapping long after next Christmas over the lady of the House of Towers riding like that into town.'

Her smile faded as a thought struck her. 'Talking of local chatter, perhaps you've heard about the poor chap who died the night we arrived? Up at the abbey. Maybe someone has mentioned who he was?'

Corcoran rubbed his whiskers thoughtfully. 'I heard as someone had passed. But what a fellow was doing in the abbey would be a mystery fit for combing the longest beard over. The Mother Superior never lets a man in the place, save for Father Quinn.'

'The gentleman was found prior to that on the road some way beyond this last mile stretch,' Clifford said.

Corcoran's brows rose to where his hairline probably was ten years before. 'A body in the road, you say? Mind, not the first I've seen, or heard of here.'

'Gracious,' Eleanor gasped. 'Do a lot of people get struck by cars or... similar then?' She mentally slapped her forehead and lowered her voice. 'Or perhaps it's been on account of the national troubles?'

The old retainer's shoulders stiffened. 'But, for sure, you'll be after getting out of your wet clothes after braving the wrath of the weather. I'll be leaving you to it.' He tugged his forelock and shuffled off towards the gatehouse.

Eleanor watched him go. 'Well, it seems we'll have to leave the Rolls to its fate until tomorrow.'

Clifford sighed. 'Unfortunately so, my lady.'

In the one room they'd made more than habitable, he ducked under the carved cream stone chimney cowl that tapered up to the ceiling. There, he set to lighting the perfect pyramid of kindling and logs he'd prepared before they went out. Gladstone, recognising a fire was in the offing, collapsed at her feet on the thick rug.

She perched on the arm of the nearest blue settee. 'Now, you rashly promised something about us passing a delightful time exploring Hennelly Towers, which I haven't forgotten you've never seen either. Funny though, even though it is supposed to be a castle, it has more of a family home feel to it.

Assuming one had a family of fifty with which to fill it, of course.'

He rose and, having wiped his hands, busied himself arranging her wet outdoor things in a precisely spaced line along the fireguard spanning the vast fireplace.

'Yet there are but twenty-nine rooms, my lady. Considerably less than the forty-three at Henley Hall. However, perhaps that change of clothes and hot toddy mentioned earlier before exploring?'

She nodded. 'Actually, a hot bath would be welcome, but with only well water and no heating except the fire, it would take an age to prepare.' She glanced at the snow falling outside. 'Anyway, few, if any, of those children on Miss Breen's cart have gone home to a hot bath, so I can certainly do without. Besides,' she headed out of the room and up the stairs, calling behind her, 'it would delay finding out if there really is a ghost of Hennelly Towers!'

12

Ten minutes later, wrapped in three layers of cashmere jumpers over her favourite grey silk house pyjamas, she bounded back down the staircase and into their improvised dining-cum-sitting-cum-everything room. The fresh coffee smelt heavenly as she settled down to enjoy several extra-warming cups. Finally, having persuaded her butler she was thoroughly warmed even to her insides, they started their tour of the castle in the grand hall. Eleanor stood in the centre and gazed up at the ornately carved ceiling.

'There's something of the theatrical about this space, wouldn't you say, Clifford?'

Clifford cast his eye around. 'I would concur, my lady.'

The hall was the size of a ballroom. Lit by several oil lamps, three enormous crimson settees dominated the centre, while suits of armour stood ready for battle along the walls. Above the leaded windows' pelmets hung vibrant tapestries of mediaeval village scenes. Adorning the chimney and presiding over each of the five doors leading off were proud reliefs of the Hennelly family coat of arms. He read the motto underneath.

'"*Propositum et perseverantia in perpetuum.*" Determined purpose and perseverance forever.'

'Well, I'm determined to explore, but my perseverance might fade, so let's go.'

He lit them both an oil lamp, which reminded her again of the children on Miss Breen's cart who had only peat for heating, cooking and lighting. And sometimes, as the headmistress had said, not even that. Counting her blessings once more, she set off, the heels of her stout Oxford flats echoing across the stone flooring and down the shadowy corridor. She'd chosen them for warmth since they had space for thick socks. Clifford followed, his footsteps as silent as ever. She often wondered if he just floated along, rather than walking.

In the first room, she peered around, her eyes struggling to see even with the oil lamps as the whole space seemed to be clad in black oak panelling. She put a hand on the back of the nearest throne of a dining chair and placed the lamp on the long, bare table, the light dancing off the walls. Clifford stepped to the end of the room and, after some grumbling from the ancient shutter hinges, the space was flooded with the best illumination a grey December afternoon could offer.

'Gracious, this feels decidedly mediaeval as well.'

'Yet the house dates closer to the early eighteen hundreds, I believe, from the pointed cinquefoil detailing.' He traced the five scallops of the nearest window's arch.

She looked around again, still having to blink to see any details. 'Given that West Ireland's climate probably hasn't changed much in centuries, it might have been sensible to put less stained glass in the windows. It looks lovely, but it doesn't allow enough light through. Certainly not on a day like today.'

'Although that appears to be a theme in several of the rooms, my lady.' Opening the far door, he waited for her to join him.

'What? We're back in the hallway. No disrespect to the

architect, but why would you have the dining room just off the main hall? And likely the furthest distance from the kitchens?'

'From the panelling, my lady, I conjecture this was never intended to be used as such. Rather, it was to be the gentleman's study.'

She smiled. 'A brandy and cigar retreat, you mean?'

He bowed. 'One and the same, in his lordship's case. Onwards?'

More mediaeval-themed rooms passed in a blur until she paused at the seventh. Here, cream stone, pink-and-blue wallpaper and heavy curtains covered the walls, and mismatched rugs the floor. Scattered around the room, richly coloured settees, ash-wood tables, side stands and bureaus abounded.

Their tour of the second floor was accompanied by a great deal of creaking floorboards and hinges as they peeked into the numerous bedrooms. Each room had a colourful variation of last century's elaborate, hand-blocked wallpaper with swathes of matching drapes adorning the four-poster beds and windows. Incongruously, mismatched wardrobes and drawer-chests also proliferated in every room. Eleanor pointed above the door of one.

'I do love these pretty frilled arches everywhere. And there's an overriding smell I can't place. Henley Hall is always awaft with beeswax, leather polish or flowers from the garden. Or Mrs Trotman's expert ministrations in the kitchen but here, whilst not unpleasant' – she sniffed the air – 'it's like decades of wood smoke, probably peat, and...' She threw her arms out questioningly.

'West Ireland.' Clifford nodded while running an appreciative finger over the large glass bevel of a clock set so snugly in the wall, its numbered face appeared to be straining to be noticed. 'However, the plethora of mounted clocks is even more intriguing. This being the eleventh I have counted already.'

She smiled. Her butler was obsessive about timekeeping,

perhaps because he'd been brought up by a clockmaker for some of his childhood. 'Well, so far I haven't seen any sign of the infamous Hennelly Towers ghost. Maybe we'll bump into him as we continue exploring?'

A short while later, she had completely lost her bearings due to the seemingly looping corridor. 'Are we back where we started yet?'

'Not quite, my lady. This floor seems to have been designed around a central sitting room, on one side of which are the family bedrooms, and the other, the guest ones, I imagine.'

'If you say so. That's eleven bedrooms in total we've seen, all cosy enough if anyone were to inhabit them for a while and breathe some life into them. Twelve, if you include mine. Although, naturally, you won't countenance stepping over the threshold now I've unpacked my things in there.'

He threw her a hopeful look. 'Unpacked? As in items of attire hung neatly or placed in drawers, perfectly folded?'

'Not a bit. Mostly tipped out onto the long pink velvet settee only my room has been graced with, or spread across any available space.' She hid a smile at his groan. 'Actually, would you be uncomfortable if I just peeped into the staff quarters?' She held up a hasty hand. 'Except whichever room or rooms you've chosen, naturally?'

'Of course, my lady.'

Having climbed the staff stairs at the end of the corridor, she emerged onto a small landing with several doors off.

'Clifford?' she murmured after peering into the last but one diminutive bedroom, which, like the others, held only a single bed, an empty open-fronted wardrobe and a bare nightstand. 'I don't want you to feel uncomfortable by my observation, since you've installed yourself up here most respectfully, but isn't there a strange air along this entire floor? A feeling, I mean.'

'Such as one would expect on entering the *Mary Celeste,*

the infamous ghost ship found abandoned in the Atlantic in 1872?'

She nodded. 'Exactly. It seems the staff did just up and flee. There's even an odd shoe left here and there. Maybe they were as terrified as Corcoran said.'

'If you say so, my lady,' he replied noncommittally.

Back down on the ground floor, he opened one last door. 'Since you wish to view the entire house, there is a corridor here which leads to the rear of the kitchen and the pantry.' He led the way, opening the door at the end for her.

'Corcoran!' he muttered.

Eleanor eyed the voluminous piles of berry-laden holly, spliced hazel and ivy trails in confusion. Among them were also three large baskets filled with moss and what looked like a hundred ancient shepherds' beards. Two sawn-off silver birch branches leaned against the whitewashed wall, while a pot of red paint and another of green sat on top of a box filled with sticks and pebbles. That all of it had clearly been thrown in from the threshold of the outer door made Clifford steeple his hands over his nose.

She shrugged. 'He did say he wouldn't step into the house.' Suddenly, the penny dropped. 'Ah! So this is what your note asked him for, was it?'

'If one were to ignore that every item has been substituted by another and hurled into the wrong room, yes, my lady.'

'Clifford, you old softie!' she breathed through the lump in her throat. 'Tell me you weren't going to sit up all night as a surprise so I could come down to the place adorned with beautiful handmade Christmas decorations in the morning?'

He tutted. 'Indeed, I was not.'

'Fibber!'

'Most assuredly. However, the "surprise" element has been rather lost.'

She noticed his slightly deflated tone. 'I've a suggestion. If my lack of being meticulous won't drive you too potty, we could sit up in the kitchen, and...' She tailed off, feeling foolish.

'Make them together, my lady?' His eyes twinkled. 'Thankfully, I brought enough of his lordship's favourite port that any lack of craftsmanship will soon go unnoticed by either party. Shall we?'

13

Even the cold nipping through her bed socks couldn't keep Eleanor huddled under the blankets after she'd opened her eyes. She bounded up and smiled at Gladstone and Tomkins in the bulldog's bed, curled as they were together, one paw around the other.

'Morning, chaps. It's, umm...' She looked around the rose-and-cream flowered walls for one of the inset clocks Clifford had been so intent on observing the night before.

'Coffee o'clock, my lady,' Clifford's measured tone came through the door.

Grabbing her robe, she hurried over and wrenched it open.

Her butler stood facing the opposite wall so as not to catch a glimpse of her, despite her being swathed head-to-toe in night-wear. She smiled at his rigid standards of decorum, even in rural Ireland. 'I am, Clifford, absolutely filled with festive joy this morning!'

'Heartening news, my lady,' the back of his head seemed to say. 'Three minutes, if you will.'

'Tsk,' she teased, 'is that a butler's three minutes? Or a lady's?'

'A butler's.' His amused tone echoed back along the corridor to her. 'So three minutes, not thirty.'

Fifteen minutes later, in their impromptu breakfast room, she paused to admire the festive decorations. They'd taken longer to make than either she or Clifford had allowed for, a slight excess of port being partly to blame. That, and their rivalry as they both tried to trump each other's creativity. However, the results were worth it. The silver birch branches made the perfect substitute Christmas trees, replete with artfully woven hazel twig stars and shepherd's beard snowflakes. Festively painted pebbles and a raft of other impromptu garlands and wreaths spanned the walls around the room.

At the table, she took a sip of coffee, the hot liquid warming her insides.

'I have news,' Clifford said. 'Corcoran has procured us transportation – of sorts – until the Rolls is repaired.'

'Oh, that's wonderful! Even though we haven't yet worked out why someone disabled it at least we can now go and get it towed back here. And if we leave early enough, we can call in at Murphy's for breakfast and then the abbey to ask a few more questions before we meet this farmer—'

'A Mr Sheeply Walsh, I recall.'

'Yes. Him.' She took another sip, hoping the warmth would reach her toes. 'And even you must think Corcoran has redeemed himself by somehow securing us a car to use?'

'Ahem, with apologies for the correction, my lady, it is not quite as I suspect you are imagining.'

Gladstone padding in interrupted their conversation. He trotted over to Eleanor and sat, his head in her lap, his doleful eyes looking up at her. She patted him on the back. 'Sorry, old fellow, but you'll have to wait until we're in the village. We're fresh out of food here. The hens have mysteriously stopped laying. Maybe it's the ghost putting them off!' She turned back to Clifford. 'But surely anything will suffice to get us around?'

He arched a brow. 'Perhaps, once you have finished your drink, you might like to be the judge of that?'

Her curiosity eating her up, she gulped down her remaining coffee and followed him outside where the sky was an unbroken vista of snow clouds. On the top step, she shivered as she scanned the empty driveway in confusion. 'Funny joke on your part, Clifford? No car at all. Just Shanks' pony, is it?'

'Around the side of the house, my lady, if you would be so gracious.'

Her hands flew to her mouth as she rounded the corner. 'Oh my! That looks, umm... snug.'

'A euphemism for rickety? Or ridiculous? Or both? However, may I introduce your "jaunting" car?'

He shuddered while gesturing at a tiny, two-wheeled cart, which was barely wide enough for the both of them. She stepped over and stared at the plank of wood that served as a seat.

'It's not that bad, Clifford. Although, where do we put our legs? I mean, there's no room in front of the seat?' He tapped the footplate she'd thought was merely for stepping aboard. 'Oh, it's a side-saddle sort of ride, I see. And it's really called a "jaunting car"?'

'It is.'

'Then, in the spirit of doing the local thing,' she said, swinging herself up onto the right-hand seat and patting the other one, 'I suggest a-jaunting we go.'

He didn't move. 'Have you noticed something is missing, perchance? Such as our means of propulsion?'

'Ah!'

It was just shy of half an hour later their charabanc was ready. Eleanor had eventually coaxed Gladstone from his slumbers in the morning room on to the jaunting car where he palpably didn't fit. Wedged between them both, his look of disdain left them in no doubt about his opinion of their new mode of transport. Tomkins, on the other hand, had bounded out and only been persuaded to return inside by bribing him with the promise of a fish head or two on their return.

Sitting inelegantly on the minuscule seat, wrapped in as many layers as she'd packed, she stared back at the creature now standing staring contemptuously over its shoulder at her. It had taken them the best part of twenty minutes to persuade it to stop eating the small, formal garden at the front of the castle, and another ten to cajole it between the long wooden breeching bars that attached it to the cart. At least it hadn't bitten either of them.

'Are donkeys really as stubborn as people say, Clifford?' she whispered.

'I believe so, my lady. However, that is a mule. Technically, the offspring of a male donkey and a female horse.' He shook his head at her optimistic look. 'Known for being equally stubborn. Or "mulish", hence the derivation of the adjective.'

'Well, we're going to have to make friends with him, or her, on this little sojourn into Derrydee.'

'Him. Or Mullaney, as he may answer to, if we are particularly fortunate.'

Whether it was Clifford having finally hit upon the appropriate word, or clucking noise, or flick of the reins, they didn't know. Perhaps Mullaney had simply tired of waiting. But after five minutes of futile effort, with a jerk the cart lurched forward, and they were off.

Eleanor failed to stifle the laughter that erupted at the ludicrousness of their situation. Her ever-impeccably suited butler was huddled sideways, clinging to the reins. She was trying to restrain Gladstone's now excited desire to ride on the very front edge of the cart. And all three of them were at the mercy of a mule with a mind of its own. Thankfully, it seemed to have decided a trip to the village was likely to result in something tasty to nibble and trotted out that way.

Eleanor grabbed the rail as one of the wooden wheels hit a pothole and she was jerked out of her seat and back down. Hard. She could only shrug at Clifford and hang on to Gladstone as the other wheel hit an even bigger hole.

'Well,' she panted, 'I'd say this is way better than the Rolls. We were far too conspicuous.'

'Unlike the spectacle we are cutting now,' he replied drily.

'Oh, I don't think anyone will notice,' she said airily as Gladstone, having spotted a bevvy of ducks by the side of the road, stood up on his stiff front legs with a rally of exuberant woofs.

Murphy slapped his thigh, grinning widely, as he happened out just as they arrived at the pub.

'Surely, my eyes are still swimming in dreams? Or whiskey, maybe?' Sliding a hand under the neck strap of their steed, he brought it to a stop and leaned a forearm along the mule's hindquarters. 'The lady of the House of Towers taking a lesson in the local life, is it?'

'Absolutely,' she said, declining Clifford's – and Murphy's – offer of help, as she climbed stiffly down. 'Although I do think the addition of a cushion for one's posterior might be advisable.'

Laughing equally at her remark and Clifford pinching the bridge of his nose at her mentioning inappropriate parts of her anatomy, Murphy looped the trailing strap of the cart over a post. Turning, he sauntered back in to the pub, calling over his shoulder, 'Breakfast'll be ready in a shout, seeing as we thought you'd be along. But you'll have to make do with what we've left in. Rashers and clutch cake with colcannon farls be the only choice.'

'Sounds delicious,' she said eagerly, beating Gladstone in leading the charge into the snug.

'Thank you, Kathleen,' she called a few minutes later, as Clifford set two generously loaded plates down on the table. Staring at the three-inch-high crust of the pie in front of her, she tapped the golden-brown top with her fork. 'I genuinely didn't know one could do something so spectacular-looking with mostly just eggs and bacon.'

'Ah, see if you can't work out the rest of the ingredients, then,' Kathleen said. 'Seeing as I can't give away the secret every Murphy grandma has passed down.' With a wave, she disappeared.

Eleanor inspected hers closely, then tasted it.

'It holds together like proper cake. And it tastes divine.' She tried some more. 'It's got a slightly sweet and salty base, interspersed with hints of cheese and lashings of the tastiest bacon I've ever eaten.'

'An ingenious blend of bread-and-butter pudding with overtones of omelette?'

'Either way' – she cut another large forkful – 'please take your notebook out and describe this for Mrs Trotman so she can make it when we get home to Henley Hall.'

'As you wish.' Looking up from jotting several lines, he shook his head at Gladstone, who was wistfully staring at the basket of farls. 'Kathleen's griddle cakes are not intended for a greedy bulldog, Master Gladstone.'

Eleanor nodded and passed the dog a piece. 'So "colcannon" is some form of cabbage and potato.' She took a bite and moaned with delight. Tapping his page with her fork, she ignored his tut. 'Please add these as well. They are beyond sublime. Chewy, but soft, a hint of cabbagey bitterness wrapped in buttery heaven. And this isn't even proper Christmas fayre yet!'

Back on the cart, she almost regretted the amount she'd eaten as they wallowed and bumped along, Mullaney seemingly oblivious to the rough road. A moment later, she frowned.

'You said the farmer would meet you at eleven o'clock at the Rolls. And it's only about...'

He peered up at the blanket of snow cloud. 'Five and ten past nine.'

'How can you tell that when the sun is entirely hidden? Anyway, we've plenty of time for a detour to the abbey as planned. We're both sure the Mother Superior knows more than she's confessed to.'

'Indeed, my lady.' Clifford tugged on the right-hand rein to turn the cart down a narrow track. 'Might one enquire what one's plan is on reaching the abbey?'

'You can, but as I'm sure you've worked out, I don't have one yet. Other than to try and get even one straight answer out of the Mother Superior, that is. So, while we each think of a plan' – she avoided his gaze – 'I say we see if we can spy a farmhouse on the way. Somewhere someone might have seen something regarding our poor deceased friend that night. Mind you, I admit, I've only noticed a handful of buildings of any sort and they are all set back miles from the road.' She leaned forward and called, 'Speed up there!' The mule stopped abruptly, almost throwing all three of them out of their seats. She shrugged sheepishly at Clifford as he got them moving again. 'Sorry. Perhaps I'd better keep quiet and watch and learn.'

But only a moment later he reined Mullaney back in and pointed down a track they had just drawn level with.

A few hundred feet from the road was a low thatched cottage, barely longer than it was wide, its stone blackened with age. But it wasn't the cottage that had caught Clifford's attention, she realised.

It was the two men climbing into a car parked outside. Before Clifford could urge Mullaney down the track, the car bounced away into the woods. She turned to him, a questioning look on her face.

He nodded. 'I think, my lady, we should pay this cottage a visit. It may contain some items from the Rolls I was careless enough to "misplace"!'

14

'I can't imagine you'll need your picklocks,' Eleanor said in a hushed tone as they crept up to the cottage's austere entrance. 'That door looks like it might fall in if you just breathed hard enough on it.'

'Indeed, my lady.' He held his ear to the worm-eaten wood for a second, then straightened up. Placing his shoulder on the door, he shoved gently and was instantly swallowed up by the gloomy interior.

'Oh my!' Eleanor gasped as she darted in behind him. She blinked along the row of wide-eyed faces of what had to be a family in front of her. *Why did we assume it was empty, Ellie!* A lean-cheeked woman wrapped in a holey brown shawl and a gaunt man dressed in a desperately patched suit sat on two stools. The only other form of seating in the room was three tattered sacks of straw on which six ragged children were perched, their bare feet hanging above the cobbled stone floor. A three-legged table was perched against the opposite wall, while a row of mismatched crates covered with rough blankets occupied the far side. A black pot hung from a chain over the fireplace grate, which had no evidence of having seen wood, coal or even peat in a very long while. There was no sign of water, washing facilities or even a cupboard for storing food.

Eleanor winced but tried to cover it up with her best smile. 'Please do excuse our very impolite intrusion. We thought, umm... someone else lived here.'

The man and woman shared a bemused look while the children stared between Eleanor and Clifford, the four smallest drawing their knees up slowly as if cowering into the sacking. The man stood and raked his cap off, his tone somewhere between confused and suspicious. 'Perhaps you're in need of something?'

Eleanor, unusually, was at a complete loss to know what to say in reply. Behind her, Clifford cleared his throat.

'Too kind, sir. But I shall repeat her ladyship's profuse apology and ask for nothing more than the answer to one question, if it isn't too much trouble?' The man eyed him warily but jerked his chin as if answering tentatively in the affirmative. 'Thank you. The question is: who were those men? The two who just left here. In the car. You see, her ladyship wishes to find—'

'No one!' The man's voice was unnaturally loud. The whole family, including the children, shook their heads vociferously. 'No one,' the man repeated. 'Not a soul! There's been no one in here, save us.'

Back in the jaunting car, Eleanor shook her head. 'That was an uncomfortable meeting of two worlds. What a tragically hard existence they seem to lead, Clifford.'

'Quite,' he replied gently. 'However, poverty is not usually the nurturer of such ready fear. Besides, I am undecided if it was not *us* they felt threatened by.'

'We did barge in ever so boorishly, I suppose. And maybe those two men who disabled the Rolls are part of their family. Maybe they were just protecting them?'

'Rather than our initial impression that they were the ones

in need of protection? Hmm, more confusion to ponder en route.'

She nodded. 'Either way, it was obvious we weren't going to get anything out of them, so let's hope we have more luck at our next port of call.'

As the abbey loomed into view, she let out a long whistle. 'Gracious! I had no idea it was so enormous. In the dark, it didn't seem even one tenth as vast as the castle-cum-palace it is. Just look at those,' she said, her mittened forefinger moving up through the cold air as she counted, 'five, six, no... seven storeys in parts, two beautiful towers at the rear and one imposing affair at the front. And in such white stone, not the cream-coloured one which Hennelly Towers is built in.'

Clifford looked it over with the critical air of an art expert. 'Slate-grey brick quoins running up each corner, carved spandrels, highly-detailed gables over the leaded mullioned windows, plus castellations to the towers' parapet rooflines.'

'Save it for later, Mister Architecture,' she said as the cart came to a stop. 'We might need your infuriating attention to detail inside.'

As she climbed the abbey's steps, her sharp hearing caught his muttered, 'Aren't I the fortunate one, Master Gladstone!'

The nun who opened the door to them was a fresh-faced young woman of fewer years than Eleanor. Wide-eyed below her black head covering, she gaped at their request to see the Mother Superior. After a few moments, it seemed to dawn on her that her unexpected visitors were still staring at her expectantly. After asking them to wait, she closed the door, leaving them outside.

Clifford's attempts to draw some hitherto undiscovered patience from Eleanor by remarking on the admirable extent and quality of the formal gardens they could glimpse through the gated arches failed entirely.

'We aren't here to admire the roses, Clifford!' she hissed. 'And it's freezing out here!'

'Then what is the purpose of your visit, child?' a sharp voice called from behind them.

'Ah, Reverend Mother. Good morning.' Eleanor beamed, despite being rather unnerved by the diminutive woman's intense blue-eyed stare through her spectacles.

'An unnecessary observation since every one is good, each day being a gift from the Lord.'

'Yes, of course. Well, please forgive us not calling ahead but I... *we* felt the need to talk with you again.'

'On points of faith?'

'Not exactly.'

After her direct approach with Constable Doyle had failed, Clifford had persuaded her to adopt a more 'oblique' tack with her questioning. Before Eleanor could expand on the reason for their visit, however, the Mother Superior shook her head.

'Our horary is prescriptive for a reason.'

Evidently thinking that was clear, she gestured for them to return to their waiting cart.

'The abbey's elected liturgy of hours and additions,' Clifford translated. At Eleanor's blank look, he bowed respectfully to the Mother Superior. 'The incumbents' daily schedule for prayers, silence, spiritual works, reading and meals, I believe.'

'Together with specific hours for sleep.' The Mother Superior nodded appreciatively at him. 'Hence every minute is spent as it should be, engaged entirely in the consecrated life we have vowed to. Not' – she looked sharply at Eleanor – 'spent in unworthy pursuits. If you will therefore excuse me.' She turned to go.

'Then my ignorance of religious matters tripped me up, Reverend Mother,' Eleanor said quickly. 'I only hoped supporting a rather lost soul might fall under your truly noble umbrella.' Secretly cheering as the Mother Superior turned back to her, she added, 'My sincere apologies, therefore.'

'It's called faith, child.'

'But that doesn't stop it hurting,' Eleanor said quietly.

For a moment, the nun stared between them. Then she seemed to make up her mind. 'I must continue about my duties, so you will have to walk and talk. And I' – she held up a finger – 'I will listen but I do not promise to reply.' She turned and started off down the corridor, Eleanor and Clifford hurrying after her.

Eleanor looked around her with fresh eyes, albeit hurriedly dragging her gaze forward as even her longer than average legs were no match for the fiercely spirited ones of the elderly nun. What she did have time to notice in the softly lit corridors and vast vaulted hallways they hurried through was the exquisite quality of the wood doors, swirling banister rails and decorated ceilings. Which struck her as odd for those dedicated to a life of simplicity in devotion. Likewise, the intricately carved stone window seats peppering so many corridors seemed out of place.

'I had no idea the abbey was so beautiful, Reverend Mother. Would it be rude to ask how your order came to be here?'

'A rich Irishman had it built for his family many years ago,' came the terse reply.

'It must have been a charming, if enormous, family home.'

'They never lived here.'

'After all the trouble, expense and incredible design! Why ever not?'

Their guide merely motioned for them to halt and disappeared through a narrow, arched door, framed by carved stonework

Eleanor pursed her lips. *This softly-softly approach is getting you nowhere.*

A frustratingly long few minutes later, the Mother Superior

reappeared further down the corridor and beckoned them to continue following her.

'Now, my child, how exactly can I help a "lost soul" as you described yourself?'

Deciding there was no more time for her, so far, futile efforts at subtlety she came straight to the point.

'By helping me find the truth.'

The Mother Superior kept walking. 'The truth is at the very heart of all we uphold, child. However, this truth you speak of concerns what?'

'The truth about the man we brought here that night, Reverend Mother. The one who died in this abbey.'

The Mother Superior's step faltered, but she continued on. 'That soul is now in the next phase of life. Death is not the end.'

You're still getting nowhere, Ellie. She changed tack again.

'Constable Doyle, Father Quinn and Doctor O'Sullivan whom we met that night. They are all Derrydee men, born and bred?'

The Mother Superior shook her head. 'Not a bit. The doctor lives in the nearest town, Kiltyross, where his practice is based. And Father Quinn was sent here only about six months ago by the church board from another county. His predecessor in Derrydee passed without having a novice under his wing who could take over. Only the constable is truly local, being born and raised in the village.'

Eleanor's eyes strayed right, despite still hurrying forward, making her catch the nun's heel. 'I'm so sorry. It's just that window caught my eye again.'

'The abbey has many. Please keep moving if you wish any further discussion with me.'

'I do, sincerely,' Eleanor said, still remaining on the spot. 'But this one is particularly pretty. And so different from the others.' She peered more closely at the pattern of the stained glass. 'It's like a family group above a coat of arms.'

With a poorly disguised huff, their hostess came back to them. 'It is the only remaining original stained-glass window. All the others have been replaced with those bearing more fitting religious depictions.'

'It's delightful that you've allowed it to remain. And despite its picture, you can still see through it. As I did that night when a man passed the other side.'

'Do not be fooled, child. The glass is most distorting. And to the over-imaginative' – she gave Eleanor an extra pointed look – 'it can deceive the mind to see that which it seeks to find. Now, come.' These last words were delivered as a barked command. Eleanor dared one more peep before adhering to her butler's discreet cough from behind.

For someone so unobservant about art as Clifford delights in reminding you, why is it that something in that particular window has struck such a vaguely familiar chord, Ellie? Something to do with the colours? Or that, what is it, signature in the bottom corner?

She had no more time to consider the matter as they'd arrived back at the door by which they'd entered. The Mother Superior spun around.

'You have a good heart, child. And good intentions.' The intensity of the woman's stare increased even further. 'But return back to England. Nothing good comes of raking up the past and its troubles.'

'I didn't know I was!' Eleanor muttered as they were ushered out.

15

'My lady, the farmer will be here in a moment. To avoid a protracted discourse in his presence, your answer, if I may?' They had left the abbey a while ago and were now waiting with the Rolls. 'Which of the two necessities is the least unattractive to you? Trying to pilot the Rolls whilst it is towed, or' – he waved a gloved hand towards the mule – 'trying to pilot Mullaney?'

Eleanor looked thoughtful. 'I hadn't thought of that. Mmm. Definitely the car.' As he swallowed hard, she smiled. 'Only teasing. Actually, Mullaney sounds the better option. And with less chance of inflicting any more damage on my wonderful butler's already harried nerves.'

'Too gracious, my lady.'

'On the plus side, at least the Rolls is still here. After seeing those two men again, I rather feared the worst.' She peered sideways at the man who had cared for her uncle for more years than she had been alive. And who now applied himself every inch as dutifully where she was concerned. 'In fact, if it hadn't meant leaving me alone at Hennelly Towers, you would probably have walked all the way back here at dusk and spent the night in the Rolls. And sat bolt upright, vigilantly looking out for those two troublemakers until the farmer came along this morning.'

'Unquestionably, my lady.'

'Well, our initial fear that it could have been the work of petty thieves planning to return and strip the vehicle once we had been forced to abandon it proved otherwise. At least, since there's no further damage, it looks that way.'

'True. However, the thieves may have fully intended to further dismantle the Rolls, but their plans were derailed.'

'A good thought, but they had all night to strip her bare. How badly awry would a plan have to go not to manage at least a bit more thievery within that time?'

'A better conjecture on your part, I concede. So, it does seem that the Rolls was put out of commission for another reason. What, we are yet not sure.' He glanced at his watch again. 'It is somewhat past the agreed time to meet. However, punctuality is not a trait one necessarily associates with the general population of rural Ireland.'

Eleanor shrugged. 'I suppose we'll just have to wait...'

Half an hour later, Clifford pointed down the road. 'Aha! Our tow, I believe.' He strode into the middle of the road and waved. 'Mr Walsh!'

The stocky man on the tractor waved back. A minute later he juddered to a noisy halt next to them. The farmer wore green overalls, the top half of which he wore undone and tied around his waist by the arms. He appeared to have put his grey jumper and rough brown cotton shirt on in reverse order, since the latter was done up loosely on the outside. A wide-ribbed scarf was looped twice around his neck, the ends flapping in the stiff icy breeze. The tractor itself was little more than an engine mounted directly onto two large rear wheels and two tiny front ones. To Eleanor's mind it looked more a study in unpainted scrap parts than an agricultural workhorse.

The farmer climbed off his seat. 'Morning. And Sheeply'll do fine enough.' As he came over to join them, he removed his worn worsted cap, revealing a soft-knit hat beneath. He bent down and patted Gladstone who had lumbered up to greet him with his customary licky welcome. 'Hello there, old boy.' He straightened up and nodded in Eleanor's direction. 'Lady Swift, I've heard.'

She smiled. 'Yes, that's right. And I'm immensely grateful for your tow. Oh, I say!' She started as a small furry face appeared from under the farmer's scarf. It was chestnut brown with a button nose and black eyes like bright, curious currants. Gladstone let out a growl, then stretched up on his back legs to sniff the mysterious creature.

'An Irish stoat, my lady.' Clifford raised a warning eyebrow as she attempted to stroke its head. 'A fiendish hunter of prey easily twice its size.'

'That's true.' Sheeply tickled the animal's white throat. 'You won't find so much as a whiff of rats in my barns. She's good for a few rabbits a week for the pot, too. And young trout and elvers if I take her down to the river.' He nodded at the Rolls. 'So, it's a towing to the House of Towers for this shiny beast you'll be needing?'

'For appropriate recompense, of course.' Clifford pulled out his wallet and pressed several notes into the now eager-eyed man's hand. Reaching into his inside jacket pocket, he then produced a half bottle of whiskey, which he held back. 'If we might aim for the smoothest stretches?'

'Whatever you say.' Sheeply nodded, pocketing the bottle and then brandishing a coil of thick rope. While Clifford dropped to his haunches to attach the rope under the front of the Rolls, he effortlessly engaged the farmer in easy chatter.

'Your trusty steed. A Fordson 1919 from the works in Cork, is she? Twenty horsepower with the inline four-cylinder engine.'

'That she be,' came the impressed reply. 'We farmers clubbed together and found a second-hand one. We share her, you see. Still cost a pretty penny and everything besides, but she's worth it. Mind, trick is in learning early how she likes to be cranked or the winter days'll see you breaking your arm with the starting handle.'

Eleanor left them to their baffling exchange over axle stresses, and, most confusingly, worm drive gears and wandered back over to their mule.

'Hello, Mullaney. It's just you and me to Hennelly Towers. Well, with Gladstone too. And as I've had lots of practice with horses, camels and even elephants during my travels' – she ran a hand along its neck – 'it will be fun, yes?' Receiving nothing but a rebellious toss of the mule's head and a dark-eyed stare, she sighed and climbed into the driving seat. 'We *will* become friends, you know.'

Clifford stepped over and lifted Gladstone in beside her. Deftly securing the bulldog's lead to the cart's front rail, his eyes twinkled mischievously. 'Do we need to agree on a distress signal, my lady?'

'Absolutely not!' she said over the roar of the tractor starting. 'Mullaney and I shall be streaks ahead of you and your worm gears or whatever you and Sheeply are so enamoured over.' She waved a mock imperious hand. 'Step aside!'

Four minutes later, her butler was still standing patiently as Sheeply's wheezy chuckle filtered through the cold air to her.

'Alright,' she grumbled. 'Please start us off and then we'll show you what's what.'

'As you wish, my lady.' Taking the reins, he clucked his tongue and tapped them four times against the mule's back, stepping aside as the cart moved forward.

· · ·

If they had cut a ridiculous spectacle on their way through the village earlier that morning, they now reached new heights in being the ultimate fairground attraction as they returned. Doors flew open, children and adults alike tumbling out. The women shoved their hands into their aprons, shoulders shaking with laughter as the men slapped their legs or each other's backs. The children mostly gravitated to Eleanor and Gladstone, where they were bringing up the rear, some of whom she recognised from Miss Breen's peat-cutting cart.

Sheeply seemed to be enjoying spearheading the whole procession as he saluted everyone through the puffs of black smoke from his tractor. Behind in the Rolls, Clifford ignored the wolf whistles, preoccupied with avoiding the numerous potholes in the road and the numerous feet trotting alongside. Long before they'd reached the square, Eleanor's minimal command over the capricious mule failed entirely as the beast stopped abruptly, refusing to be coaxed forward whatever she tried. The ring of giggling children parted as the one she recognised as being Cornelius stepped up.

'You've a foot jaunt ahead of you now for sure, miss. Old Mullaney won't move otherwise.'

'Oh, I don't know,' she said. 'There must be something else I can try.' But almost as if the mule had understood, it laid its ears back and set to chomping on the straw poking from a calico sling across the nearest man's shoulders.

'Oy!' he cried, spinning around to eye Eleanor darkly.

'Sorry!' She jumped down and took hold of the mule's neck strap, whispering, 'Please move, Mullaney. You can have all the carrots, oats or apples or whatever Clifford can rustle up when we get to Hennelly Towers. Please!' After a snort, the mule surged forwards, making her trot to keep up.

'Lovely day for a stroll,' she called airily to the laughing faces around her. Drawing level with Clifford, she threw a hand out at his amused look. 'What now? I'm doing just fine, thank you.'

'Indeed you are, my lady. And how well you are taking it in your stride, albeit an enforced, lengthened and hurried one. It seems that you may have finally met your match in the' – he pointed at the mule – 'ahem, independent-spirited stakes.'

'Or stubborn, as you actually mean?'

At that moment, Sheeply gave the tractor's throttle an extra blip, and the Rolls pulled further ahead.

'I really couldn't say, my lady,' Clifford's amused tone wafted back to her.

By the time she reached the start of the rutted rise up to Hennelly Towers, the tail end of the Rolls was just clearing the top of it. Determined to keep her best foot forward, she took a deep breath, which only resulted in what felt like icy shards of cold air penetrating her lungs. It didn't help when Sheeply gave her a cheery wave on his return before she'd covered even the first quarter to the top of the rise.

Hot on the tractor's heels, however, was her ever-faithful butler, his long strides making short work of the distance. With his assistance, Mullaney was soon chomping on some straw in the stable, while Eleanor sprawled on the settee in the entrance hall. Still wrapped in all her bulky layers plus her hat and coat, it was probably the least elegant figure she'd cut in a while. Clifford, however, let it go with nothing more than a quiet tut to himself as he furnished her with a reviving cup of hot coffee. As he added a nip of warming brandy, she heaved herself up onto one elbow and took a grateful sip.

'Did Corcoran help with storing the Rolls away somewhere safe?'

He pursed his lips. 'Regrettably not as he has yet to appear since first thing this morn—'

He stopped at the sharp rat-a-tat-tat on the large brass ring on the other side of the oak front door.

'Ah, Corcoran,' he said stiffly, on opening it. A streak of ginger shot past him and skittered over to jump up beside Gladstone. 'And Master Tomkins, it would seem.'

'Sheeply saw you right then, Mr Clifford,' Corcoran said chirpily. 'And Mullaney behaved himself, it seems.' He shrugged. 'It's a rare enough day you'll see that often times.'

Clifford nodded. 'Yes to both.' Then, with a sideways glance to catch Eleanor's eye, he added, 'Albeit, after a fashion, where the latter was concerned.'

Corcoran grinned. 'Ah, there's a knack to most things, so there is. Well, I just thought to check if there is anything her ladyship is needing?'

'No. That will be all, Corcoran.'

'Actually,' she called, rolling onto her stomach to try and disentangle herself from Gladstone and the now loudly purring ginger tom, 'there is one thing.'

The old retainer's eyes crinkled with humour as he watched her struggle upright, tugging her coat belt out from the bulldog's bulky form. She paused, momentarily forgetting he wouldn't step across the threshold to her. When he didn't, she hauled herself over to him. 'Corcoran, you must know the history of almost everyone and everything in the area, yes?'

His chest puffed. 'Ah, m'lady is too kind. But I'm not one for gossip.'

'Of course not,' she said, unconvinced. 'However, what I'm curious about is Ballykieran Abbey.'

He rolled his eyes. 'Sure, I've never set foot in the place. Like all the normal menfolk since Benedictine time began up there, we wouldn't get so much as a toe over the doorstep.'

'It's always been a female order, then? Just nuns?'

'Right ye be on that score, m'lady. Only the priest they allow in when needs be.'

'But what about before the nuns took it over? The family it was built for. Did you know of them?'

He shook his head, which made his remaining forelock of white hair swing back and forth. 'That'd be even before my time. I'm not as ancient as the wise-old hundred-and-twenty I look.' She had to hide a smile as he managed four steps of an exuberant jig before he caught Clifford's firm stare. 'All I know, m'lady,' he continued contritely, 'is that it was a very wealthy fella who wanted his family to live in the luxury of a fairy tale that had it built. But then he up and left it all to the Benedictine sisters on his deathbed.'

She nodded. 'That's what I heard. But after going to all that trouble and expense and then not leaving it to anyone in his family? That's curious, isn't it?'

He opened his mouth as if to contradict her, but slid his eyes right to Clifford first. On receiving a nod, the old retainer spoke up. 'It'll be on account of the deviousness, m'lady. Oh, it's fiercest in their kind, alright.'

She frowned. 'Whose kind?'

'Why, the nuns, of course,' he whispered at a volume far louder than if he had continued speaking normally. 'Them nuns have devious down to an art. For sure, they got themselves a palace in Ballykieran when the man who owned it was at his weakest. On his deathbed!' He tapped his nose. 'All I'm saying, m'lady, is that there's praying.' He put his hands together reverently, and then pounced forward like a tiger. 'And then there's *preying!*'

Eleanor was still musing over Corcoran's words as she wound her way upstairs with the oil lamp. She needed to change for the funeral of the very man who had caused her to first visit the abbey. The man they hadn't managed to save. That thought pulled her up in sad reverie on the landing beside the arched alcove as Gladstone and Tomkins joined her. She sighed, her breath frosting the window. Tomkins let out a soft mew and rubbed himself back and forth between his new bulldog friend and the hand she offered.

'Hello, chaps. It's very cute to see you're such firm friends already.' She sighed again and turned to rub her sleeve over the misted-up window, knocking over an old brass cigarette lighter on the small shelf below. She set it upright again and noticed for the first time that the majority of the window's tiny panes were of coloured glass. 'No wonder one needs to carry a lantern everywhere,' she said to her two furry companions. 'This stained glass doesn't let in much light. It's pretty though. Rather like the only original one left at the abbey, if I have any memory for patterns. Which I probably don't.' She frowned again. 'Isn't that...?'

Before she could look any closer, her butler's silent form appeared halfway along the corridor to her room, a solemn grey shirt having replaced his customary white one. In his hand, he held his pocket watch.

'My lady, forgive my interrupting whatever is occupying your thoughts...'

'Mostly our poor friend.'

'As I suspected,' he said gently. 'However, we need to factor in our reduced rate of travel to the church if we are not to arrive too late for our adieu to accompany him to his final resting place.'

She nodded. 'I know. And we were just in the village, but we could hardly ask Sheeply to leave the Rolls there. We had to get it back here first.' A thought struck her. 'Oh gracious. I only came thinking of Christmas, Clifford. I didn't ask Mrs Butters to pack anything suitable for a funeral.'

'Underneath the silk compression compartment in the smallest of your three cases, my lady.' He bowed at her questioning look. 'Call it sombre experience again that prompted my instruction to your housekeeper to pack some less... festive clothing at this,' he finished with a sigh, 'most festive of times!'

16

Eleanor shook her head in bewilderment as Clifford brought their jaunting car to a halt. 'Gracious, Clifford! We're miles early for the funeral, surely?' Hindered by her thick gloves and Gladstone balanced on her lap, Eleanor fumbled under the black lace overlay of her matching velvet dress for her late uncle's pocket watch.

Scanning her cherry-red nose and shoulders hunched against the biting cold, he said, 'Forgive me, my lady. I thought you might at least enjoy a fortifying plate of something hot and comforting before you attended the funeral.'

She smiled. 'Which is why you deviously chivvied me to get ready so swiftly, isn't it? Not because Mullaney could be unpredictable, as you suggested.'

He nodded.

'You old softie. Thank you.' The uncommon clatter of an engine made her crane her neck around. 'Clifford!' she hissed, spinning back. 'Look!'

'Hmm. Doctor O'Sullivan's motor vehicle.'

The car passed them and turned into the rear of the pub. A moment later the sound of a car door closing reached them, but the occupant didn't pass their cart to enter by the main entrance.

'Quite a jaunt from Kiltyross where the Mother Superior insisted he lives to partake of a nip of Guinness and a bite to eat?' Clifford's tone was sceptical.

'Well, I doubt he's here to make a house call.'

Nodding in unison, they both climbed down and hurried after Gladstone, who immediately headed around to the snug's entrance.

Inside, the snug was empty but the main pub was packed. Through the open hatch, she could see four occupied tables, the rest being hidden from her. The occupants of the first couple were engaged in a fiendish round of either cards or backgammon, while she had no idea what was being played on the remaining two.

'The board of three concentric squares with several sets of different coloured buttons in place of counters is "Nine Men's Morris", my lady,' Clifford said. 'And the significantly reduced chessboard is, in fact, "Ficheal" or "Fidchell", a game of ancient Celtic derivation.'

'Fascinating. And the ring board, or whatever it's called at the end there, seems very intense.'

Kathleen appeared with a bright-eyed smile. 'I saw you hurrying in, so I've set a couple of pies to heat. A proper treat today. Shin and stout they are. And here's a Guinness each to be going on with.'

'How well you read our minds, Kathleen.' He shrugged out of his coat, folded it precisely so over the arm of his chair, and reached for their drinks as the barmaid left.

'Mmm, delicious.' Eleanor sipped hers quietly, one ear straining for chatter filtering in from the larger, out-of-bounds bar. 'You know, it's just struck me. Everyone saw us parading through the village and yet no one has asked us a thing. In most rural villages, news travels like lightning.'

'By which you mean gossip is as hungrily sought as hard currency?'

'Spot on. We shouldn't be able to move for being pestered by a queue of locals desperate to hear our first-hand account of what happened with the Rolls and why we needed a tow.'

'Indeed. I had the same thought. Mr Walsh, or "Sheeply" as he prefers, made no reference to why the Rolls needed towing either. And we have had the same unexpected reticence concerning us finding the gentleman in the road.'

A few moments later Kathleen appeared again at the hatch with their steaming plates of delectable-smelling lunch. She waved a woven basket. 'Jars of chutney to go with your pies.'

'Perfect, thank you.'

They both tucked in, Gladstone being treated to his own portion under the table. After a moment's chewing, Eleanor swallowed. 'Given that I'm sure Murphy can't afford top quality meat, the beef is surprisingly tender under this savoury mustard potato crust.' She took another mouthful. 'And there's parsnips. And, I think, that's mushroom. All in the richest gravy.'

As she held up two of the chutney jars from the basket to the oil light beside her, Clifford gave a disapproving sniff.

'There is nothing more dangerous inside than redcurrant, greengage and plum, I assure you, my lady.'

'It's not more tasting notes I'm interested in, actually, Mr Sniffy. The reason I was compelled to stare at these jars is the colours of the chutney up against the light. They reminded me of something, especially the red and the green.' She looked again. 'That's it!' Hushed by the discreet flap of his hand, she whispered, 'The stained-glass window at the abbey had a signature below the coat of arms. There's one rather similar, if not the same, at Hennelly Towers. On the landing in the alcove.'

'Possibly the same builders were employed for Hennelly Towers and the building which is now Ballykieran Abbey.'

'But the abbey seems somehow more modern even though it's overlain with the time-immemorial feel of a religious order.'

'Yet the dates of construction I would wager are no more than twenty-five years apart, given the similarity of several architectural features such as—'

She raised a hand. 'You can fascinate me with all that later when we're back at Hennelly Towers, I promise. Do Irish builders usually leave their signature, though?'

'Perhaps the more pertinent question is, do stained-glass makers do so? I would be surprised for any master builder to have found time to become proficient in both skills.'

'Even here, where being a baker and a cobbler is normal?'

'Or a publican and an undertaker.'

As if on cue, Murphy's unusually anxious tone out in the main bar interrupted them.

'So, what do you think?'

They both strained their ears to hear who would respond.

'Have you discussed it with Doyle? And lower your voice, man!'

'Doctor O'Sullivan!' she mouthed.

Clifford nodded. Murphy's hissed reply filtered through to them.

'You know I haven't, Sullivan!'

'Well, either way, there's likely to be a couple more that'll need preparing down in your cellar if you don't get that idea out of your head! Another whiskey, and then I'll leave you to see sense.'

Murphy's reply was terse. 'You can't keep burying your problems, Sullivan.'

'Oh, can't I? Well, you're wrong.' The sound of a glass being banged on the bar made Eleanor wince. 'Because either you bury them or they'll bury you!'

. . .

A while later, out in the street, she turned to her butler. 'Yes. We can discuss what we heard later. For now, let's concentrate on the matter in hand. I really can't cope with the awful notion of this poor chap being buried with no one there to wish him farewell.'

'I know, my lady,' he said gently, passing her a spotless handkerchief. They continued in silence, arriving at the church-yard a few minutes later. They clambered down from the cart and Clifford slung the reins over a low-hanging branch.

'Best behaviour, Master Gladstone,' he said, tying a slim black band around the bulldog's collar. From somewhere hidden in the tiny cart, he slid out a beautiful wreath of woven yew, ferns and soft yellow and purple blooms tied at the top with an emerald-green velvet ribbon.

'Oh, Clifford, it's perfect,' she breathed as she took it gently.

'Wild celandines, speedwell, gorse and exceptionally late winter heliotrope. Although, no doubt, the local names are far more evocative. Shall we?'

They walked down the short, winding path to the church with its circular rose centrepiece window and low flint and limestone gabled porches on either side of the tiny arched red door.

Inside, the walls were whitewashed in parts, highlighting the uneven pattern of exposed wonky wood beams. Between each of the eight tall keyhole windows hung a tapestry, so vibrantly coloured she marvelled that they must have been woven yesterday. An enormous Bible lay open on the linen-covered table that seemed to serve as the pulpit.

'I believe the burial party may already be at the grave, my lady.'

They left the church and walked around to the back, where she scanned the graveyard.

'There's no one, Clifford. Except those three men standing

outside.' At his look, she gasped. 'Oh gracious! He isn't even going to be buried in the church grounds, is he?'

She hurried to the gate leading out beyond the graveyard. At her arrival, Father Quinn turned around, his white surplus fanning out behind him. The look on her face obviously betrayed her thoughts.

'With no next of kin, Lady Swift, and no one to vouch for a deceased's faith, it is tradition to bury them outside in unconsecrated ground. However, a pauper's burial does not rob a soul of their right to a Requiem Mass.' Taking in the wreath she held and their joint funeral attire, he beckoned them forward. 'If you have come to pay your respects for whatever reason makes sense to you, hurry hither that we might begin.'

The two men in rough overalls she took to be the gravediggers shared a look before stepping back and leaning on their spade handles.

At the edge of the roughly cut hole in the overgrown meadow of snow-covered soft-speared grasses, she pulled down the black lace veil of her silk hat and stared down at the simple pine box. The steel plate pinned to the front bore only one line of a Latin inscription, no name, no tribute and no date of birth.

'May rest be peaceful and eternal. If God wills,' Clifford translated in a reverent whisper.

Gladstone let out a low whine and nuzzled her leg. She bowed her head, sliding the wreath's ribbon over her wrist so she could put her hands together, willing the hot prick of tears not to release into a stream. Immensely grateful that Clifford was standing closer than he would normally countenance, she silently offered her own jumbled words for the man whose name she didn't even know. After a beat, she glanced up at Father Quinn as, despite his apparent impatience to begin, he still hadn't started. Instead, he was staring between her and the grave. With a deep breath, he flipped open the black-covered book in his hands. '*Requiem aeternam dona eis Domine...*' The rest of his sombre words spilled out into the frosty air until, without pause, he switched to English. 'Unknown, unnamed, and unbowed to the end. We send you onwards with the blessing of strangers. Amen.'

'Amen,' she chorused with Clifford. One of the gravediggers casually put his cigarette out on the flat of his spade, which, for some reason, saddened her more than the lack of mourners or hymns. She tuned in to the fact that Father Quinn appeared to be waiting for her. Clifford bent and scooped up a gloved handful of earth from the graveside mound and slid half into her palm. 'Sleep well,' she murmured through the tears that now fell as she sprinkled it along the length of the coffin. 'May you be with people who love you.'

They watched as the gravediggers filled in the grave with no more ceremony than if they were repairing a hole in the road. Then she laid the wreath.

'Beyond commendable, my lady,' Clifford said softly as he opened the gate through to the graveyard proper. But as she stepped through, a flash of orange off to the right caught her tear-streaked eye. It was the thinning ginger head of Constable Doyle. He was leaning with one arm on the roof of a grey vehicle, talking to whoever was sitting in the back but equally obscuring them at the same time.

'Parked so as to spectate on the funeral, would you say, Clifford?' she whispered, pretending to look elsewhere.

'Most assuredly, my lady,' he replied, staring forward. 'And I couldn't swear, but that car looks quite familiar.'

Eleanor glanced again, unfortunately just as Constable Doyle looked up. Catching her eye, he leaned in through the window before tapping the roof of the car, which quickly drove off. With a firm glare, he straddled his motorbike and disappeared in the opposite direction. She turned back to Clifford.

'I couldn't tell for sure, but it did look like the one at the cottage the two men got into.'

He nodded as they made their way to their cart. 'And as Corcoran informed us that only Doctor O'Sullivan has a car in this area...'

Father Quinn caught them up. 'I hope solace be yours now,' he said without slowing down.

'Father, one moment, if you will?' At his pause, she stepped around to stand in front of him. 'Thank you. Both for the service and for all you did in his final moments.'

He held his hands out. 'I am a priest. Both are my duty. And my privilege in serving our Lord.'

'I'm sure. How are you finding Derrydee after, what is it, six months?'

'Eight,' he said sharply. 'Now, there is work to be done. A duty to which I must return.' He went as if to leave, but his gaze strayed over her shoulder to the grave. A shadow crossed his face, the small black Bible's soft leather cover denting at the force of his grip. She went to speak, but he interrupted her.

'I'm sorry, but as I said, I have matters to attend to.'

He strode off towards the church. For a moment, she hesitated, and then set off after him. A man was dead, and not by God's hand, and she needed answers.

By the time she entered the church, there was no sign of the priest. She walked around the pews, thinking in two days they'd be back there at midnight listening to Christmas Eve Mass. At the back of the church an open door revealed a small anteroom. The priest's cassock and Bible lay on a chair.

She frowned. The cover of the Bible wasn't lying flat. There was something under it. Inquisitiveness got the better of her and she nipped in and flipped the cover up with one finger.

For a moment she just blinked. Then it fell into place. *That's what was different! When you found the man in the road and examined him for injuries, Ellie, he was wearing some sort of religious medallion – a St Christopher. But when you examined him in Murphy's cellar it had gone.*

Footsteps! She dropped the cover back and spun around.

Father Quinn stood behind her, glowering. Before he could speak, she held up a hand.

'Father, I know you believe in divine justice. Well, I believe in human justice just as strongly.'

His rich-timbred tone was harsh. 'What would it take for you to leave well alone, woman, and return to England?'

The anger in his voice momentarily surprised her. 'The truth. Nothing more.'

He shook his head. 'The truth is that I am a man busy striving to embody the vow I took and have no desire to preside over another funeral!'

He grabbed his cassock and Bible and strode past her. She followed him out and watched him go through the small gate at the end of the churchyard and down the lane.

There are secrets buried deeper than any grave in this seemingly quiet village, Ellie. Secrets someone is willing to kill to keep!

17

To Eleanor's mind, it was a hideously early morning walk out to the main road where Corcoran had told them they might catch a lift into Kiltyross, the nearest town. The ground was thick with a heavy frost, making it a struggle to even stay upright in patches. And even more of a struggle to run as the lorry careered past them, coming to a stop several hundred yards from the turning to Derrydee.

Ignoring any ladylike pretence, she grabbed the fur trim of her sage calf-length coat and broke into a sprint.

'We can't miss it. Corcoran said there's only one a day!'

'I say! Wait up, man!' Clifford hollered through cupped hands, his frosted breath pluming out in front of him like a steam pipe. Scooping a bemused Gladstone under his arm, he lengthened his stride and swiftly caught her up without losing an inch of the impeccably elegant figure he always cut.

Eleanor, on the other hand, had abandoned elegance altogether as her woollen scarf flew out behind her and her hair flapped across her eyes. Ahead, a straggle of villagers with sacks and parcels scrambled into the open-back lorry, followed by a small farm's worth of poultry. A horrendous clatter of metal devouring metal signalled the driver was pulling away.

'Two more for Kiltyross!' Clifford hailed, as he disappeared in a cloud of oily fumes. He doffed his bowler hat at the comely sixty-ish woman swathed in a brown wool shawl hammering on the thin metal partition of the cab to halt the driver.

'Ah, too kind, madam.'

The lorry lurched to a stop, and a moment later Clifford stepped back from the driver's window and re-pocketed his wallet.

The woman in the brown shawl patted the seat beside her with a glint in her lively blue eyes. 'Don't be after minding the hissing from me goose. Plenty room aside me here.'

'After you,' Eleanor said, barely stifling her laughter at her butler's horror. Two sinewy young men in worn grey trousers that flapped above their ankles both jumped down. Adroitly forming a brace with their forearms, the tallest shrugged good-naturedly at Clifford.

'A step for the lady, seeing as you'll be busy chasing after her fancy bonnet.'

Eleanor groaned at the sight of her favourite velvet tam-o'shanter tumbling back down the road in the icy breeze. Hat retrieved, the lorry graunched its way onwards towards Kiltyross.

Fascinated as she was by her fellow passengers, the slow, bumpy journey past fields peppered with more squat brown sheep and tracts of oily-looking peat bog dotted with scrubby bushes passed her by. While gripping tightly to the lorry side as it wallowed in and out of various potholes, she looked around, imagining the stories the villagers in front of her could tell. The men were dressed in patterned homespun jumpers, mismatched trousers and patched jackets, while the women wore wool shawls and several layers of skirts against the cold. The sacks she'd seen loaded were full of militant-looking, earth-covered vegetables, large jars of pickles, eggs nestled in cloths and the odd dried ham. The veritable farm that also accompanied them consisted of ducks and chickens clucking and squawking in competition with the hissing of the one solitary goose.

A middle-aged man balancing a crate of buff-brown hens on his lap nodded at them. 'How's Ireland treating you?' He popped one of the mint humbugs Clifford had handed around into his mouth.

'Like absolute royalty,' Eleanor gasped as she was smacked back down onto her hard wooden perch as the lorry bounced in and out of the deepest pothole yet. She grimaced. 'Although royalty whose rear parts aren't quite sufficiently padded to withstand bumps like that.'

The whole wagon roared with laughter, except for her butler, who closed his eyes while shaking his head in despair.

Half an hour later, Kiltyross hove into view. Despite the discomfort, she was disappointed the journey was over as she was enjoying chatting with the villagers. Clifford, however, couldn't disembark quickly enough. Nimbly swinging himself off the lorry, he lifted Gladstone off the tailgate and threw her a beseeching look. Mystified, she took the hand he offered and jumped down beside him, waving a reluctant farewell to the villagers.

'What's the hurry?' she whispered.

'I'll save you the seat aside me for the way back, Mr Clifford!' the comely woman called over the lorry's side.

'Ah!' Eleanor hid a smile. 'Tsk, tsk, Clifford. Leading the poor lady on like that. It's your own fault, you know. Stepping out everywhere, looking far too distinguished and handsome for your own good. Can't you tone it down a bit?'

He steepled his gloved hands over his nose and shuddered. 'I believe we have a matter to attend to, my lady?'

Kiltyross turned out to be a single snaking main street of terraced stone houses and narrow-fronted shops. Displays of goods were strung outside every flaking shop window. White, grey and pink linen, knitwear, aprons and overalls hung beside rows of pigs' trotters, ears, belly strips, mutton, necks and shanks. Interspersed were signs promising cow-tails and tongues would soon be in stock. But what really made her breath catch were the long swags of moss-green dyed hessian, festooned with lace ribbon bows, twists of red-berry holly and crowns of dried crab apples. Spanning the top of every shop front on either side of the street, the overall effect of endless winter festive bunting kindled her never-lost childhood love of Christmas.

To her frost-cheeked delight, inside, the shopkeepers hadn't forgotten Christmas either. Lit candles, crocheted angels and whittled nativity figurines adorned the counters, while wreaths of intricately knotted reeds bejewelled with clusters of dried rosy-red rowan berries and snow-white guelder rose flowers decorated the walls. In the more upmarket establishments, goose feather snowflakes and stars twirled down from the ceilings. They mesmerised Gladstone, who spun beneath them in wobbly circles, his tongue lolling excitedly.

Having bought him a knuckle bone as a Christmas morning treat in the butcher's, she emerged back onto the high street.

'Clifford, isn't this all just too magical?'

'Indeed, my lady. The Irish appear to be as relentlessly resourceful as they are admirably jocund, however, ahem...' He arched a brow.

'Yes, yes, we need to find the garage to sort out the cable things for the Rolls, I know.' She shrugged. 'It almost seems a shame, though. To go back to the Rolls, I mean, wonderful vehicle though it is. Jaunting about with you in our ridiculous little cart behind Mullaney and catching a lift in that lorry with the locals has been surprisingly...' She paused, searching for the right word.

'Unladylike?' he teased. 'Uncomfortable? Undignified?' At her amused huff, he held up his hands. 'Perhaps delightfully unconventional for a lady whose heart skips at the mere whisper of the word "adventure"?'

She nodded. 'Insidiously bewitching, if you must know.'

His brow furrowed. 'Mmm. And yet, once again, it was noticeable that not one of the villagers asked why we were going to the main town?'

She pursed her lips. 'Or shared any gossip about the events of the last few days. It's like they're all colluding together.'

'Or are too scared to ask?'

She shook her head. 'I still haven't got over finding that Father Quinn has our poor dead friend's St Christopher medallion. Why would he have taken it?'

'Assuming it was the same medallion. It is a very common one, being the patron saint of travellers – and children. Many people wear such a medallion.'

'True. But the chain it hung on was very distinctive. And, if it wasn't, why was Father Quinn so angry?'

'Perhaps, my lady, because you were "snooping about" in the church?'

She shrugged. 'Fair point. But Murphy swore that he hadn't taken anything off the body in his cellar. Which means, if he was telling the truth, that someone must have removed the medallion from the body before it was brought to the pub. And as it was brought straight from the abbey as far as we know—'

'It must have been removed there.'

'Yes! By Father Quinn, I'll warrant! Anyway,' she said, looking around, 'we can't do anything about it at the moment and we have a garage to find.'

It took several futile attempts to locate the place Corcoran had mentioned for the shilling to drop. Stepping past another huddle of donkeys, bicycles and carts, she gestured around them.

'There are so few cars or vehicles here, Clifford, wherever

this chap's workshop is, it isn't going to be in the high street, is it?'

'Now I reflect upon it, most likely not, my lady.'

The lanky streak of a youth who had been following them in amazement for the last few minutes raked off his cap and swung down a cloth sling tied to a stout hazel rod. Through prominent front teeth and a pronounced stutter, he said, 'Y-y-you'll be a-a-fter Wrenchman, is it?'

'Does he fix motor vehicles?' Clifford said.

'N-n-no, not him.'

Clifford frowned. 'Then he is of no use to us.'

The young man shook his head. 'H-h-he don't r-r-repair 'em, b-b-but he b-b-builds them better than n-n-n-ew! I'll t-t-take you for a g-g-go of your little f-f-friend there.'

Relieved payment appeared to be nothing more than patting Gladstone and ruffling his coat, they followed the youth down a side street. The bulldog, having loved the attention, strained on his lead to walk next to his new best friend.

'Talk about fickle affections!' Eleanor whispered to Clifford.

'Indeed. However, I imagine Master Gladstone will switch his loyalty back to us on learning that the young man's bindle contains only tired-looking vegetables. Which, I suspect, has none of the allure of the disgraceful array of Christmas treats you have purchased for Master Greedy.'

'Bindle? Oh, his little bag on a stick. I didn't realise.' She peeped up at her butler. 'How I would love to spend a day in your observant brain. Well, at least until your maddening methodicalness and irritating exactitude drove me to escape screaming.'

A few minutes later, after trailing their guide down a rough track between two pubs, they arrived at an open-fronted workshop. With its dirt floor, huddle of metal pails filled with feculent black oil and old tools on a dented bench, it certainly didn't have the air of a garage that dealt with luxury cars. Clifford nudged her away from the half-dismantled engine she hadn't spotted hanging from a fraying rope looped over the central roof joist just above her head.

'Chin up, Clifford,' she said. 'Maybe it's better equipped than it looks.'

'Perhaps, my lady.' He reached for his wallet and dropped several coins into the waiting youth's hand.

'C-c-cor! It m-m-must be Christmas.' He doffed his cap to both of them and yelled, 'W-w-w-renchman! Shop!' before giving Gladstone one last pat and disappearing back up the path.

Left alone, they both looked about the deserted workshop again. A noise outside caught her attention. She peered out at the bushes. *Is there someone there watching us, Ellie?*

Before she could check, a door at the rear of the workshop screeched open. She spun around to see a sinister stooping figure silhouetted in the light shuffling towards them...

18

The figure that emerged from the door actually turned out to be a rather unthreatening man in his early fifties. As wide as he was tall, swamped in ragged blue, oil-streaked overalls, he was a good seven or eight inches shorter than Eleanor. Peering up at them through bottle-bottom spectacles, he blinked and then shrugged.

'Morning be, folks, welcome whoever you are. Though, I can't say as there's anything leaping out from me toolbox' – he tapped his forehead – 'as to how I could help fancy types as scrubbed as you?'

Eleanor let out the breath she'd been holding and glanced towards the bushes. But if someone had been there, they'd gone now. She mentally shook her head. *Probably nothing.* She turned her attention back to the man in front of her.

'Good morning, Mr, er, Wrenchman?'

The man cocked his head. 'Young tike! Flannery's me name. And what could the likes of you be needing off me garage?'

Clifford stepped forward. 'Our requirements, Mr Flannery, are quite simple, being merely a set of ignition leads for a Rolls Royce Silver Ghost. The year of manufacture being 1909.'

Flannery snorted so loudly he rocked on his heels. 'Do I look like a monkey's cousin to you? Be off with your tall tales. You'll see one of them engineered beauties in these parts when the peat turns to gold. Until then, I've work to do.'

He swished them towards the door, but Eleanor stood firm. 'Look, Mr, er, Flannery, we really do need the cables. The car was my uncle's, Lord Henley. He left it to me along with the House of Towers over in Derrydee. Perhaps you've heard of the place?'

Flannery whistled and looked at her with fresh eyes. 'Even those born with no ears has heard of it, miss. I mean, ma'am.' Switching to appraising Clifford, he ran a black-fingernailed hand over his jaw. 'So, maybe the peat *has* turned to gold?' He tapped his chin. 'And what if I could get them leads, mister?'

Clifford withdrew his wallet. 'Then, as well as payment, naturally, it would be her ladyship's delight to allow me to drive the Rolls over here and introduce you to the motor's breathtakingly intricate design. Once it is in running order, of course.'

Flannery's eyes lit up. With his fingers drumming his chin, he looked past both of them. 'I'll have to talk nice to the reverend, mind.' He nodded to himself. 'Wait here, folks. Pull up a bucket to perch on.' He scurried off, only to trip over Gladstone. Righting himself, he patted the disgruntled bulldog and disappeared down the road.

Eleanor shook her head. 'Fancy the vicar having a Rolls Royce? I mean—'

'I suspect not, my lady.'

'Then what did he...' She tailed off as her butler mimed making a telephone call. 'Ah! Not a Rolls, but one of the few telephones in the town, I see.'

Feeling quite the blunt brick, she tried to muster some patience while awaiting the return of the Wrenchman, or Flannery as he seemed to prefer to be called. Thankfully, she didn't have to wait long. But when he did return, her joy was short-lived.

'A week minimum? Surely not?'

''Fraid so, ma'am. They needs be shipped from the Manchester works, you see.'

She grimaced. 'And I suppose it *is* Christmas.'

Flannery nodded at Clifford's wallet.

'Ah yes, a deposit, naturally.' Clifford passed him several notes. 'Until next week then. Thank you.'

Having left the garage, they retraced their steps and, even with Gladstone eagerly sniffing everything in his path, were soon back in the town proper. Eleanor stopped and turned to Clifford.

'Don't worry about the Rolls. And I'm not saying that flippantly because I fully appreciate all the love and expert care you've lavished on her for Uncle Byron and, subsequently, for me. It's just that someone, or something, always turns up trumps. Even in the Himalayas, when the frame of my bicycle simply split in two with all the rough going, a knight in shining armour arrived. Well, yak skins and striped blankets, actually. The point is, he saved the day by fashioning a lasting repair for my broken frame. Flannery will secure those cables, I'm sure.'

He bowed. 'Despondency suitably admonished from my thoughts, my lady. Now, if you are able to steer your own thoughts away from luncheon for a moment longer?' He pulled out the key they had discovered in the dead man's heel and gestured with it down a passageway barely wider than his shoulders. 'I made enquiries as to the presence or otherwise of a locksmith whilst you were engaged in shopping.'

'Top-notch, Clifford. Sufficiently so, that I shall overlook your thinly veiled dig that my mind is usually fixated on food. So, lead the way and let's find out what that key fits!'

But on arriving at the tiny brick-fronted enclosure that served as the locksmith's shop, all was in darkness. She pressed her face to the small oval of glass in a loose collection of wood masquerading as a door. 'Dash it! He's gone for lunch himself.' She tutted. 'Well, I suppose we'd better follow suit.'

A moment later, her frustration lifted as they turned into a bustling square.

'A market, Clifford!' She stared at the colourful squares of cloth on the ground, each covered with a display of home-grown vegetables or homespun clothing. She recognised some of the goods –and sellers – from the truck. Men and women, laden with bags and baskets, surged around the sellers, while donkeys with their carts stood patiently waiting. The busy scene rang with the clamour of sellers and customers as they haggled over the price of the goods on offer.

'For sure. Where else are folks to sell enough to buy a few Christmas spoils, miss?' a chirpy Irish lilt called.

The explanation came from a gaunt-faced, unshaven middle-aged man. He whispered something in Clifford's ear.

Her butler flinched. 'A little racy for our milder tastes, but thank you.'

As the man melted into the crowd, Clifford shook his head at her questioning look. 'He was trying to sell us some "poitín", my lady. An alcoholic concoction made from a mash of chiefly barley and potatoes, together with whatever else is to hand, including bark on occasion. It has been illegal to distil it since the introduction of taxation on alcohol in 1661. Invariably, it is a lethal brew of up to ninety per cent proof. To my mind, useful only if one has a life-threatening wound to disinfect.'

'Well, thank you for gallantly saving my head from the morning after. Now, we need to take some provisions to the Christmas celebrations in the village hall, naturally. And surely we could buy something to add to our meagre festive provisions so far for this evening?'

He eyed her sideways. 'Purely in the name of supporting the local economy, of course?'

'Of course.' Smiling at each of the now extra eager sellers eyeing their smart clothes, she pointed along the first line. 'Proper butter. And just look at that cheese! Fresh bread rolls too. And we positively must have some of those little jars of relish. What do you say?' She spun back around to find her butler, however, was looking uncharacteristically furtive, his bowler hat pulled down over his face, collar turned up.

'What are you doing?' she hissed.

He gestured to a small flurry of tables outside a bakery in the far corner of the square. 'Given our reduced timeframe, perhaps we should partake of luncheon first? That café looks eminently suitable.' His eyes darted back over his shoulder at the row of poultry sellers behind them.

'Ah!' She laughed, and then lowered her voice. 'And a sufficiently safe distance from your female admirer with the goose you were flirting with in the truck, eh?'

Before he could refute her remark, she was halfway to the café. Once there, Gladstone woofed an exuberant agreement as she ordered a plate of the golden brown, hand-crimped pastries the couple at the nearby table were enjoying. Clifford's eyes followed the young, waif-like waitress back into the café, nodding in approval at her pristine white apron.

'Hot they be, like the tea,' the waitress said on her return with a tinkling laugh. 'Mind your tongue or you'll be panting harder than your darling hound there.'

'Ooh, too divine, Clifford!' Eleanor puffed through her admittedly far-too-hot mouthful. 'Potatoes and onions with a herb I don't recognise, all in a sort of solid but beautifully rich beefy-tasting gravy.' She reached for the cup of milkless, barely yellow liquid that passed for tea and took a gulp. 'The tea's delicious too, if a bit odd. Smells like rosemary and it's slightly bitter and sweet at the same time.'

He discreetly peered at the couple at the next table under

the guise of sniffing his own cup. '"Heart-of-the-earth". Or "self-heal", my lady.'

'Oh, come on, Clifford.' She waved her half-eaten pastry at his still untouched plate. 'A hearty snack won't hurt you just for once.'

'A hearty appetite may indeed be *key*, my lady.' He jerked his head towards the couple's table.

She glanced over and gasped. 'Crumbs! You clever bean!'

Between the plates on the opposite table lay a small key, identical to the one they had found hidden in the heel of the stranger's shoe.

'Perhaps this might be yours?' Clifford appeared at the surprised man's elbow, holding out a tattered coin purse, his eyes flicking over the fob attached to the key.

'Oh, you clumsy lunkhead!' the woman cried, slapping the man's hand hard enough to leave a mark. 'We saved for ages for our one night away. Some treat it would have been with you throwing our last pennies away in the street.' She turned to Clifford. 'Thank you, sir. For sure, it is too honest of you.'

With a bow, Clifford returned to Eleanor, who waved an admonishing finger at him as she whispered, 'Honest? Really? I'd say you have the expert sleight of the most scallywag of hands. Picking his pocket and then handing him his own purse as if he'd dropped it in the street. His wife will never let him hear the end of it.'

He looked suitably contrite. 'True, my lady. But on the other hand, we now know not only what our mysterious key opens – a hotel room door – but also which hotel!'

19

'Two Fires Hovel?' she said through frosted breath, gesturing for Clifford to walk alongside her rather than his usual respectful distance behind. 'What kind of name is that for a hotel?'

'Hobble, my lady. *Hob-ble.*'

Her nose wrinkled. 'Not much better. I wonder they get any customers. Why would they call it that?'

'I suspect the establishment is named such as a mark of respect to the thousands of tragic souls who passed this way. It was a hundred-and-thirty-mile trek from here up to Sligo on the more northerly west coast some seventy-seven years ago during the famine. Hence the "hobbling".'

'And two fires?'

'A reference to the equally fatal options of remaining to unquestionably starve or, in their already hopelessly weakened state, to almost certainly pass away aboard their supposed salvation – one of the over-packed and squalid ships bound for America. Disease abounded.'

'Oh, Clifford.' Her heart clenched, the lump in her throat stopping her from asking what was burning on her tongue.

'Yes, my lady,' he said softly. 'Rest assured, I will assist you in finding an appropriate way to provide something for the people of the area. At least for those of Derrydee.'

She nodded gratefully. 'Now I understand. That's why you asked the waitress in the café to look after my disgracefully outrageous shopping, wasn't it? Talk about the English princess lauding her entirely unearned privileges over everyone's heart-breaking history.'

'In truth, I left it in part for that reason, as I feared guilt would otherwise be your companion. Unfounded, if I might add, as the Ireland of now is more wealthy – and independent – than then. But I also did so in part because experience tells me a swift, unencumbered exit from the hotel may be required. Ah! Speaking of which, here we are.'

In front of them, the part-brick, part-stone building struck her as having been built as a low barn, which someone had then confusingly tacked a chapel onto the back of. A sloping door of washed-out green was flanked on either side by frosted glass, which ran up to the blackened thatch of the roof. The rear of the hotel, however, was covered with mossy grey slate and sported a tiny central bell tower. The age-old walls were peppered with a sprinkling of church-like arches, half now glassed-in, the others boarded over. Despite the door being a good two feet above the height of the road, there were no steps, merely a wooden post to heave oneself up with.

Eleanor shook her head. 'Just when I thought Ireland couldn't get any more surprising. This is the most unusual hotel I've ever seen.'

'Shelter does appear to have been offered in a variety of forms over the years, my lady.' He stared up at the building. 'Hmm, a far more guileful ruse will be required than I had anticipated to gain entrance and search the corridors to find which room the key might unlock.'

'Right!' She mimed rolling her sleeves up. 'I've a plan.'

He eyed her with trepidation. 'I must ask if you are suggesting I take second fiddle in the orchestration of this perturbingly unrehearsed investigative minuet?'

She laughed. 'Nicely put. And, yes, I am. So, you follow my lead. Ready?' She grabbed the wooden post to swing herself upwards.

'Not in the wildest stretch of even a lady's imagination,' he murmured. Nevertheless, he picked up Gladstone and followed suit.

'Whatever must you think? It's terribly embarrassing.'

The scarlet-faced manager mopped his brow with the hand-kerchief he'd pulled from his striped burgundy-and-blue waistcoat.

'For sure, miss. But these things can let go on any of us without warning. Evidently, even those of, umm, fancy ladies it seems.' He coughed awkwardly and hastily looked away. 'Not that I've stumbled over a lady having your, umm... difficulty though in fifteen years of running the place.'

He continued hurrying her down the long and gloomy corridor from the reception desk, which also appeared to be the hotel's bar. Beside him, she made a great show of holding her skirt tightly to one side.

'Oh, it's not the first time I've had to make an unprecedented stop because of such a... mortifying predicament. It must be that the lace is too delicate or some such. Poor fellow.' She gestured at her butler trailing behind them in horrified silence, Gladstone's lead hanging from one wrist as his hands strayed to his ears to blot out her words. 'He's had to play guardian several times outside a hotel room door whilst I mend my—'

'Up there, miss!' the manager squeaked. 'Number seven is empty just now, as it's been all week. And it's safest on account of there being no window to speak of.' He pointed up an uncarpeted set of worn stairs, flanked on one side by peeling, over-busy floral wallpaper and on the other by a handrail missing several spindles.

'So kind. And so gentlemanly of you to spare my blushes in letting me find the way, thank you.' She held a handkerchief to her lips. 'Are any of your guests in, though? I'd hate to have to explain to anyone else why I'm here.'

The manager shook his head vigorously. 'No, you're alright on that score, miss. Everyone left after their tea and egg this morning.'

'Very reassuring, thank you. I'll be down in a trice with news that all is mended.'

'Then I'll be in the cellar!' he mumbled and shot off back the way they'd come.

'Oh, do stop fretting about a lady's precious reputation, Clifford,' she whispered as they rounded the corner at the top of the stairs.

He sighed. 'How can I fret over something that is entirely in absentia, presumed lost forever?'

'Much like the manager imagines my underthings are as good as.' She smiled apologetically. 'Sorry, my ever-chivalrous-knight, but it was all I could think of on the spot. It worked though, didn't it? We're in and upstairs with a few minutes to play for. After all, he's not going to come knocking to help me with the little sewing kit he believes I carry in my handbag, is he?'

Clifford busied himself unnecessarily adjusting Gladstone's collar. The bulldog, however, shook himself free and scampered ahead, clearly thinking this a tremendous extra adventure in his already exciting day. His nails clattered against the scratched wooden floorboards, except when they scrabbled on a thread-bare, frayed rug that then shot out behind him.

Eleanor blinked hard, trying to adjust her eyes to the gloomy light on the landing. She could make out ten – no, eleven – doors, the nearest bearing a shakily hand-painted '2'. 'Well, we know our poor tragic friend wasn't staying in number seven if it's been empty all week.'

'And the couple in the market square are occupying room four as it was marked on their fob,' Clifford said, having momentarily subdued her panting bulldog.

'With those discounted, then, what would appease your unwavering sense of order most? Starting with the evens, or' – she waved a hand left – 'the odds?'

'Singularly, on this occasion, my lady' – he whipped out the key they had retrieved from the dead man's heel – 'neither. Let's just start with the nearest.'

'No success here,' he whispered a minute later, checking over his shoulder before stepping gingerly across to the opposite side, even his delicate tread drawing creaks of betrayal from the bowed flooring.

She bit her lip as she stood up from peeping through one more keyhole. 'That woman in the square said they'd saved for ages to have a night away here, but the rooms are terribly basic. Just an iron-framed bed, a bedside table, plain wash jug and bowl and a wardrobe so meagre I wouldn't get even a quarter of a case's worth of things in there.'

'But each has a chair. Plus, there are curtains, of a fashion.'

'If they have a window to hang them over, which half of them haven't. Mind you, some have wallpaper on at least some of the walls. I guess those are considered the luxury rooms.'

He paused in trying the key in the next lock. 'My lady, perhaps focus on the matter in hand?'

'Yes, yes,' she said, still feeling bad for having so much when others had so little. 'You're right. Hurry up and stay focused, I hear you. If we do find the room—'

'*When*.' He straightened up. 'If you will forgive the correction.' He turned the handle, both of them wincing at the groan it let out.

'Well done! Come on, we'll be in and out in a trice.'

He arched a brow. '*We?* My lady, you distinctly told the manager I would be waiting outside.' His lips pursed. 'The only even vaguely decorous sentence in the entire discourse.'

'I did. But how is that going to help if someone comes and you're standing outside number seven where I'm supposed to be mending my...' she caught his eye, 'my you-know-whats. Suppose they come barging into' – she glanced at the door – 'number eleven while I'm rooting through here?'

'An excellent point.' He gestured for her to lead the way, pressing a quieting finger to Gladstone's muzzle. 'However, my lady, if there is one more mention of your "you-know-whats", you will find me standing outside not the room, but the hotel!'

20

If the handle had creaked, the door hinges positively wailed.

'Dash it!' she said more loudly than intended as they hurried into the room.

Clifford pressed the door shut behind him, finger to his lips. 'If we might prioritise speed – and stealth – above all else?' He was clearly uncomfortable at being in the room with her, particularly given their supposed pretext for being in the hotel at all.

She glanced around. 'Well, I doubt it will take long. We're unlikely to miss anything. It's as bare as all the others I peered through the keyhole into.'

The room was indeed furnished with the absolute minimum. But being at the back of the hotel, it did have a window – an arched, church-like affair. It had been boarded up, but the boarding had rotted out in parts, allowing shards of grey December light to enter. Unhelpfully though, that, combined with the whitewashed stone walls, made it freezing. Clifford pressed a slim torch into her shivering hand, clicking his own on at the same time.

'Nothing in the drawers in the bedside table or washstand,'

she said a moment later, turning back from checking both. 'Just
the wardrobe and the bed then, I guess. Or we'll have to resort
to taking up the floorboards!' She tutted at Gladstone as he got
in the way a third time. 'At least try and use your nose, boy!
We're in a hurry.' But her urgent tone drew only a woof she
hurriedly silenced.

Clifford was already inspecting the skinny wool blanket,
and the faded pink sheet on the bed, each of which he held at
arm's length. He checked under the uncomfortably thin
mattress and then dropped to his haunches, sweeping his torch
under the bed.

'Nothing, my lady.'

'Over here!' she hissed.

In a single stride he was beside her, staring at the solitary
jacket hanging on the otherwise empty rail. He reached for it,
then froze at an aggrieved female voice in the corridor.

'Speed up or else, he said!'

Eleanor's eyes flew to the door handle, willing it not to turn.
She mentally thanked Clifford for having the presence of mind
to wrap a silencing hand gently around Gladstone's muzzle.

'With my knees so swollen as well!' the vociferous grumble
came again. Eleanor held her breath. 'And them the size of tree
trunks purely on account of having scrubbed his floors all these
fifteen years. Gratitude, my eye!'

The last words echoed from further down the corridor.
Eleanor breathed out.

'That was close!' she whispered.

Clifford nodded. 'Time for that swift' – he scooped a
bemused Gladstone under his arm – 'if not unencumbered,
exit.'

'But the coat!' she hissed. 'We haven't checked the pockets...
Oh my! Quick thinking.'

Opening the door a crack, he mouthed, 'Not gone, but
facing the other way.'

'Right,' she mouthed back, 'go!'

As they rounded the end of the corridor and started down the stairs, she heard the woman's voice again. But it was the voice that answered that stopped her in her stride. She darted a look at Clifford, who nodded vigorously, but pointed even more vehemently down the stairs. She hesitated for a moment, and then hurried after him.

In the back of the surprisingly empty lorry, Eleanor ruffled Gladstone's ears where he was sprawled on her lap, snoring loudly despite the endless bumps threatening to launch him onto the floor. She looked across to Clifford.

'At least we didn't miss our lift home.'

'But only by the skin of our teeth.' He pursed his lips. 'And only after a distressingly inelegant display of sprinting down the main street by a certain party.'

'Dashed exhilarating, though. And maybe just a little like the good old days, when you were entangled in all manner of invigorating antics with Uncle Byron?' She held his firm gaze, imitating his customary impassive expression. After a minute, he rolled his eyes.

'Touché, my lady.' His lips quirked. 'Perhaps it was. Though a great deal more swathed in impropriety.'

She shook her head. 'That I don't believe. Two dashing chaps like you two, with all manner of dubious skills, let loose in foreign lands on rafts of, no doubt, noble and vital missions. I'm not that green. But I shall endeavour to be more ladylike from here on in and to drag you into less uncomfortable situations.'

'Thank you, my lady.'

'Truce then?'

'Truce.'

'Good. Now,' she said, gesturing around the otherwise

empty back of the truck, 'I wonder how everyone else from this morning will get home to Derrydee?'

'Hmm, I trust it is not in a later vehicle and we risked twisted ankles and making a spectacle of ourselves for nothing.'

'Well, Corcoran seemed very certain this was the only one. He should know. He told us he's lived in the village since he was a boy. Gracious, probably in the same gatehouse, I assume. Anyway,' – she pointed to her butler's less-than-usually slim fitting black coat – 'with just us here, we can have a good old rifle through our poor deceased friend's pockets now, since you pulled the best ruse ever!'

This drew an arched brow. 'And the ladylike element within that image is...?'

'Says the scallywag who stole a dead man's coat by whipping it on under his own, which shockingly involved him disrobing in a closed room with his mistress present!'

At his quiet groan, she turned away to spare the last of his blushes. 'And I'd like to know what someone as smart as Doctor O'Sullivan was doing at that hotel! It was definitely his voice I heard. Not making house – or hotel – calls, that's for sure. Not on that floor. The manager told us all the guests had left after... what was it?'

'Tea and egg, my lady. And I concur. You may turn around, thank you.'

He held out what she could now see properly for the first time was a worn brown leather jacket with deep front pockets. The inside had no lining, just an extra flap on either side to create the pockets.

She slid her hand into the first pocket, and then the second. 'Nothing, as you must already know. Save for more of this, that is.' He held out his gloved palm, into which she dropped the small mats of lint her deeply rummaging fingers had collected.

He examined it closely. 'That certainly qualifies the jacket as our deceased gentleman's I would say, seeing as it is the same blue and white threads as you unearthed previously from his clothing.'

'While he was on Murphy's mortuary slab!' She shivered, turning the jacket in her hand. 'Actually, our poor dead friend must have worn this permanently buttoned up to the neck against the cold. Even your starched shirt collars aren't as stiff as this. Must have been very uncomfortable, I'd say.'

'I confess, in the heat of the moment and then with our hurried journey to catch the truck back to Derrydee, I failed to notice that.' Clifford's brows flinched. 'However, a gentleman's collar on a jacket as informally styled as this has no need of stiffening. Most uncommon.'

He produced his pocketknife and flicked out two of the slimmest blades.

'Oh, they make little scissors!'

She held the collar taut, hiding her impatience as he methodically cut the stitching.

'Paper?' He looked at her in puzzlement.

'Newspaper, in fact. I can see some print. And old. It's yellowed. Keep going.'

Despite her now growing itchiness to slash the last run of stitching herself, she let him maintain his careful pace of slow snipping until, finally, he slid out a section of newspaper, folded lengthwise several times.

'Most unexpected. Both it being hidden and folded with such precision to fit into the collar so as to be worn unnoticed by anyone less eager-eyed than yourself, my lady.'

She waved at it. 'Well, go on, unravel it!'

But even before he'd unfolded the paper halfway, he pressed it to his coat front, his face paling.

'Oh gracious,' she breathed, 'whatever is it about for you to look so worried?'

'It is not *what* it is about, my lady.' He swallowed hard. 'But *who*.' He shook his head at her outstretched hand.

'You'll have to show me sooner or later.' Reluctantly, he passed it over. 'Now,' she said, staring at the cutting, her brow furrowing, 'what is...?' She looked up in astonishment. 'Clifford! Why would a total stranger in another country have cut out a newspaper story about...' she glanced back down at the clipping, shaking her head, 'about *me*?'

21

A glorious fire blazed in the grate, the tiered stand of nibbles beside her smelled delectable, and the hot mulled wine let out tantalising wafts of spice and orange. The festive decorations they'd jointly made hung from every portrait and photograph on the walls, while Clifford had also quietly created a breathtaking shimmering star to span the long oak bureau. Crafted from meticulously stacked crystal whiskey glasses, each filled with a swirl of red berries swimming below a flickering, floating candle, it bathed the wall and ceiling in a warm glow. And on the opposite wall, a family of crocheted snow-white angels, which Eleanor had purchased from the wool shop in Kiltyross, cosied up to each other along the mantelpiece.

On the thick rose-coloured hearthrug, his soft round belly rising and falling with his deep snores, Gladstone was happily chasing dream rabbits. Tomkins was cuddled around his neck, purring contentedly, their whiskers intertwined.

And under the silver birch branches that improvised as a Christmas tree, exquisitely wrapped presents awaited. It should have been the perfect Christmas scene, but one thing was missing...

'Clifford?'

He arched an admonishing brow. 'Sitting with the mistress is not bending the rules, it is breaking them beyond all hope of repair.' As she went to argue, he waggled a white-gloved finger. 'It is, however, nothing compared to the ignominious transgression of joining her in a tipple and her favourite savoury treats into the disgraceful hours.' He sniffed. 'Which I fear she is also angling for.'

'Which is why, tomorrow, we shan't tell anyone that's how we spent the evening, I agree. Not even the staff back at Henley Hall.'

He shook his head, his lips quirking. 'How did I fail to notice his lordship's wily nine-year-old niece hiding in the Rolls when leaving England?'

She laughed. 'I really couldn't say, Clifford, but I'll definitely insist on an eye test for you when we return. Now, let's start with a toast. To Christmas in Ireland, no matter what.'

He raised his mulled wine. 'Amen to that.'

The clink of their glasses drew a snort from a half-roused Gladstone as he stretched his stiff legs out and then buried his face back against the softness of Tomkins' front paws.

'It is rather odd,' she mused aloud before she could stop her words flying out. 'I mean, we find a man unconscious on the very road to the house I've inherited here in remotest Ireland. It then turns out he has bought a newspaper years ago and cut out a clipping of me on my travels. And to top it all off, he's then hidden it in his clothes.'

Clifford put down his glass. 'If you are asking my opinion?' She nodded. 'Then, my lady, yes. But, in truth, far more so than I conjecture you are imagining.'

She paused in sipping her mulled wine. 'What do you mean?'

'I agree, it is odd, to the point of disturbing, that he had the clipping of you at all. All the more so that it was secreted into his clothing. However, what is more odd – and more disturbing – is that he did not purchase the newspaper. Nor cut out the clipping himself.'

She gawped at him. 'Clifford! Even with your infallible knowledge and unfathomable wizardry, you can't possibly know that.' After a long moment of silence from the opposite settee, she leaned forward. 'But somehow you do, don't you?'

'Yes, my lady.' He sighed. 'However, this is all too vexing since I wished for nothing but a truly restful Christmas sojourn for you.'

'I know, with only thoughts of how I could possibly have eaten so much and lost so often to you at chess again.'

Without replying, he rose and strode from the room.

'Ah, that's evidently the end of any talk of our investigation for tonight, then,' she whispered to the once again comatose Gladstone and ear-twitching Tomkins. 'Poor chap. He's gone for the chess set to stop me waffling on about our deceased friend any more, I presume.'

But as she took another long savouring sip of her drink, he reappeared carrying something else.

'Photograph albums, Clifford?' He placed three on the inlaid coffee table between them. 'Which of the morass of rooms here did you ferret these out from? And how many of my Irish relatives are in the pictures?'

'None, and none, my lady. I brought these from his lordship's collection in the library at Henley Hall. I imagined you might enjoy perusing them in your' – he permitted himself the luxury of a small sigh – 'supposedly uneventful evenings here. I believe you have not yet managed to do so since arriving back in England.'

'Thank you, Clifford. And you're right. I've only had a cursory glance now and then. That was beyond thoughtful of you.'

'More, as it turns out, useful than thoughtful.'

Mystified by the enigmatic statement, she took the middle album he handed her. Leaning over, he flicked carefully through to a page that had several photographs of her as a child. One was her at about four years old laughing in her uncle's lap, the others her aged nine to thirteen, mostly in her hateful school uniform. She tapped one of her deep in remonstration with Clifford in the apple orchard.

'I didn't know Uncle Byron had caught you and I squabbling?'

His eyes twinkled. 'I imagine his lordship found it tricky to capture us in any other sort of exchange, my lady.'

She laughed, but quickly sobered as his expression fell grave.

'What's really bothering you, Clifford?'

'If you would be so gracious as to turn to the next page?'

She did as he bid. 'Oh, there's one missing from here.' She ran her finger over each of the four corner mounts now framing only the discoloured cream backing paper of the album itself. 'What a shame. We'll probably never know what it was. Unless, that is, you can remember?'

'I can.'

From his inside pocket, he produced the newspaper clipping they had found hidden in the dead man's jacket collar and slid it under the four corners. For a moment she could only stare at it in shock. Then she slowly shook her head.

'It fits perfectly!' It took a moment longer for her to process what she was seeing. 'But Clifford, before, I was merely baffled. Why would a stranger, in another country, have a newspaper clipping of me? And why would he have secreted it so carefully in his jacket?' She threw her arms out, spilling a trickle of wine on Gladstone's upturned tummy. 'But now. Now, I'm not baffled, I'm completely bamboozled! I mean, how could he have got hold of the clipping from Uncle Byron's album?'

'The "how" I believe I can explain. Certainly, in part. It is, however, the "why" that is troubling me.'

With their glasses topped up, she couldn't fail to notice her butler's eyes, normally so unreadable, were filled with a mixture of sadness and... *anger, Ellie?*

He cleared his throat. 'I need to take us back to the day of his lordship's funeral.' Her heart faltered as her bulldog jerked awake with a soft whine and hauled himself up to lumber over and lay his head in her butler's lap. 'It's alright, Master Gladstone.' Clifford ran a slow hand over each of the bulldog's stiff little ears.

She peered at him over the top of her glass. 'We don't have to continue—'

He held up a halting hand, his tone softening. 'Best let it tumble out, as you so often say, my lady. Anyway, as you are aware, the funeral itself was conducted by our own Reverend Gaskell in Little Buckford's Church of St Winifred's. The reception however—'

'Was held at Langham Manor, since Harold and Augusta Fenwick-Langham were very old friends of Uncle Byron's. And they insisted you all attend in honour of uncle's fondness for you all, even the ladies and Joseph.'

He nodded. 'And indeed Silas, as they wanted all his lordship's staff to be present. But Silas' attendance is, I believe, what allowed this to occur.' He leaned over and tapped the empty space in the photo album balanced across her lap.

'How? I know he's the most fiendish and secret security guard ever employed. So secret, I still haven't met him, actually, although you assure me he is constantly patrolling the house and grounds.'

'He was. And is. Except for this one occasion when he was at the funeral reception at Langham Manor. Anyway, approximately an hour after our collective return from the Manor, Polly reported to Mrs Butters that one of the windows in the library "looked a bit funny". She relayed this to me, so I immediately checked and found the third window along had been jimmied open.'

'Gracious! Burglars being so callous as to profit during someone's funeral. That's terrible!'

'My sentiments entirely. But after an extensive search of the house, nothing could be identified as missing.'

She shrugged. 'They must have been interrupted then. Perhaps you all arrived back just as they started to break in?'

'At the time, my conclusion also.' He tapped his forehead sharply. 'Which now seems particularly foolish, for which I apologise profusely to you and his lordship.'

She shook her head. 'Not accepted, as you did everything above and beyond for Uncle Byron, exactly as you do for me. Besides, I imagine that day you could barely think straight with the grief you were going through. So please move onto the next part of the story, if it isn't too distressing for you?'

'Thank you. It was on the Wednesday of the following week that we received the developed photographs from the funeral. Handkerchief supplies ran perilously low, I must admit. At one point Mrs Butters exclaimed that in one of the photographs she and Mrs Trotman were crying over, there was a man seemingly watching the funeral from afar. A lone mourner unwilling to join the main party, I hazarded. However, Mrs Butters informed me that she had seen the same man outside the gates of Henley Hall the day before.' He picked up the third album on the table and turned through the pages. 'As you know, his lordship assisted a great many people over the years, of all walks of life and, ahem, careers.'

'Including reformed criminals, yes.'

'Quite. I therefore concluded the man was another of these whom I had not personally had recourse to meet.' He reached across to place the open album in her lap then stood patiently.

Starting with the first of the images, she shook her head

sadly as she moved down the page. 'Gracious, I realise now just how little I knew of Uncle Byron's life. And his friends, or even acquaintances. I don't recognise anyone really except you and the other staff. And the Langhams, of course.'

'Not the man Mrs Butters identified?' He tapped a figure in the background.

As she peered harder, her hand flew to her mouth. 'It's him! Isn't it? The man we found in the road?'

'The very conclusion I drew, on checking when we returned late this afternoon, my lady.'

'But that's why you had that sense of déjà vu that night out in the lashing rain as we struggled to heave him into the back of the Rolls. Some deep part of your memory recognised him.'

'Regrettably, without alerting my conscious thoughts until a few hours ago.'

He returned to his perched seat and steepled his fingers over his nose.

'That's not the end of the tale, is it?' she said tentatively.

'No. There are more witless mistakes on my part to confess to.'

'Clifford, what's that William Blake quote you've repeated on occasions. "Hindsight is a wonderful thing...?"'

'"But foresight is better"?'

'Precisely. So, with what you can share now, we'll have the best chance of working out how to solve this whole puzzling episode. But not if you're caught up in berating yourself over things you couldn't possibly have known then.' At his contrite nod, she smiled. 'So, after the kitchen table conversation with the ladies...?'

'It was some weeks later that I was engaged in mounting the photographs in one of the albums.' He tapped the third one in front of her. 'But on finishing, it seems a waft of wistful nostalgia must have blown in through the window, as I found myself looking back through all of them. From the earliest days with his lordship through to those when his irrepressibly determined young niece first became his ward. However, my reminiscing was sadly cut short by an odd discovery.'

'That the newspaper clipping of me was missing?' At his nod, she gasped. 'Clifford, do you think the dead man could be the one responsible for poor Uncle Byron having been poisoned?'

'Very possibly.'

'But if he was responsible for Uncle Byron's death, why would he then have taken a newspaper clipping, of all things? Especially one of me?'

He shook his head. 'I wish that I could answer with any certainty, my lady. All I do know is the last time he appeared, there was a funeral. And when he appeared again, albeit barely conscious, there was shortly after another funeral. *His.*' He faltered. 'But maybe it was supposed to be...'

'Mine?'

His reply was drowned out by her scream.

22

'Clifford! The gatehouse!'

'Corcoran!' they cried in unison.

She flew across the main hall with Clifford on her heels. Wrenching the front door open, she tore down the driveway. But the harder she ran, the more time felt like it was slowing. Beside her, Clifford's suit tails seemed to be flying behind him in slow motion.

The scene that greeted them as they finally rounded the head of the drive was even worse than she'd feared. At the base of the billowing plume of smoke that she'd seen from the window, it seemed the entire gatehouse was ablaze. Spitting tongues of flames reared out from the now glassless ground floor windows. Below the racing funnel of fire pouring up from the roof, a menacing cloud of thick black smoke billowed around the upper floor.

Shielding her face from the fierce heat with her arm, her lungs filled with the stench of acrid smoke, she ran along the front of the building yelling, 'Corcoran! CORCORAN!' But her voice was lost in the incandescent howl of the dying building.

Clifford dashed to the single burning plank that was left of the front door and tried to force his way inside but was instantly driven back by the white heat.

'Too dangerous,' he hollered through cupped hands. 'Stay back.'

'No! We have to find him.'

'My lady, NO!'

But her legs were already propelling her back to where he'd tried. As if to show her who was in charge, the fire gave an extra bullish roar as the leaded upstairs windows blew out, covering them in glass.

Retreating to a safer distance, Clifford shouted, 'There's the back door, but the fire's too strong that side as well.'

'Water, Clifford. Where is there water?'

A flash of inspiration told her to sprint to the gutter down-pipe now leaning forwards precariously from the remains of the blazing fascia board. However, the two tin pails of rainwater she found and threw achieved nothing but a spiteful hiss from the nearest ball of roiling flames.

'Dammit!' She cast around. 'There must be a well!'

Clifford disappeared into the dark. Instantly he returned, clutching two more buckets and gesturing for her to follow him back around the corner. Unhelpfully, the well was a distance from the house. Fortuitously, however, it was not a bucket on a rope as she'd expected. Somewhere over the last century, it had been upgraded to a sturdy iron hand pump. Juggling the buckets they'd found between them, she sprang to the outlet end as he seized the long tapering handle.

'Corcoran!' she cried with each bucket of water she ran with and hurled through the windows. Spinning back after the fourth one, she bounced off something square and solid. A strong hand took the pail from hers, piercing blue eyes blinking hard between a thick dark hat and scarf.

'Murphy! Oh, thank goodness. We need a human chain.'

He nodded and raked his coat sleeves back revealing the muscular forearms she'd noted previously. 'We'll form a line with the three of us to pass the water along and the empty buckets back to the pumper.'

She shook her head. 'It will have to be just you and I.' They ducked at the crash of a falling roof beam somewhere around the other side. 'Because if we three make a line, there won't be a pumper.' She beckoned him urgently back to the pump and shoved his bucket under the outlet.

Murphy raised his voice over the fire. 'Sure there will be. Smithy makes us three. Your man there is four.'

At that moment Clifford pointed over her shoulder at the man hurrying towards them. As he reached her and scooped a bucket from the ground, in the glow of the blaze she recognised him as the man who had directed them to Murphy's pub that first morning.

'We'll do all we can, miss,' he hollered in her ear.

Scanning the house for a sign they were starting to gain control of the blaze, she sent a prayer heavenwards that Corcoran wasn't inside and took up her position.

In a trice the four of them had an efficient chain in place. Filled buckets flew up the line to Murphy, then Smithy, then her, the empty ones deftly hurled back to Clifford.

'Change!' Clifford's measured call reached her burning ears. Her face smarting from the scorching flames, she ran to take the pump handle as he hurried to the front.

'Good call,' Smithy shouted. 'For sure, the heat's fierce on the hands and face at the front even for a blacksmith of all my years.'

Despite the increased number of buckets, the water still failed to douse the flames to any noticeable degree. In fact, if anything, the fire seemed to be taking greater hold.

'We need more help!' she shouted to Murphy as they exchanged buckets.

He shook his head. 'None of the village'll see this. Not with your House of Towers being this far out. The night's too black.'

Keeping the chain going, she refused to give up hope. 'But you saw it. And your pub is right in the thick of the village.'

He raised his eyebrows, which intensified the reflection of the fire dancing in his eyes. 'Not to stick a spade in your hopes there, but I was just passing.'

As Smithy took the head of the chain once more, he ran a blackened hand along his jaw. 'Lucky thing we were two more for the fray.'

'Yes,' she called back more brightly than she felt. Something about their story had sent a shiver down her spine despite the unrelenting heat of the fire.

She glanced back at Murphy stoically working the pump, then jumped as Clifford whispered in her ear, 'Just passing, my lady? On a dead-end track that leads only to Hennelly Towers and then out to peat bog?'

'And this late in the evening?' she whispered back.

'And I wager you could see – and hear – this fire over in Kiltyross itself. Let alone Derrydee.'

She nodded, understanding the cautionary look in his gaze to say nothing.

'Change!' Clifford shouted, discreetly gesturing that she was not to leave his sight.

As they continued to fight the fire, with every bucket of water thrown on the flames she repeated to herself, *Let Corcoran be alright. And then we'll find out what Murphy and Smithy were really doing out here!*

23

In the grey, brooding light of dawn, the smouldering remains of the gatehouse looked even more desolate than in the depths of the night.

Murphy and Smithy had stayed at their firefighting posts until the well had sputtered out its final bucket load with an empty belch. Clifford had declared the fire was as extinguished as it could be, she had reluctantly conceded, and they had left. Standing around in the bitter cold, with drenched feet couldn't help anyone, she knew. Especially after the last of the gatehouse roof had collapsed, making it futile – and too dangerous – to search the smouldering ruin until full light. Staring up at the sky blanketed in cloud, however, she wondered if it would ever be light.

She jumped. 'Oh, Constable Doyle. Good morning. I didn't see you there.'

The policeman had arrived a while ago, followed by Doctor O'Sullivan. Since then, he had poked around the ruins while the doctor waited for him to signal that it was safe to enter. Having eventually done so, they had both disappeared inside what remained of the building. Whatever they'd found, however, hadn't removed the scowl from the policeman's face. Fearful of hearing about the morbid scene they'd had probably encountered, she tried to lighten the mood.

'I'm afraid every time we meet, it seems I've got you out of bed. You do a great job of—'

An authoritative wave of a podgy hand silenced her.

'I've no need of platitudes for doing my job, thank you.'

She smiled wearily. 'Constable, I fear we may have got off on the wrong foot that night at Ballykieran Abbey. Genuinely, I want nothing less than to have no involvement in any further unpleasant matters. And to indulge in nothing more subversive or troublesome to the Irish authorities than enjoying a traditional Christmas in my lately inherited ancestral home.'

Doyle shuffled his feet and busied himself with his notebook, avoiding her gaze. 'I've a report to write if you want to be getting along to the main hou—' He broke off at the sound of the blackened front door hinge being batted aside.

'Doctor O'Sullivan.' Eleanor swallowed hard as he came over. She couldn't keep putting it off any longer. She needed to know. 'Is it…?'

He put his brown leather bag down on the ground and tapped one set of long pale fingers over his green wool suit jacket. With the other hand, he removed his unlit pipe from between his teeth.

'The body in there is as I expected.'

Her heart lurched. 'Corcoran?'

'What do you think?' Doctor O'Sullivan held her gaze longer than was comfortable, then indicated to Doyle that they needed to move off to one side. As the two men talked in an inaudible tone, she tried to ignore that they both kept glancing over at her.

Clifford handed her a handkerchief. 'I can only offer the

thin comfort that we believe Corcoran would have passed in his sleep due to smoke inhalation long before the fire...' He tailed off and glanced sharply at the doctor and policeman.

The two men stared back, exchanged some more muttered words, and rejoined them.

'The undertaker will be along to collect the remains shortly,' Doyle said.

'Murphy?' At the policeman's nod, she shook her head. *Poor old Murphy. He's probably only just got to bed.* She turned to the doctor. 'Obviously I'll pay for the funeral and any other costs.'

O'Sullivan spun on his heels and returned to the gatehouse without a word.

Let it go, Ellie. Everyone's upset and tired.

Now alone with Doyle, something in his firm glare whisked her back to the last time she'd seen him.

'It was a shame you got waylaid and missed Father Quinn's Requiem service for the man who died up at the abbey, Constable.' She kept her tone even. 'It felt quite the sad affair, given there was no one to attend from his family.'

'If you say so,' he said noncommittally.

She shrugged. 'I really know very little about the workings of the police in Ireland, but I would very much like to improve my knowledge. And as you have noted to us each time we've met, you are extremely conscientious about your official duties. Which is why I thought it rather harsh. Harsh enough to feel compelled to write and complain.'

She turned as if to walk over to the remains of the gatehouse, their conversation over.

'Complain?' Doyle's eyes narrowed. 'About me?'

'Gracious, no. On your behalf. Really, I thought it most off that you were being checked up on by a superior.'

Doyle frowned in confusion. 'What superior?'

'The person you were talking to in the car at the funeral. So few people have a vehicle around here. Which, together with the fact they were sitting in the back, made me realise just now that it must have been one of your superiors.' She leaned forward. 'It doesn't feel nice not being trusted, does it?'

Doyle's neck flushed to the colour of his cheeks as his mouth flapped like a fish. 'I've no need of being checked up on! The very notion.' He puffed his chest hard, then tugged his jacket back down over his exposed waistline. 'I was attending the funeral in an official capacity to make sure you English weren't getting up to any more shenanigans! And my superiors have no need to check up on *me*.'

'Oh, marvellous. A good friend of yours then, planning an evening together perhaps?' she said airily.

'It was no one. Just... just someone passing.' He strode over to his motorbike, yanked his helmet on and putted off without another word.

She caught Clifford's eye and nodded. *Passing? Through a dead-end village, Ellie?* She frowned. *Where have you heard that excuse before?*

The sound of wooden wheels on the gravel made them both turn around. Steering the donkey cart approaching them was the headmistress. The wagon was empty of children this time, much to Gladstone's disappointment, as he scrabbled up against the nearest wheel once it had stopped, looking for his new-found friends.

'Miss Breen. An unexpected but very welcome surprise,' Eleanor said as Clifford offered the woman a hand down.

She shook her head. 'No need of that, thank you, Mr Clifford. I shan't stop longer than it takes to say my piece of consolation.'

'Gracious, how kind.' Eleanor was touched. 'To come all this way from the village to offer your condolences.' She sighed. 'You must have known Corcoran far better than I. My deepest sympathies to you. Perhaps you were long-standing friends?'

'Friends!' Miss Breen muttered, tightening the collar of her grey wool jacket.

Eleanor coloured, fearing she had upset the woman. 'Oh, I just meant that Derrydee is such a close-knit village, it feels as though everyone knows everyone. And has done so forever.' She felt a wash of wistfulness. 'If only you knew how absolutely delightful that sounds.'

'I reserve fairy tales only for the very youngest of my pupils,' Miss Breen said stiffly.

Trying to lighten the conversation, Eleanor smiled. 'I'm sure everywhere has its drawbacks. Even tropical paradise has biting insects, after all.'

Miss Breen fixed her with a scrutinising look. There was a hint of something Eleanor couldn't place behind it. 'Lady Swift, I'm of the firm conviction there's more merit in the sawdust on the bakery floor than the gossip that's served up in there. So, it's probably utter nonsense but well, from when we met before...' She paused as if struggling to remember what she was going to say.

Oh dear, perhaps she's having one of those forgetful days.

'What was the gossip?' Eleanor prompted in a kindly tone.

'That' – Miss Breen jerked to – 'that you stayed up all night with the menfolk and worked as hard as them in fighting the fire.'

'Well, I did all I could, naturally.' Eleanor was puzzled the woman would think otherwise. Then it dawned. As Clifford had said so pointedly to Doyle minutes beforehand, that was hardly the province of titled ladies. She shrugged and then ran her hands down her arms. 'It's such a tragedy though that we didn't realise earlier. If only I'd seen the flames sooner and we'd found the buckets more quickly, we might have been able to save him. Poor Corc—'

'Lady Swift,' Miss Breen said sharply. 'Do not upset your-self mourning the man who perished in that fire because—'

'—because,' interrupted the equally educated voice of Doctor O'Sullivan, 'mourning is not the Irish way. There will be a proper wake, a celebration evening, immediately after Christmas. On this side of the water which separates our two sets of beliefs, we rejoice the life, not mourn the passing.'

Eleanor nodded. 'Of course. It's a wonderful approach. I'm sure Corcoran will look down with his endearing joviality, which I had too few chances to enjoy. However, it is still my heartfelt wish that I'd got to the gatehouse sooner.'

The doctor shrugged. 'It would have made no difference. Corcoran is... *was* famous for being impossible to rouse from his slumbers. If it offers any salve, he was most certainly asleep and the smoke would have done for him unawares, long before the flames.'

As we hoped, Ellie.

The doctor glanced up at Miss Breen. 'I'm sure you've a host of preparations ahead of the children singing tonight. Don't let us keep you, Headmistress.'

'It was so kind of you to call, Miss Breen,' Eleanor said. 'We're looking forward to hearing Midnight Mass. We'll be there for twelve.'

The headmistress glanced over her shoulder at the doctor who was striding over to his car and then said in a low voice, 'Meet me at a quarter to at the back of the church!' Darting a look over her shoulder again as Murphy appeared behind them, she tapped the reins on the donkeys' backs and set off to the village.

Intrigued by her words, Eleanor waved distractedly at the retreating headmistress and then the doctor as he climbed into his car. Out of the corner of her eye, she noticed Murphy hovering behind her, his cart a few feet away, Smithy at the reins. *Was Murphy eavesdropping on your conversation with Miss Breen, Ellie? Or just waiting to talk to you?*

'Thank you for coming, Murphy,' she called over her shoulder. 'Just a moment.'

She hurried after the doctor, determined to ask what he was doing in the hotel in Kiltyross. But as she drew level with the car, O'Sullivan climbed back out.

'Lady Swift, plans can be adjusted for the better.'

She stopped, confused. 'I've no doubt. However, forgive me, I don't understand—'

'Let me make myself clear. Perhaps you'll be good enough to consider an early return home?'

She was dumbstruck. 'But—'

'Lady Swift, I have been called to attend one too many accidents since your arrival.'

She stared at him. 'But I've merely been unwittingly – and very reluctantly – caught up in both tragic occasions. I didn't come to make trouble, any more than I'm the cause of any. All I've tried to do is help two men who were in trouble themselves.'

The doctor's face reddened. 'Then leave the village to bury them!'

He climbed back into his car and started the engine. Exhausted physically and emotionally after the events of the night and the discovery of Corcoran's body, his words riled her. She strode up to his side window.

'Like their other problems?' she said angrily, noting him flinch. 'Doctor O'Sullivan, tell me, what were you doing at that hotel in Kiltyross?'

His eyes widened, but he said nothing. She folded her arms. 'Alright, then, what is your official diagnosis of' – she waved in the direction of the charred remains of the gatehouse, unable to bring herself to say Corcoran's name – 'the body in there?'

He shrugged his shoulders. 'What do you think? Death by fire, obviously. Specifically burns or smoke inhalation.'

'Ah! Not "death by water", then?' Her gaze bore into his. 'Like the man we found *half-drowned* in the road and rushed to the abbey in the hope he could be saved?'

The sound of tyres spinning on the rough track and the doctor's car receding into the distance was her only answer.

24

'Gracious, Clifford! There's a positive stream of people surging into Murphy's pub. And on a Sunday!'

Clifford brought their jaunting car to a halt to let a group of five men hotfoot it in front of them and on into the bar.

'Indeed, my lady. That is in order to beat Sunday's "Holy Hour" as the law is called. Anyone inside a public house in Ireland at two o'clock is allowed to remain there and continue drinking. However, no one else is allowed to enter the establishment until after four o'clock.'

They made their way to the snug. 'This was an excellent suggestion of yours, Clifford,' Eleanor said with heartfelt relief as she untangled Gladstone's lead from around her ankles. 'The place seems extra festive this morning. Just the pick-me-up we need.'

It seemed Kathleen had found the time to add some extra welcoming additional decorations too. Alternate paper snowflakes and angels hung from twists of silvery foliage along the walls. And each table was set with a centrepiece of gingerbread snowmen holding iced-mittened hands to form a ring under the red and green wrapped bottle bearing a white candle.

Sinking into the seat her butler had pulled closer to the fire for her, she watched him shake the shroud of snowflakes from her coat. He then did the same with his, before arranging their gloves along the fireguard. She took a deep breath. 'It feels good to be away from Hennelly Towers for a bit while we settle our thoughts. Although, I don't know if technically this is going to be breakfast or lunch after staying up all night?'

'Or supper. Or elevenses. Maybe tiffin, my lady. All and any are possible contenders, as breakfast is traditionally taken upon rising after a pleasant repose in the arms of Morpheus, that is, sleep. And luncheon...' He gazed wearily at the open page of his slim leather pocketbook before striking his meticulous hand-written list through with a haphazard line from his fountain pen. She gaped at him, never having witnessed such a sloppy display, then tuned into the mischievous twinkle in his eyes. 'My lady, given that the meal schedule since our arrival has lurched along on one bent wheel with a hindward bias, why don't we simply declare it a free-for-all? And at the same time, delight in more tasting notes over Kathleen's moreish fare?'

This lifted the last of the pall dogging her thoughts. 'Excellent idea. While we do, instead of taking a leaf from the Irish's book, I shall take an entire tree and adopt their refreshingly stoic and sanguine approach to life.'

'And death,' he muttered as he disappeared down the corridor. He returned a few moments later just as Murphy opened the hatch and hailed them both even more brightly than usual.

'Welcome be, folks. A long glass of the tastiest Guinness you'll ever drink, for sure. And a whiskey chaser' – he waved at Eleanor – 'as a medicinal rubdown from the inside.'

She waved back. 'Thank you, Murphy. Especially for all your tireless help last night. You must be exhausted.'

A fleeting shadow crossed his face. 'Word to the wise. Never put your hand up to be a publican if a pillow and eider-down are your persuasion.' He let out a chuckle, which sounded forced to her ears. 'Cleaning pumps and sweeping out folks who can't hold their drink are my usual bedfellows at crowing time.'

'But you've still got a full day ahead of you, so I'm all the more grateful. If there's any way I can repay you, please—'

He flapped a bar towel at her. 'We'll call it even for you teaching me a sharp lesson last eve.' At her questioning look, he grunted. 'Never underestimate an English lady on account of her having a title as lofty as the towers guarding her house. Fair play, you've more grit than the rocks that make up the Crag!' The hatch closed noisily. Not noisily enough, though, to hide his uncharacteristic bark. 'Kathleen! Jig to it, girl. Folks need to eat!'

I imagine he's more tired than he let on, Ellie. And maybe he also knew Corcoran better than he let on. She turned to Clifford.

'I don't suppose we could jump between two discussions, could we? Tasting notes and... ah!' She took what had inadvertently become her investigation notebook that he held out. 'Sure it won't spoil your meal? It's a rare treat to see you eat at all, let alone positively relish one as you have each time in here.'

'After three long years in service to a mistress with an unfathomable magnetism for food and murder? No, my lady.'

'Three *long* years, is it now?'

He pressed a finger to his lips. 'Given our joint disquiet over the landlord's sudden appearance last night, if I might suggest lowering our voices?'

She nodded and smoothed her page open with the base of her Guinness mug, which made the notebook's spine groan sufficiently for Clifford to shudder. Heading the top line with 'Fire – accident or arson?', she paused, then underlined the question mark several times.

'I want to believe it had nothing to do with us trying to find out what happened to the man we found and rushed to the abbey, but what do you think?'

He rubbed his chin. 'I am leaning significantly towards the fire being an accident.'

'And not just because you want me to feel better about it?'

'No, my lady. Though that would be sufficient enough reason.'

'But what kind of accident could have occurred? Think about it. Corcoran has... *had* lived in the gatehouse for decades. He must have known every grate, chimney brick and oil lamp better than his oldest friend.'

Clifford sniffed. 'Not wishing to malign a man who cannot be present to defend himself, but a cigarette end imprudently cast towards the hearth without checking it had reached the safety of the grate? And the subsequent flames unnoticed due to being under the influence of one alcoholic beverage too many, perhaps?'

'Or he could have been under the weather and fallen asleep too early to tamp down the fire. O'Sullivan said what a heavy sleeper he was.' She sighed. 'At least it seems certain according to the doctor the smoke would have got to Corcoran well before the... the flames.'

He nodded. 'I do not believe Corcoran woke up, my lady, and thus did not suffer as I mentioned. Had he woken, there are many ways to exit the gatehouse swiftly. I...' He frowned.

She leaned forward, mindful to keep her voice down. 'What is it?'

'I have just realised the error in my summation of the possible chain of events. Corcoran cannot have been a smoker.'

'How can you be so sure?'

'The only aroma of smoke ever about his person was that of peat from the fire, and the lack of cigarette ends littering the area around the gatehouse makes it a certainty.' At her admonishing look, he shook his head. 'My lady, without wishing to speak ill of the deceased, Corcoran was not the sort of man to snuff out his cigarette only when a suitable receptacle was to hand.'

'Fair point. He would have flicked it to the ground. But there are other ways for the fire to have started accidentally, as we said. And if it wasn't an accident, why would someone set the gatehouse ablaze in the first place?'

He cleared his throat. 'I'm afraid, my lady, I can think of only one answer.'

She nodded slowly. 'I know. But why would anyone want to kill Corcoran?'

His brows flinched. 'Because they were concerned that he might divulge some information they wished to remain hidden?'

She gasped. 'You mean divulge it to *us*? About the man we found on the road, perhaps?'

They looked up as Kathleen appeared at the hatch. 'Food's only three minutes from your plates. Sorry to keep you.'

'Oh, we're in no hurry.' Eleanor smiled broadly. But it faded as she took in Kathleen's hesitation. The hatch closed hurriedly as her dark hair swung out of view. 'She's not her usual self, either, Clifford.'

'Indeed not.'

'Well, whatever feast or otherwise she has dutifully prepared for us, it will no doubt include some sort of delicious potato bread or farls. Which it would be unforgivably rude not to dunk in the main dish, so I'd better go wash my hands.'

'Dunk?' Clifford gave her a withering look as he came around to slide out her chair. 'Please allow me to accompany you.'

'To the ladies'!'

He ran a horrified finger round his starched collar. 'To the decorous vantage point of the top of the stairs only, naturally.'

'Why? In case there's another body downstairs?'

He shook his head. 'There is no body. Rest assured, I checked on our arrival. I conjectured Murphy would likely have anticipated our coming in to eat and placed any, ahem, deceased persons out of view.'

'You mean Corcoran? So that's where you disappeared to when we arrived. But then why accompany me?' Both their gazes slid towards the hatch. 'Because we aren't at all sure about Murphy, now?' she whispered.

He nodded in agreement.

On her return, she seized the pen and wrote "Murphy" in smaller, more scrawled lettering on her page. Clifford peered over. 'Your usual hand would likely have sufficed to disguise the subject matter. However, bravo for bringing Prudence back to the table with you.'

'Ugh! You know she's not my favourite companion. That would be you, Gladstone old chum.' She ruffled one of her bull-dog's ears and pretended to whisper in it, 'And the world's most respectfully, disrespectful butler.' Straightening up, she tapped the page. 'It struck me on coming back up the stairs that the person I've just listed here' – she glanced at the hatch – 'could have been the man I saw through the stained-glass window. You know, in the cloisters at the abbey.'

'Likewise, however, Smithy, perchance?'

'Gracious, yes. I noticed last night they're of a similar build.'

'And gait too, I witnessed.'

She added Smithy's name to the list with a groan. 'It feels horribly ungracious to include among our suspects the names of the only two people who helped us last night. Especially as we have no motive for either of them wanting the man we found in the road – or Corcoran – dead.'

'I agree, my lady. However, we both felt their story of just passing rang false and what better way to cover one's guilt at having started a fire—'

'Than by turning up and helping to put it out!'

'Exactly. It also did not escape my attention that they did not show until the blaze had taken hold.'

She peered out the window at the swirling flurry of snowflakes and shook her head. 'Like our poor friend in the road, I feel like a drowning man – or woman.' She leaned back in her seat and groaned. 'Is there anyone we can trust?'

He nodded. 'Yes, my lady, I believe there is.'

25

'Food's ready, Mr Clifford,' Kathleen called over the sound of the tin tray being slid through the hatch.

Eleanor and Clifford glanced at each other in consternation.

'And beyond delicious it will assuredly be,' he said calmly as he cleared the space in two long strides. 'Ah, perfect! Fish, perchance, since it is Christmas Eve?'

'Right you be on that. Gravelled Ailish.' She darted off, closing the hatch as she went.

Eleanor grimaced. 'We'll have to be more careful. I was so caught up in our discussion I didn't hear her open the hatch again. Do you think she heard us?'

He frowned. 'I do not know, my lady. Either way, all we can do is make sure we are more vigilant in the future.'

She nodded and took a long sniff of her food as he wrestled a now overeager Gladstone under the table. 'I love how unfathomable the names are. It makes every dish a challenge to get to the bottom of.'

Clifford's lips twitched. 'Yet, no doubt, you will easily get to the bottom of yours.'

'Hilarious. And true. Come on then. What's behind this amazing aroma?'

Having peeled back a corner of the golden-brown topping, he sniffed. 'Freshwater shad or "Allis", which shares characteristics of the herring family in that it has a slight oiliness to its meat. It offers a mildly sweet flavour. Generously stewed with leeks and celery in this case, which is fortuitous, as it is also renowned for being a militantly bony fish.'

'And the "gravelled" part of the dish's name I assume is from this remarkable crumble topping of potato' – she forked it a few times – 'flour and oats.'

He turned the dish back and forth slowly, inhaling. 'With wood sorrel, parsley and mustard, I believe.'

'And finely chopped bacon morsels, which is an absolute masterstroke to my mind.'

They ate in silence, both savouring every mouthful of the stew alongside the potato farls.

'Perhaps we should return to our discussion?' Clifford said as he sat down from passing the empty dishes through the hatch to Kathleen and making sure it was closed afterwards.

Eleanor nodded. 'Before we were interrupted, I was drowning in this case and you threw me a lifeline. So, who exactly can we trust?'

'Ourselves.'

She cocked her head. 'Explain, please.'

'What I mean, my lady, is we have been in these predicaments before. The one thing we do know is that we can rely on our combined skill – and intuition – to break through an impasse such as this. If I might be so bold as to make a suggestion?'

'Willingly.'

'It seems that since arriving here and stumbling over the gentleman we found in the road we have unwittingly set in motion a series of chain reactions. If we were to list each of these reactions, perhaps a clearer picture might emerge as to why?'

She nodded. 'That's an excellent idea.' She wiped her mouth on a napkin and marshalled her thoughts. 'Well, the very first reaction it set off, as it were, was us trying to find help for the poor man.'

'Indeed. Which led us to Ballykieran Abbey.'

'Which is where things really kicked off. Not only did the poor man die – under suspicious circumstances for sure – but we also fell foul to one degree or another of the Mother Superior, Father Quinn, Doctor O'Sullivan and Constable Doyle – four of our now five or six suspects. Although, neither of us really think the Mother Superior is guilty. Or is that just wishful thinking?'

He arched a brow. 'I would rather not comment at the moment, my lady. Perhaps continue before we lose our thread?'

'Alright. Now, having unknowingly put ourselves on the killer's radar, it would seem, the Rolls being disabled was the next reaction in the chain. If, that is, you ignore the staff having the wind put up them by the ghost of Hennelly Towers, which I think we can?'

'I believe so, too, my lady. Perhaps the staff had their own reasons for leaving. Possibly they hadn't been paid. I believe I mentioned that the Hennellys were rather fiscally challenged by the time his lordship inherited the estate. He did provide money to pay the staff through a local agency, but it's possible they recently began pocketing the money instead. I confess, his lordship – and myself – were, perhaps, too reliant on instructions being consistently actioned without the pressure of regular scrutiny.'

'Either way, there's no point in berating yourself now. But if it is the case, why would Corcoran have made up all that nonsense about a ghost?'

'I imagine to give his story credence. And as to why, he may have fabricated the tale to spare your blushes over our conjectured financial irregularities. Or maybe he was fearful he himself might be accused of having had a hand in misappropriating the staff's wages?'

She frowned. 'I can see that. But why would he stay if he wasn't being paid himself?' She tutted. 'Ah! Of course, he was still able to live in the gatehouse. As he said, where else was an old retainer like him going to go?'

'And, again, not wishing to malign the dead, he was not the sort of man, I feel, to hesitate in taking certain liberties in lieu of pay, shall we say?'

She snorted. 'Personally, if he did, I don't blame him. Either way, let's agree to ignore matters relating to the staff and real – or imagined – ghosts and take the Rolls being disabled as the next event in our chain reaction.'

'Exactly, my lady. It adds up so far. We discover the gentleman in the road. He isn't quite dead, unbeknown to the killer. We take the gentleman to the abbey where the killer is alerted to the fact that not only wasn't his victim dead, but that two English visitors found him alive. The killer finishes the job at the abbey, but is concerned about those nosey English.'

'Perhaps the killer was worried his victim may have told us some damning information before we brought him to the abbey?'

'Astutely reasoned. Which means the killer needs to find out. But it needs to be done without revealing themselves. So, to keep us here and render us all but immobile, thus easier to track, he has the Rolls disabled.'

She tapped her chin with the pen. 'This was an excellent idea of yours, Clifford. By leaving out unrelated events, I feel the true picture is emerging.'

'Hopefully, my lady. There is the final matter of the fire at the gatehouse though, which I am still leaning towards being an unrelated accident.'

'I agree.' Eleanor coaxed her grumbling bulldog out from under the table where he was very comfortable. 'Sorry, Gladstone old chum, you'll have to wait until we're back at the house to have some titbits. Since' – she glanced sideways at Clifford – 'even your master has devoured all his share of Kathleen's wondrous fare, can you believe it?'

At the bar, Clifford paid their dues to Murphy. 'Our compliments to Kathleen for that lovely meal, if you will.'

Murphy nodded. 'And may the rest of the day lay down for you both.'

As they rounded the corner of the pub, the icy wind whipped Eleanor's scarf harshly against her face. Frowning, she almost missed the beauty of the snowflakes having settled into a carpet of glistening white. 'Fire, then ice. More contradictions, Clifford!'

But as he went to answer, she shushed him, her sharp hearing catching two disembodied male voices coming from behind the pub. They were exchanging exasperated words. Words that made her breath catch.

26

The overheard conversation came to an abrupt end as one set of heavy boots clomped away. She motioned a mystified-looking Clifford to hurry after her, hoping they hadn't missed the owner of the last and most disgruntled of the two voices.

She was in luck. A man stood in front of them, taking a deep breath through his gnarled hands, which he was running over his lean weathered cheeks. The top half of his stained coveralls were faded blue, but the legs patched with green. An enormous wiry-coated wolfhound sat next to him, leaning against a broken wooden post.

'Good morning,' she said cheerily. 'What pretty weather for Christmas Eve, wouldn't you say?'

The wolfhound gave Gladstone a bemused sniff as the bulldog padded up, his stumpy tail wagging.

'Pretty, miss?' The man whipped off his cap and let his head fall back as he peered up at the heavy snow clouds while scratching his shock of thick grey curls. 'For sure, I've never taken the time to consider the beauty of the freezing weather I'm working to keep body and soul together in.' He looked at her with a genial glint breaking through the milkiness marring his still striking blue eyes. 'But thank you kindly for the lesson that I've likely missed many a treat.'

She coloured in embarrassment. 'Gracious, no lesson intended. I shall leave all of that to your wonderful village head-mistress, Miss Breen. In fact, her delightful pupils put me straight on a most important matter.' She smiled as he leaned forward, charmed by his guileless display of curiosity. 'That, unlike your magnificent dog there, my rather ungainly hound falls short of the mark in this neck of the woods.'

The man laughed and waved a calloused hand in Glad-stone's direction. 'Keep him for rounding up the mice in the kitchen, do you? Though I doubt he'd manage even that. That belly tells its own story. Send him home with me, mind, and my sheep'll chase the fat off him for you.'

She laughed. 'A most generous offer. What do you say, old chum?' Gladstone eyed her with disdain at the suggestion and huffed down pointedly beside his new friend, his stiff back legs sticking out sideways.

'Mind,' the man said, 'granted he's better in the leg depart-ment than Carrick, my wolfhound. He's just got the three now, having lost a hind, but that doesn't stop him earning his keep.'

'Ah, you're a farmer,' she said as if she'd surmised he could equally have been a cabinetmaker or an accountant. 'Clifford, how fortuitous is that!'

'Most, my lady,' her butler said without hesitation, though she knew he still had no idea where she was steering the conver-sation to. She turned back to the farmer. 'So fortunate, as I said, because I would like to ask your advice.'

'Advice?' He rolled his eyes. 'The likes of me advising the lady of the House of Towers! Best be getting along we should. Carrick!' He tapped his dog on the head. 'Fields are a'calling.'

'I wonder if news travels as fast in Derrydee as it does in my village in England?' she said quickly as the wolfhound leaped lithely to his three feet.

'Faster than flames fanned by the devil.' As the words left his lips, the farmer looked down at the ground. 'Apologies, miss, didn't mean to be thoughtless after your trouble of yester night. Sixty-seven years with no one but dim-witted sheep to talk to all of the day's hours does that to a man.'

'Please don't apologise. Accidents happen. Even house fires,' she said, observing his reaction. That he looked away failed to put her mind at rest. 'However, it was most fortuitous bumping into you today because you're probably just the man who knows how I can ensure we'll never have a repeat issue. Of running out of water, that is, as we did last night, sadly.'

'Water, you say, miss?' He seemed even more uncomfortable.

Clifford nodded. 'The well for the gatehouse ran dry before the four of us could extinguish the blaze.'

The farmer held out his hands to Eleanor. 'Fair play, miss, you did all you could, I heard.'

'We all tried. But Clifford here realised this morning, it's probably a good idea to have a water store in conjunction with a well, you see.'

'Right you be on that score. Least for folks with a scrap of land blessed enough to have one on.'

'As you must have. Mind, I can't imagine your well ever runs dry if you farm, though?'

The farmer shook his head wearily. 'Not the case. Even my land runs out sometimes.'

'I'm sorry to hear that. What on earth do you do when your well *and* your water store run out then?'

His expression clouded. 'Pay through my teeth to have some delivered, as I'll have to this evening. In December! Well's fine, but water store,' the sinews of his neck stood out, 'was vandalised. Robbery it be. Pumped straight out of the river and then driven a few miles, yet you'd think it was liquid gold for the price they charge as well!'

'Ah! So whoever delivers is a little sharp in their business practice, perhaps?' Clifford said.

The farmer nodded vehemently. 'Disgusting it be, especially when folks have scraped through having nothing to eat all those years.' He gestured down the road. 'Funny enough, I was just telling Shaun to stop wasting his breath. The price ain't coming down. In fact, it's soared on account of them having the only truck in the village now.' He lowered his voice. 'Since, that is, they wrecked the only other one!'

'Them?' Eleanor asked casually, having overheard this part of the conversation, but not a hint of anyone's name. 'Who are they, these water delivery people? I shall have to contact them no matter how much they might be profiteering.'

The farmer's jaw fell. 'Oh, no, no. They're not folk I'd recommend dealing with unless you've no option but to die of thirst or lose your livestock!'

'Your cautions are greatly appreciated,' Clifford said. 'However, her ladyship wishes most ardently to replenish the water at Hennelly Towers in case of any future fires. Rest assured, I shall intervene at the merest whiff of a further exaggeration of the price.'

'Don't!' he blurted out. 'Don't intervene. In fact, don't go. The Gilligan brothers are...' he said, swallowing hard, 'best left alone, let's say. Especially by folks from elsewhere.'

Eleanor took a step closer and looked at him imploringly. 'Please tell us where to find them? Hennelly Towers is all that remains of my Irish heritage. I can't risk leaving it unprotected.'

The farmer stared at her. Finally, he sighed heavily. 'If as you can't be told, miss, follow the track that swings off at Three Collops Wall. Then same again at St Colum's Crop. You'll find their yard right enough.'

As they set off, she felt a surge of hope. 'I know we both think that the farmer was suggesting these Gilligan brothers vandalised his water store so he'd have to buy more water off them, which is beyond reprehensible. But they also might have seen something the night we found the man in the road. If they're the only people with a truck, they are also the only people likely to have been out and about on that lonely stretch. And they do late evening deliveries as our helpful farmer unwittingly just told us, since he's expecting them tonight.'

Clifford nodded. 'It's a tenuous hope, perhaps, but the best we have at the moment.'

Back on the cart with Mullaney trotting along at a slow, but steady, pace, she peered forward and shook her head.

'You know, I'm not at all convinced now we'll find this yard where these Gilligan brothers apparently run their business. What kind of directions were they our farmer friend gave? Right at the cod something or other, and then again at the horsewhip of a... a saint, was it?'

'"St Colum's Crop", my lady. Which I am imagining will actually be a rocky projection, gracing the otherwise predominant bog.'

'Ah, well worked out, Clifford. And the other thing?'

'"Three Collops Wall". A collop being a century-old Irish measurement of grazing land. One collop would be sufficient to accommodate one cow or twelve goats or six sheep, for example.'

'Marvellously impressive knowledge, my most-learned butler, but how big is that, then?'

'That depends entirely on the sustaining qualities of the land, naturally.' He pointed at the remains of a drystone wall enclosing a small rectangle field. 'I believe we turn here, however.'

The track turned out to be a tortuous affair to start with and positive purgatory after that. As they bounced along, the increasing presence of barbed wire strung randomly between a forbidding regiment of thick wooden posts on either side added to the already uneasy air.

He frowned. 'Deemed illegal on public highways in 1893, if memory serves. Unlike the right to strew one's land with all manner of detritus, as it seems the Gilligans have a penchant for.'

She couldn't deny the burgeoning heaps of rusting metal, smashed barrels and rotting household rubbish hardly encouraged them to push onwards.

A moment later, Clifford drew the mule to a stop next to a partially collapsed wooden shelter and shook his head in disgust.

'I fear that if we continue, Mullaney may lame himself on a nail or other sharp or rusty item scattered on the ground.'

She nodded and swung herself down, telling Gladstone to stay put. As she turned around, she jumped in surprise as Clifford shot out a restraining arm, pressing her against the shelter. His jaw was taut, his brows thunderous.

'Clifford, you look positively... furious?'

'Would that I could refute that, my lady. However, I have just spotted who I can only assume are the Gilligan brothers.'

She risked a peek, immediately flattening herself against the shelter again.

'It's them!' she whispered.

He nodded grimly. 'The same two reprobates who disabled the Rolls!' Pressing the bulldog to his chest, he covered the dog's wrinkled muzzle with one hand. 'Not a sound, Master Gladstone.'

Eleanor nudged his elbow. 'We need to snout around and see what we can spot or overhear.'

'Snout around?' He grimaced at the insanitary surroundings.

She nodded. 'Just a quick in and out. Then straight to Hennelly Towers for a bath!'

Next to the outbuilding they were sheltering against were piles of rusting water tanks, dented milk churns and peat-black-

·

ened tin baths. Creeping along behind them kept them concealed, but their best attempts at stealth were repeatedly threatened by the heaps of stones waiting to trip them unawares. After carefully checking around for hazards, Eleanor stopped and peered through a gap in the milk churns. She could make out a central area of compacted dirt under a frosting of snow. Her gaze followed the littering of discarded beer bottles, which led to a low stone building. Despite its diminutive size, it didn't preclude it being the Gilligans' home as few of the family cottages were any larger.

A movement at the corner of the yard caught her eye. A mean-jawed thirty-ish man shuffled out from what she realised with a shudder was not a set of precariously stacked doors but a makeshift lavatory. He raked a hand through the lank black hair brushing his collar and dragged on the end of the smouldering cigarette hanging from his bottom lip. With a grunt, he straggled across the snow-flecked dirt in his unlaced boots. Hauling the waistband of his grubby grey trousers up his beefy frame, he kicked a five-gallon tin jug upright from where it had been lying next to a metal tank. After a barked call of 'Mick!' to no one she could see, he sucked on the end of the patched hose attached to a large rusting tank. He quickly removed it from his mouth as a stream of what she assumed was petrol shot out. A fair amount soaked his trousers before he managed to shove the hose into the neck of the jug.

With a horrified but muted sniff at the scene, Clifford whipped his coat-tails up and dropped to his haunches beside her. She shrunk back as the door of the house opened and a taller, but no less presentable, version of the first man appeared.

'For the love of all that isn't holy, can't a brother grab a minute to himself!' he growled.

The first man flicked his still-glowing cigarette end at the grumbling newcomer with a sly grin. 'Maybe, when he's no trouble to be after causing. Which he has.'

'Aha, is that so!' Mick rubbed his hands together. 'Then we'll fall a-bed tonight righteous that the day wasn't wasted. For sure, it's about time the sport got worth going after!' Mick produced a cigarette from somewhere under his patched jumper and threw it in the air before catching it between his lips. Imitating his brother's sly grin, he fished in his grubby trouser pockets and pulled out a handful of matches. Running one along the tank until it spurted into flame, he pretended to lick the burning end, then flicked it at his brother. Laughing uproariously, he sped up, repeating his apparently hilarious joke as the other man struggled to dodge the barrage of flaming missiles while guffawing.

'I'd have thought you'd have had enough of playing with fire for now, Mick, especially after the last BIG one!'

She gasped and motioned towards the stone building, but Clifford shook his head vehemently. Too late, as the toe of her boot knocked against the precarious pile of milk churns in front of her. She gasped and lunged for the lower ones as Clifford grabbed the others with his free hand. There was silence for a moment, neither of them daring to peer again through the flurry of rust that now floated down. But then more oblivious laughter rolled across to them. Exhaling in unison, they shared a relieved look.

And then Gladstone sneezed.

'Intruders, Mick!' the first brother yelled as he jerked around, scanning the area. 'Me shotgun's in the truck!'

In a flash, Eleanor whipped up a stone and skimmed it at a deft angle to strike a tin bath on the other side of the yard.

'There!' the brothers chorused.

'Run!' Clifford hissed.

27

Not daring to interrupt the unfathomable understanding between her butler and their mule in case Mullaney mutinied and stopped, Eleanor contained her thoughts all the way back to Hennelly Towers. As they reached the gatehouse, her neck spasmed as she craned around for the hundredth time to check the Gilligan brothers weren't following them. Satisfied, she breathed a sigh of relief as Clifford drew the cart to a stop, sprung lithely down and patted Mullaney's velvet muzzle.

'Good work, sir. A highly deserved late luncheon?'

He produced a long-handled soft cloth bag, which he placed over the mule's head to much eager braying and whinnying.

Stepping around to Eleanor's side of the jaunting car, he offered her a hand to alight. Avoiding his gaze, she accepted, but then knelt down to scour the ground around his feet. 'Dash it, Clifford! You must have dropped it here somewhere.'

Gladstone joined in, digging a helpful hole close enough to shower her in snow-slushed mud and stones.

'Dropped what, my lady?' Clifford spun on his heel to watch as she moved to search behind him.

'Your long list of reprimands and future cautions you're itching to scold me with.'

He pursed his lips. 'Long and *justified* list. But is that why you believe I halted Mullaney at the head of the drive?'

'Well, obviously. Because otherwise' – she stood up and smiled innocently at him – 'you would have deposited me in the main house so you could ensure I was suitably regaled with a raft of delectable refreshments before you started.'

He stared back with his ever-inscrutable expression. 'Rest assured, the list awaits. However, I stopped here to follow up the clue you perspicaciously, if most imprudently, led us to.'

She pretended to whisper behind her hand. 'See, now I'm confused. Has the telling-off begun or not?'

'Not' – his lips quirked – 'by a very lengthy margin. That's for later. In the meantime, shall we?'

He gestured to the rear of the gatehouse and beyond the well that had run dry the night of the blaze. To her surprise, never having seen it in the light, the area was covered in a swathe of snow-flecked grass flanked by tended shrubs.

She scratched her head through her thick woollen hat. 'Funny how we jump to conclusions about people, isn't it? I hadn't imagined Corcoran to be a tidy gardener.'

Clifford gave a softer sniff than his usually sharp mark of disapproval. 'One would hope he was precisely what he was engaged and recompensed to be. Which included being the custodian of the gatehouse and its immediate surroundings. However, in his regrettable absence...' He tailed off, a flicker of discomfort crossing his face.

'It's alright, Clifford. You were never too hard on Corcoran. Genuinely.'

Heartened by his appreciative nod, she continued. 'Now, it's Christmas, so what say we crack on here with whatever brilliant idea you've had? And then let's celebrate in the warmth of

Hennelly Towers until it's time to head back to the village for Midnight Mass?'

'Most acceptable, my lady. In short, I noticed whilst watching the Gilligan brothers' reckless, and wasteful, antics with the lit matches, that their footwear' – a spasm crossed his face – 'was entirely unlaced.'

Her eyes widened. 'Footprints! Clifford, you clever bean. They didn't walk as a result, so much as both shuffled. Which would leave distinctive footprints which we should be able to spot if they were here the night of the fire.'

He held his hands up at her expectant gaze. 'Indeed. However, I had underestimated the concealing efficacy of this morning's snow.'

'It's still the best plan we've got. Gladstone! Where are you, boy?' Whipping off her mittens, she pressed two sets of fingers in her mouth to let out a piercing whistle, which made her butler wince. 'Oh, Clifford, look!' The bulldog had ambled out from behind a log pile, Tomkins lying along his back, his front feet draped over Gladstone's head like the ear flaps of a furry ginger hat. She laughed. 'So pussy cats don't like to get their paws too cold and wet, is that it, Tomkins?' The tom meowed loudly and then fell into a soft purring, his chin buried in Gladstone's wrinkled forehead. Shaking her head, she waved a hand at the ground. 'It looks like it's just you and me, then, Clifford. Footprint spotting we go!'

Bending from the waist, she set off along the rear of the gatehouse, sweeping the fresh snow aside with the toe of her boot.

'Here's the front half of one!' she called almost immediately. He was beside her in two long strides.

'Hmm. Perhaps you might be so gracious as to place your foot on top of it.'

'But that will deface some of the... oh, dash it, it's one of mine, isn't it?'

He nodded, but his expression faltered as he tapped the charred remains of the thick wooden lintel of what had been one of the rear windows. 'And far too close to the heart of the blaze it is.'

'Just as all those of yours we find will be. Although you catch me unawares so often by silently appearing from nowhere, I'm not sure you actually leave footprints.'

'Says the lady who has yet to master gliding elegantly in an evening gown and heels.'

She straightened up. 'Well, until it warms up, I'll practise gliding elegantly in my thick coat and boots.'

'Mmm.' He hunched down and stared at something squashed into the mud next to the footprint. His frown turned to a look of disgust. He stood up with a grunt.

She stared at it. 'What is it?'

'The remains of a lighter. And if our initial assessment was wrong and the fire was not an accident, possibly the means by which it was started, I'd warrant. Let us return to our hunt.'

She continued her search until Clifford called her over a few minutes later. He was crouched over the shrubbery, which ran on to a copse.

'More prints?'

He nodded. 'Yes. Although they are rather faint and muddled together. They are also too far from the well for it to have been any of us trying to extinguish the fire or deal with its aftermath.' He produced his pocket magnifying glass and held it out to her.

She dropped down and scrutinised the area. 'Mmm, I'd say they look like the prints of someone who dragged their feet rather than walked properly. Like the Gilligan brothers?'

'My thoughts too. However, I did not wish to colour your evaluation. And someone? Or some... two?'

She looked again, tracing every indent with her mittens.

'Two! The toes are definitely larger in one set of prints. And Mick was taller than his as yet nameless sibling, I noticed. Which means he may have had slightly bigger feet.'

'Quite.'

They rose and followed the hedged path with Gladstone alongside, still carrying Tomkins.

'Wait! Look along that line of bushes. They've been trodden down.'

'Most observant, my lady. But why would someone leave the path?'

'Let's find out!'

Ahead, the track was little more than an indent in the scrubby low undergrowth of winter-worn rough grasses.

'A deer path, I would conjecture, my lady.'

'Gracious! They did well to survive not being eaten through the generations when people basically had nothing to eat.'

'A subsequent natural migration back into the area in the years after things had thankfully improved, I assume.'

She looked at Gladstone and Tomkins. 'You'd best wait here. That looks horribly prickly through there.'

'Master Gladstone,' Clifford said in an authoritative voice. 'On guard!'

With an animated woof, the bulldog sat, the cat sliding off his back onto the ground in one graceful motion.

She glanced at Clifford enquiringly.

'A command I have been working on with your otherwise unruly bulldog, my lady. Given the frequency of the, ahem, situations we find ourselves in.'

'Top-notch initiative, Clifford. Now let's find out where this track comes out.'

It soon emerged onto a dirt road, with more footprints visible in a large patch of mud where it met the path. But footprints weren't the only thing visible.

Clifford dropped to his haunches again. 'Mmm. The mud shows the imprint of heavy truck tyres.' He ran his eye down the road. 'Heading east-south-east, my lady. That is, back towards the village.'

'Or beyond to Three Collops Wall and St Colum's whatever it was?'

'In all probability.'

Something tugged at her brain. 'The farmer we spoke to said the Gilligan brothers deliver water, didn't he?'

'Indeed, that being our ruse to venture out there. I noted a raft of barrels lashed to the rear of their truck just before we fled their yard. And, my lady?'

'The man we found unconscious in the road. If the brothers are the murderers...'

His thick gloves muffled the sound of his fingers clicking. 'Then that is how he was drowned! In a barrel on the back of their lorry. Brilliant deduction. Bravo!'

'And then they dumped him on that lonely stretch of road, poor fellow. Without even checking he was actually dead.'

'Hmm. Or, was he trying to hitch a lift out of the village to safety—'

'And they caught up with him first! Oh, Clifford.'

He backed up and cocked his head, muttering to himself as he stared at the mud. 'Prints there and back, curious?'

Her brow furrowed. 'There's nothing curious about them going both ways. If the brothers parked their truck here and lumbered along the path to start the fire, they'd have returned to it, naturally.'

'True. But there are two sets of prints heading towards the gatehouse, but three back.'

She gasped. 'Another person! Gracious, I think you're right. There. That's smaller and longer, more slender even, like a man's shoe rather than a boot. But it's the depth of winter. Everyone is in boots. Including the women.'

'Not everyone, my lady.' He mimed sucking on a pipe.
'Doctor O'Sullivan!'

Midnight Mass couldn't have been held on a more picture-book night. The falling snow iced every inch of Derrydee church's entrance, glistening white in the hundred lit candles set in any available receptacle. Eleanor nodded at the villagers still outside and motioned for Clifford to hasten Gladstone along and follow her around to the back.

'Miss Breen asked to meet us here fifteen minutes before the service started, remember?' she whispered.

He arched a brow. 'Appointments are not items which tend to slip *my* mind.'

But after twenty minutes, Eleanor's feet were numb and there was no sign of the headmistress. She had also developed the same uncomfortable frisson of being watched as she'd felt in the workshop in Kiltyross.

Clifford's brows finally twitched. 'If I might urge you to go inside, my lady. The night is too bitter for you to linger any longer and Mass is about to commence.'

She cast her eyes around for the elusive headmistress once more and then nodded. 'I agree. I don't think she's coming. We're both freezing our—' She caught his warning eye. 'I was only going to say "freezing our noses off" out here for no purpose.' She uncrossed her fingers inside her mittens. 'Let's go.'

Inside, the wooden pews were densely packed with rows of hushed men, women and children, the air thick with the smell of candle wax and damp. The overlying atmosphere was of an age-old community joined in celebrating a most revered tradition.

'Ah, there she is.' Eleanor hurried along the rear of the pews where the headmistress in a grey wool jacket stood gesturing to a line of eager pupils above in the choir loft. At their arrival, the children leaned over and waved excitedly at Gladstone. Miss Breen turned and acknowledged their presence with a polite nod.

'Good evening, Lady Swift, Mr Clifford. You made it through the weather, I see. But don't be deceived into incaution. Last time it snowed on Christmas Eve, the village was cut off until New Year.' She pointed at the choir. 'I hope you enjoy our school's little contribution this evening.'

With a quick scan along the pews, she waved them towards two free spaces in the front row. Eleanor, however, stayed where she was.

'Thank you, Miss Breen.' She lowered her voice. 'But why didn't you meet me fifteen minutes ago as we arranged?'

The headmistress stared back at her, her wide-eyed gaze seeming to strain across a vast gulf. 'Lady Swift, what is this?' Her voice rose shrilly. 'I recall doing no such thing!'

She's obviously batty, Ellie.

'Now,' the headmistress said, pulling on the collar of her jacket, 'Derrydee are united together tonight and Mass is about to start, so kindly take your places.'

Shaking her head to herself, Eleanor went to sit, but then turned back.

'One question though, Miss Breen. The Gilligan brothers—'

The headmistress gasped and shot her a look that made her feel every inch the chastised child.

'I will say to you, Lady Swift, what I say to every one of the pupils that have ever passed through my school. Listen to your parents. Say your prayers. And stay away from the Gilligan brothers!'

She spun on her heel and held her hands up like a conductress, prompting the first wheezy bellow from the organ pipes.

As Eleanor took her seat, an icy pit formed in her stomach. The children's innocent, glass-clear voices floated over the hushed congregation as they sang the opening hymn. 'Angels we have heard on high.'

'And devils we have met on low,' she whispered to Clifford. 'But who here is an angel?'

He nodded slowly, his eyes scanning the pews. 'And who a devil?'

28

Despite having fallen into bed long after two thirty, Eleanor sprang awake at six o'clock. All the excitement of Christmas morning that had fizzled and sparkled inside her as a child had never diminished as an adult. Even with the unpleasantness they had become embroiled in since arriving in Ireland, the year's most special day held every inch of its age-old magical promise to her skipping heart. She glanced over at her bulldog, curled up in his bed with his new feline friend.

'Come on, Gladstone! And Tomkins! You're family too. Wake up! Last one downstairs makes breakfast!'

Scooping up the card from her beau that had nestled under her pillow since the morning Clifford had teasingly delivered it to her, she grabbed her robe. Sliding a hand into the pocket to check her beau's present to her was still there, she bounded over and wrenched the bedroom door open.

'Oh, my!' She pressed the card to her chest, blinking back the hot prick of happy tears. With a skip, she followed the twinkling path of tiny lit candles which ran the length of the corridor and down the stairs to where her butler stood waiting with a steaming cup of delectable-smelling coffee. Only it wasn't her butler as she normally saw him. He was wearing his dark brown dressing gown over his suit trousers and starched white shirt.

'Clifford! You remembered my saying that breakfast in dressing gowns was always the most special part of Christmas morning as a child.'

He bowed from the shoulders. 'On which note, Happy Tidings, my lady.'

'And Happy Christmas to you. And thank you for breaking your rules on being suitably attired. Though I'd say you look very distinguished in your shawl-collared robe. And thank you for the candles too. They are truly beautiful.'

'But disappointingly inedible. Shall we to breakfast?'

The telltale swish of Gladstone, still half-enveloped in his blanket, interrupted them as he lumbered sleepily down the stairs. Conversely, Tomkins appeared full of beans as he repeatedly ran down and back up, encouraging the yawning bulldog to hurry. Clifford bent to tickle the cat under its chin and then ruffled the bulldog's ears once he'd joined them.

'Trust you to appear at the mention of food, Master Gladstone,' he pretended to whisper behind his hand. 'Mind, they do say pets imitate their owners.'

Eleanor was still laughing at her butler's mischievousness as she settled cross-legged onto the now familiar high-backed pew in the alcove of their adopted morning room. Clifford helped Gladstone up beside her, standing aside to let Tomkins spring nimbly to join them. He gestured to the meticulously arranged table, cosily lit by more candles and festively dressed with pine-scented greenery and moss-green linen napkins magically folded into free-standing miniature Christmas trees.

'Comestibles or gifts first, my lady?'

'Ooh! How about both?'

Moments later she clapped her hands at the generously loaded plate, and slender flute of bubbling champagne he placed before her, along with a curve of exquisitely wrapped presents. Glancing across the table, she shook her head at his cup of tea and slice of dry toast, and the singular lack of anything to open.

'Oh no you don't!' She scrambled out from under her lap blanket and poured him a matching flute of champagne, and then ran to the sitting room to retrieve his gifts. Having done so, she slid two envelopes onto his place setting.

'Oh, Clifford,' she murmured a few minutes later, fearing the sentimental lump in her throat would choke her. 'Just look what our wonderful ladies have conjured up for me this year. And I begged them not to bother. From Mrs Trotman, a beautifully detailed book of Uncle Byron's favourite menus with all the little stories behind them. A concertinaed velvet organiser commodious enough for even my vast collection of silk scarves made lovingly by Mrs Butters. And Polly and Lizzie, bless them, they've each made a darling little woollen basket to help me be tidier on my dressing table.' She ran a finger across each of their presents. 'I really don't deserve such amazing staff.'

'Most gracious, my lady, if unfounded. I am sure your staff are learning at this very moment that their mistress has spoiled us collectively beyond all measure.' He held up the first card she'd placed at his setting as she went to protest. 'Arranging for the conversion of the two adjoining storerooms by the kitchen into a staff sitting room is too generous.'

She waved her hand. 'Nonsense. You all work so hard. Those two rooms were never used for anything even half as worthwhile. It's still your turn. Oh, unless you'd prefer to open that one later, of course?'

In reply, he reached for the other envelope beside his plate. But as he unfolded the newspaper advert inside, he seemed to hesitate.

'Oh dear,' she said gently, risking his dismay at her being the one to top up both their champagnes. 'You're so tricky to buy for. Perhaps I've got it wrong?'

He looked up, eyes alight. 'A wireless radio, my lady! And of superlative quality. Indeed not!'

She smiled in relief. 'To be installed in your rooms only though, for when you've heard enough of Mrs Trotman's bawdy chatter in the new sitting room.'

He shuddered. 'Which will be every evening!' He studied the newspaper advert again, then reached under the table. Holding out a meticulously wrapped parcel with both hands, he bowed from the shoulders. 'This is but a tiny token of my heart-felt gratitude for being in your service, my lady. Happy Christmas.'

She swept her place setting clear and unwrapped it reverently, not wishing to tear even a corner of the emerald-green tissue paper. Her breath caught as her eyes instantly swam, for inside was an incredibly life-like oil painting of Henley Hall, clearly lovingly painted by his own artistic hand. Her beloved uncle stood beaming on the top step, his arm around her. She ran a finger slowly along the bottom of the frame as her heart swelled with affection for her impossibly reserved, but ever-thoughtful butler.

'Oh, Clifford, that's the most special gift ever. Thank you! It must have taken you forever.' Too touched to trust her rushing emotions wouldn't embarrass him further, she took a sip of champagne and cleared her throat while casting around for a neutral subject.

'So, we and the village are entirely cut off by snow as Miss Breen warned us might be the case?'

He nodded. 'It would seem so.'

It had been snowing consistently all night, but the intensity had increased tenfold while they were at Mass. By the time they came out of the church, snowdrifts were already piling up and the ride back to Hennelly Towers had been a fraught affair.

Clifford swapped the now empty flutes for coffee cups, while she wiped away the condensation on the windowpanes with her pyjama sleeve. In the few hours she'd been in bed the snow now lay like a thick white eiderdown over the countryside.

Her coffee poured, Clifford popped out to assess the conditions. Returning a moment later, he brushed the snow off his coat and rejoined her at the table.

'I believe we can still reach the village as the wind of last night has blown sufficient off the track onto the fields. However, we will require extra time. So, your planned Christmas Day of joining in with Derrydee's festivities remains intact.'

'Hurrah! Now, we've still got a few hours spare before we need to leave, even with the snow. So, all I have to do is hurl myself into something warm enough...' She paused at his pained expression. 'Problem?'

'With the greatest respect, my lady, for the villagers this is the one day in the year in which their Sunday best will be on display. And will have been painstakingly mended and spruced, borrowed, sewn from scratch or even haggled for at the expense of many missed meals if necessary.'

'So rather more effort on my part is needed then?'

He nodded.

'Well, in that case, you'll have to break one more of your rules, I'm afraid.'

He arched a questioning brow.

'I've no idea what is dressy but not over-showy, given these people have so very little. So, you'll need to run the gauntlet of my fearfully untidy bedroom to help me pick something suitable.'

To her surprise, rather than recoiling in horror at the suggestion, he whipped out a note from his pocket instead.

'Thankfully as unnecessary as it would be inappropriate, my lady. I took the liberty of jotting down a couple of suitable clothing suggestions.'

'Spoilsport!' She swiped the list from his hand. 'Well then, as you've saved me time in choosing, could you bear to take the lead in quickly running over who we think may be a devil, as we said last night – and who may be an angel? Then we can put all that unpleasantness to bed until after Boxing Day and truly enjoy our first Irish Christmas.'

'Happily, my lady.' He produced her notebook from his inside pocket, handed it to her, and then waited for her to get comfortable back at the table. 'Who shall we begin with?'

She flicked to a new page. 'Let's leave aside general feelings about our suspects this time. I mean, they've all been obstructive in their own way. And they've all tried to warn us off investigating. And they've all denied knowing the identity of the man we found in the road, too.'

'But neither of us believed that from their reactions.'

'No, we don't. But, let's concentrate on specifics. Well, what specifics we have. Now, Doyle.' She wrote his name at the top of the page. 'He specifically lied about the cause of death.'

'Unless Doctor O'Sullivan misled him?'

'True. But there was also the suspicious oil leak you noticed at the scene and outside the police station. And he dodged my question as to who he was talking to at the funeral.' She looked up and shrugged. 'That's it so far. Now, Doctor O'Sullivan.'

'The only specific evidence we have, my lady, is that his car seat was wet the night of the murder. Possibly from transporting the half-drowned gentleman.'

She grimaced. 'Hardly damning. And he may not have owned up to it – but he didn't dispute it either – when I conjectured that the man we found in the road had been half-drowned.'

'Which means his lack of surprise denotes he was already aware of the fact.'

'Exactly. And we know he was at the hotel in Kiltyross, an explanation of which he dodged, just like Doyle did about the man he was talking to at the funeral.' She looked back down at her notebook. 'And it might have been O'Sullivan's footprints leading away from the gatehouse we found yesterday, along with the Gilligan brothers.' She thought hard while Clifford made notes. 'No, that's all the specific points we've got for him. So, Father Quinn. Again, if you ignore his attitude and his denying knowing the man we found in the road – oh, and his warning us off investigating like the others – all we have is that he has a medallion. Which, it happens, is very similar, if not identical, to the one I saw on the man in the road.' She winced. 'It still doesn't feel good suggesting a priest might have stolen something, though.'

'Unlike conjecturing he might have committed a murder?' Clifford replied drily.

'Don't be a scallywag. Next, Murphy. Despite his admirable and lengthy firefighting efforts over the gatehouse blaze, he appeared suspiciously quickly. And with a pathetically flimsy reason for being so readily on hand.'

'Which goes for Smithy too, my lady. And returning to Murphy, he also clearly eavesdropped on your conversation with Miss Breen at the gatehouse. But not through natural village nosiness, to my mind.'

'Maybe it was him watching us at the church last night? And at the Wrenchman's workshop in Kiltyross?'

'Very possibly. But as you suggested sticking to specifics, we have no evidence of that.'

'True. Onto the Mother Superior, then.'

'Who staunchly insisted no man other than myself could have been in the abbey, even though you are certain it was a male you glimpsed through the stained-glass window that night.'

'And she seemed quite unnerved when she saw the unconscious man.' She sighed. 'We've even less on her than the others, haven't we? Advancing to one of our newest suspects, then,

Miss Breen. She denied inviting me to Derrydee at all and then last night, denied having asked me to meet her ahead of Midnight Mass. I'm wavering between whether she is a genuine suspect or the poor woman is simply short of all her mental faculties.'

'I confess I am uncertain of the lady's lucidity at times, too.' He frowned.

She looked up at him. 'Are you trying to fathom what grudge she could have held against Corcoran?'

'Worrying though it is that you can read my thoughts, yes, my lady.'

'It's only fair, since you read mine all the time.' She smiled but sobered as she glanced at the page. 'So basically, any one of them could be a devil. Or none of them, I suppose. Maybe they're all devils! Possibly one or more of them were in it together. Or all of them!'

He frowned. 'I believe it doubtful more than two of our suspects would have been directly involved, since it is usually an uphill endeavour to commit murder and keep it concealed. The more people involved, the more likely the secret will emerge.'

'I agree. So, I've kept the best – or worst – for last. The Gilligan brothers.' She counted the points off on her finger. 'They own the only truck, and we know they deliver water on it. Our poor man died by drowning. We're half sure we've found their footprints around the gatehouse and I'm quite convinced they're capable of murder!'

His brows flinched. 'I think we both believe almost anyone is capable of murder with an extreme enough provocation or set of circumstances given our unfortunate experiences over the last few years. In the case of the Gilligan brothers, however, I do concur it seems that they would need very little provocation. If we are sticking to specifics, however...?'

She threw her hands up. 'Guilty as charged. So, going back to specifics?'

'I noted no sign of oil under their truck in their yard. Nor by the heavy tyre marks on the track at the end of the copse. Therefore, it still seems most likely the patch beside the unconscious man in the road was made by Constable Doyle's motorbike.'

'Which places him, not the Gilligan brothers, at the scene of the first murder.'

'To be clear, my lady, it does not necessarily exclude them either. Being the main road, there are numerous tyre marks from trucks that pass up and down, so one or more of them may have been theirs.'

She tapped her chin with the pen. 'Maybe, then, the three of them are in cahoots despite what we just said?' She shook her head. 'That doesn't sit right at all, now I think of it. Doyle's a policeman. Even a crooked one would be more cautious than to murder someone in league with types as untrustworthy and unsavoury as the Gilligans, surely?'

'Normally, I would agree. However, Ireland has recently been through some unsettling times that might lead to such an unsavoury alliance. Needs must, as it were.'

She stared down at the few lines she'd written and flipped the notebook closed in frustration. 'Dash it. Perhaps I should try and call Hugh? Maybe the long arm of the English police might be able to make a few enquiries on our behalf?'

He frowned. 'Unfortunately, given the current uncomfortable Anglo–Irish relations, I doubt Chief Inspector Seldon could be of any assistance even if you could reach him.' He picked up the empty coffee cups and headed for the kitchen, calling over his shoulder, 'I believe, my lady, we may be entirely on our own in this matter.'

29

'Clifford! Just listen to that!' Eleanor's breath rose in a frosted plume.

The noise of the Christmas party in Derrydee Village Hall spilled out to greet them as Clifford coaxed Mullaney to a stop alongside the crinkly tin building. Gladstone barked in excitement, his tongue hanging out like a slice of curled ham.

She cupped his wrinkled jowls and kissed his forehead. 'Why are you so excited, old chum? You've no idea why we're here, silly.'

Clifford eyed her sideways. She laughed. 'Yes, alright. Maybe he's caught it from me since I'm positively skipping with anticipation inside.'

'Though perhaps not only at the prospect of being included in such a festive community event?' he said with mischievous nonchalance.

'Clifford, you do know you're like one's best girlfriend from school? And hilariously, not that much more discreet.' She slid her wool scarf carefully from her neck and wrapped her fingers around the delicate silver pendant inset with a tiny emerald-green heart hanging from the prettiest chain she'd ever seen. 'I still don't believe you didn't have a hand in helping Hugh choose this for me. It's too perfect.'

He shook his head. 'Genuinely no, my lady. Do not do the gentleman a disservice.'

'Well, I've saved his letter to read in bed tonight. Although I might be too excited and come begging to your door to read it to me instead.'

'Assuming either of our vision is still functioning sufficiently to read at all. Which, from the raucous din inside already, I predict, is extremely unlikely.'

'Clifford! Are you actually going to let your hair down just a little? That would make my entire Christmas.'

His expression gave nothing away as he came around to take Gladstone and then help her down.

'Let's see, my lady.' He paused as they reached the door. 'However, one seed to plant, if I may?'

'Try me.'

'Given the more earthy disposition of our collective hosts, should the dance floor seem quite the lure, perhaps remember the words of the eminent Irish playwright George Bernard Shaw. A man acutely acquainted with the minds of his national brethren. "Dancing is a perpendicular expression of a horizontal desire."'

She was still laughing as they stepped inside.

'Ah, welcome be, folks!' Murphy hailed them from across the room as they entered, arms outstretched and looking far more his usual self. He gestured around the packed hall. 'Derrydee are one tonight. And one you both be with us.'

'Why, what a wonderful welcome,' she said. 'We'll try not to disappoint.'

'Did you hear that, folks?' Murphy hailed the hall over a ring of amateur musicians who seemed unable to agree on what tune they were playing. 'The lady of the House of Towers has come for a sharp lesson in the Irish art of celebrating Christmas.'

'Hurrah!' the villagers bellowed back, obviously in the mood for high jinks. Numbering around eighty people, ranging from babies to the elderly, Clifford's prediction of the display of Sunday best was indeed evident in the busy throng of smart trousers and jackets, pretty shawls and at least one ribbon adorning every little girl's hair

She gasped in surprise as Clifford then stepped forward, his distinguished bearing drawing an instant hush. Pretending to whisper behind his hand, he addressed the wide-eyed crowd. 'Actually, good people of Derrydee, my sympathies and apologies. I rather fear this festive night, you might be subjected to a course of instruction in merrymaking, Lady Swift style.'

This drew a cheer so loud, she clasped her hands over her ears.

'All the villagers are going to see is a perfectly decorous lady, you total scallywag!' she chided her butler teasingly as he passed her a minute later adroitly balancing a tall stack of trestle benches.

'While you keep Mullaney company outside?' he called back mischievously.

For a moment, she stood captivated as the inhabitants of Derrydee bustled about rearranging the hall for the main part of the Christmas Day festivities. After a life spent travelling the world, first as a child aboard her parents' wandering sailboat, and then as an adult on her trusty bicycle, the comforting feel of belonging somewhere, even temporarily, was too precious to miss.

And what a united bunch she had been welcomed into. Teams of laughing, waistcoated men, all sporting a sprig of green in their buttonhole, competed to be the first to haul their huddles of mismatched tables into the enormous rectangle being created. Under Murphy's watchful direction, crates of beer and other alcoholic beverages were being ferried to the makeshift bar, which consisted of several doors balanced on barrels. And an army of red- or green-aproned women were unpacking a sea of baskets with much discussion over every home-made offering.

Among them, Eleanor spotted Kathleen, who seemed to have the air of a far more confident young woman than she'd recently had in the pub. Clifford's arrival with two further baskets filled with the sausage meat pastries and mince pies she'd inadvertently hampered him making that afternoon by trying to help were received with delighted appreciation. And, Eleanor noted with a quiet chuckle, a fair proportion of batted lashes. Meanwhile, Gladstone lumbered between everyone getting in the way and halting progress as many curious hands reached down to stroke his wrinkled jowls or tickle his wildly wagging stumpy tail.

But it was the children who really captivated her heart. The youngest charged about the hall, chasing each other with handfuls of pine cones stolen from the centrepiece Christmas tree, while the older ones each balanced another on their shoulders, who then strung yards of ribbons around the lower roof beams. This soon, however, dissolved into good-natured battles to see who could knock who over.

Then, as if by invisible signal, the villagers parted to the sides, their rhythmic handclaps ringing out. She watched as the lads who had helped her up onto the truck to Kiltyross came together in the centre of the hall to form the same brace with their arms. To the crowd's chant of 'Finnegan! Finnegan!' a wiry youth of likely fourteen sprang like a young buck onto the brace and then somersaulted up towards the central beam, propelled by the two below. Eleanor darted forward in concern, just as Clifford did from the opposite side of the hall.

Smithy appeared at her elbow, laughing. 'You've no fears over my lad taking a tumble, miss. Ever seen a cat as has been raised by monkeys?' He pointed at the youth now swinging from one arm from the highest beam, grinning broadly.

'Gracious, that's your son?'

'One of a few handfuls.' He nodded, proudly patting his chest. 'Only,' he hollered upwards good-naturedly, 'he's forgotten the bunches of ladyluck he's up there to hang, the dozy eejit!'

For the next half an hour, Eleanor went from group to group to lend a hand with whatever was needed. The now impressive span of tables was adorned with holly rings, ivy trails and artfully wound fronds of spruce peppered by teardrop woven-reed baskets filled with dried red and silvery-white translucent berries. The hotchpotch of plates and bowls were then added just as the rousing cheer from the men attending to the bar declared it ready. Even the musicians seemed to have finally agreed on their repertoire for the evening and downed their instruments to get a drink in before they started playing in earnest.

As Murphy reached the end of hollering, 'Good neighbours, all set we be for starting,' there was a general scramble for a trestle seat at the tables which Eleanor followed along with, throwing an encouraging nod to her butler. Clifford, however, couldn't help hovering, clearly unable to countenance sitting until all the ladies were seated. Murphy slapped him on the back with a chuckle.

'You're the only one gent enough to wait for the womenfolk to park their skirts. But you needs be quicker than that, Mr Clifford. Derrydee women'll pinch the food off your plate as well if you tarry.'

He shooed the two eager-eyed women beside Eleanor further along the line to make room for her butler who perched awkwardly next to her, insisting in a whisper it would be the one and only time!

With everyone seated, the villagers scooped up whatever cutlery they'd been given and banged the table expectantly. Eleanor joined in, peeping impishly at Clifford.

'I thought we agreed, when in Rome...'

It was only as the noise died down, she spotted Miss Breen at the far end of the rectangle of tables. She still looked every inch the headmistress in her smart grey jacket and ankle-length blue skirt, despite her greying hair being pinned in loose curls. As the banging stopped, she rose and glanced through her wire-rimmed spectacles at the villagers.

'*Nollaig shona duit*, Derrydee!' Her voice carried easily around the hall. Gesturing at Eleanor and Clifford, she smiled in greeting. 'Or "Happy Christmas!" to our welcome guests.'

'And the same to you all!' Eleanor called back to the unanimously nodding villagers. 'Genuinely, I shall never forget sharing this special time with you. Thank you.'

Murphy and Kathleen filled up the glass in front of each adult with something suspiciously transparent and retook their seats. 'And so,' Miss Breen raised hers to the lines of attentive faces, 'to another year blessed of better health, stronger newborns, plentiful harvests and... peace.'

Nods and murmurs of assent accompanied the toasting. Eleanor swigged hers like the rest and immediately regretted it as she coughed most of the fiery liquid back up, to the great amusement of those sitting around her. Having drunk copious amounts of water to soothe her burning throat, she stared pointedly at Clifford's empty glass. He avoided her eye, pointing instead to the basins of stew being placed at intervals on the tables.

Once the stew had been shared out with great care – accompanied by a sausage meat pasty and a slice of bread each – Eleanor tucked into hers with relish. It seemed to be 'potluck', a mixture of various meats and root vegetables in a tasty sauce. It was followed by dessert, including a mince pie. The villagers had mistakenly assumed that the pasties and pies were entirely of Eleanor's own fair hand and took delight in thanking her profusely. So profusely, she squirmed in her seat. Clifford, however, whispered in her ear.

'Because they believe that the lady of the House of Towers made them especially for the village, they are so much more the greater treat.'

The meal finished, the plates were cleared in a trice and the tables magicked away. With the trestle seats now ringing the hall, the musicians stepped forward. As an elderly man struck what looked like a tambourine with quick strokes, they started playing.

'A traditional drum or "bow-rawn", my lady,' Clifford said. 'Ah, the tin whistles too.' His head moved to the beat. 'And now the fiddles. Perfect. Let the reel begin, it seems.'

The music had indeed turned into a haunting reel that set her swaying.

'How does one reel, then? I've never—'

She was interrupted as each of her hands were taken shyly by two of the boys from Miss Breen's peat cart, the bright-eyed Cornelius, still in his pink-bottomed jumper, and the rosy-cheeked and robust Patrick.

'We'll teach you, miss,' they chorused.

And to the collective hilarity of the room, they did. Even Gladstone's spinning in uneven circles in front of her didn't steal the show. But just as she'd almost mastered the fiendishly tricky hops, skips, and other assorted steps of the reel, she noticed her butler's eyes twinkling where he stood beside the musicians. Without warning, the tempo doubled and the entire village joined them on the dance floor. It was only then she realised the "ladyluck" Smithy's son had finally hung up was, in fact, mistletoe. And three women were steering her butler under the central one.

'Serves you right!' she said as she danced past him with one of the lads who had helped her up onto the truck to Kiltyross.

'A little help, my lady?' he said weakly.

'Too caught up here, sorry!' she called over her shoulder.

Over the next hour, the music and drink flowed as the villagers jigged and reeled around the hall, the cheers increasing in volume with each stolen kiss under the mistletoe. Clifford had escaped the women's clutches and taken refuge with the musicians. He'd even played several accomplished tunes on the fiddle, much to Eleanor's ever-growing amazement at his seemingly endless talents.

Eventually, even the hardiest among the crowd needed a pause from the dance floor. The youngest children had all been settled on a pile of blankets in the corner of the hall and amazingly slept despite the din. As Eleanor left the dance floor, Gladstone wandered over and snuggled up in the middle of them all, yawning widely.

In the main part of the hall, dancing had been replaced with singing. To her delight, it was as informal as everything else about the festive fun. Song after song was performed by anyone who stood up as the opening lines were played. She found the haunting ballads accompanied by just a single Celtic harp so stirring, each one brought on the prick of tears. Blown away by the lack of self-conscious and heartfelt singing by even the men, Eleanor wished the night would never end. A sentiment clearly echoed by the whole village because, as the singing finally finished after a good two hours, the dancing resumed with extra gusto.

'Clifford,' she panted a while later, feeling light-headed and gratefully downing the glass of water he'd produced. 'It's gone three in the morning. Do these people have no end to their stamina?'

'I fear not, my lady, because, ahem, they have somehow formed the impression that the lady of the House of Towers is up next.'

Her jaw dropped. 'What on earth have you let me in for now?'

But his only reply was to gesture behind him to where the villagers were enthusiastically beckoning her into the centre of the room. She spun back to him.

'I don't suppose... a little help?'

'Oh dear. Apologies, my lady, but I'll be too caught up,' he called over his shoulder as he picked up the fiddle he'd been lent earlier. 'Let's just hope I remember the tunes and you know the words!'

30

'No, Clifford, really. I'm not finding the bumps a problem at all.' The hard wooden wheels of their jaunting car jarred into yet another pothole. Lifted out of her seat, Eleanor tightened her grip on Gladstone and clung grimly to the rail. 'But,' she said croakily, 'it seems your prediction that last night's festivities were likely to leave one with rather hazy vision was accurate. Your pothole-dodging skills seem a tad under par this morning.'

Clifford sniffed sharply. 'Apologies, my lady. However, I'm sure any reduced faculties, or sense of balance,' he said, glancing quickly at her and away, 'on either of our parts are not due to an overindulgence at the village hall dance.'

She nodded and then thought better of it. 'Absolutely. More that, even after we finally returned to Hennelly Towers, we stayed up most of the rest of the night.'

'Morning.'

'Yes, that too. But what kind of Christmas Day would it have been if we hadn't ended with our traditional chess tournament and a few tipples of Uncle Byron's favourite port?'

'Less sleep-deprived? However, you did finally retire at six thirty this morning, so you'll be fine, I'm sure.' He stared forward, his lips twitching.

She laughed. 'Oh, alright. To salve your curiosity, yes, I did then stay up rereading the contents of Hugh's card over and over. Which was so perfectly him! Just two lines of hopeless awkwardness.' She was overtaken by the smile that always got the better of her at the thought of her far-too handsome, chestnut-curled and distressingly athletically framed beau. 'Happy now?'

His tone softened. 'If the gentleman's words made you feel so, my lady, then absolutely. Not that I meant to pry, of course.'

'Actually,' she said, her hand straying to her already treasured pendant, 'I'm floating somewhere up with the stars that he had the courage to collude with you – a second time too – to let me know he's thinking of me.'

'Heartening news. On to the Wren Boys' Parade in Derrydee then, Mullaney,' he called to the mule.

His words had made her realise that she had no idea what exactly they were heading for. 'Now, my favourite encyclopaedia on legs, what's this parade all about then?' She quickly held up a mittened hand. 'Perhaps just the short version, since I'm sure I can see the church spire already.' She pointed ahead in the distance.

'Miraculous, since the church is in fact west of us at this juncture.' He pointed in the opposite direction. 'Anyway, the Wren Parade owes its roots to the belief that the hiding place of St Stephen, the first Christian martyr, was given away to his enemies by the rapid trills of a wren. Hence, for many years, every December twenty-sixth, which is St Stephen's Day, a wren has been hunted and then paraded from door to door by costumed locals, known as Wren Boys. The bird itself is displayed on the end of a pole, decorated with ribbons or similar.'

'Poor thing! Why go from house to house with it, though?'

'To ask for money to bury the creature since its kind has been deemed evil. Money is "exhorted", as it were, by the threat that the bird might be buried outside the house of someone who did not contribute and thus bring them ill luck. Monies collected have long traditionally been put to a charitable purpose or to cover the cost of one of the celebrations of the season, such as yesterday.'

'Well, the food was delicious. Including the mince pies and sausage meat pasties you made, and I rudely got the credit for.' At his favourite word, Gladstone's head shot up from where it had been lying in her lap. She laughed. 'I did say "sausage", Mr Greedy. And I know you didn't get much, thanks to Clifford having packed you a picnic dinner of your own, so the children didn't feed you all of theirs. But don't worry, I'll make up for it tonight, I promise.'

Satisfied, Gladstone laid his head back down as they rumbled on.

A few minutes later they turned into the main square.

'Oh, my!'

Clifford's potted history of the parade had been as informative as usual, but it didn't prepare her for the large gathering that greeted them. The villagers crowded outside the houses, while in the street stood thirty or more men and boys. At least, she assumed they were men and boys by their different heights as their faces – and more – were hidden from view. She blinked twice.

'What on earth?'

Clifford slowed their jaunting car to a halt and nodded. 'Most creative. Unlike yesterday where Sunday Best needed to prevail, today, the more ragged the clothing, the more in keeping with the celebration, it seems.'

'And the masks? Some of them are positively ghoulish. Look

there, that chap is in tattered pyjamas adorned with strings of leaves and his head is completely hidden by a mask of... of what I have no idea.'

He glanced in the direction she pointed. 'Artfully applied bark, moss and tar, I would propose. The blackening effects of coal dust also seem popular, particularly when mixed with' – he stared at the Wren Boys again – 'molten wax, allowing the sculpturing of the more disfiguring features, I imagine.'

'Half of them are entirely encased in plaited straw, Clifford! I can't fathom a theme at all.'

'As it should be, my lady.'

'Because?'

'Because, what a missed treasure trove of experiences travelling would be if everything were like home.' He held her gaze. 'But hopefully that notion hasn't rekindled too brightly the wanderlust that kept you abroad for so many years?'

'Hmm, it just might have,' she teased unconvincingly. The idea of leaving the life she now had in the village of Little Buckford was unthinkable. She would miss her staff and Henley Hall itself, so imbued as it was with the spirit of her beloved late uncle. Not to mention her soppy bulldog and her beau.

A shout heralded the start of the parade as a muscular figure walked to the front. He bore a pole with the tiny frame of a dead wren swinging from the top. He was leading what was clearly another man bent from the waist, draped in the remnants of several thin brown blankets through which a wooden horse's head poked through. A bank of the smaller Wren Boys broke rank to scamper over to her.

'Oh my! Hello, Samuel, Cornelius, Connor and is that Patrick? You all look absolutely... wonderful.'

'Thank you, miss,' they chorused, spinning in circles. Pausing only to grab a quick lick from Gladstone, they shot back into line and marched on like proud soldiers.

The rest of the villagers milled along behind the Wren

Boys' procession, which stopped to knock on every door. As the entire village was already following them, there was a pause each time until someone left the crowd and stepped inside, only to then step out again in greeting.

After a slow foray up and down the main street, the line of costumes broke apart with no signal she'd spotted. They then set off in smaller groups down the winding alleyways of tiny terraced houses. With a shared shrug, she and Clifford plumped for the largest group. As they wended through the village, Eleanor got another glimpse of how simply the general population lived. Many buildings comprised only a single communal room downstairs with a peat-burning hearth and little furniture.

What also struck her were the outdoor bench seats. Long enough to accommodate at least five people, and set every twenty houses or so, most were merely rough wooden planks. Socialising was the lifeblood of the villagers, she had already realised. But running her hand along one of the seats brought home just how much it must have kept this community battling on together through generations of difficulties she couldn't begin to understand.

A flash of ginger hair broke into her thoughts. In a narrow alleyway opposite, Constable Doyle was deep in a furtive-looking conversation with one of the adult Wren Boys. She caught Clifford's eye and ducked past, using a handy bench seat as a pretext to adjust her bootlace. The rest of their group moved on.

With the two of them now left behind, his gaze followed to where she was pointing.

'My lady, it is probably nothing more than Constable Doyle delivering a caution to a person of no bearing on our investigation.'

She nodded grimly. 'Except that catching sight of the straw-and-feather costumed man he is talking to has transported me back to the figure I saw through the stained-glass window at the abbey! I'm sure it's him! Although, I know I said the same about Murphy. Either way, we can't afford not to follow it up!'

Peering down the alleyway again, she threw her arms out in frustration. 'Dash it! They've both vanished. They must have ducked inside a house.'

'Unlikely, my lady.' Clifford tapped the nearest wall of flaking bricks with his gloved hand. 'This forms the back of the houses in this alley. Their doors are on the other side.'

'Right then.' She darted forward down the passageway that was barely wider than her.

'There!' she whispered at the sound of hurrying footsteps ahead.

But then the alleyway crossed another, just as a rabble-rousing swathe of other Wren Boys swept past with a dozen or more villagers in tow. Once they had gone, she pressed on. But she could see no one.

'This is hopeless, Clifford!' At his silence, she spun around. 'Clifford?' But her butler had also disappeared. 'Clifford?' she hissed again.

Then her eyes fell on a dropped feather several yards straight across. Hurrying forward, she scooped it up and ran on. Something, however, was blocking the end of the alleyway. Or rather *someone*, she realised with a frisson of dread. It was a Wren Boy, his costume particularly wild and all-encompassing. Whoever this was, he had less than friendly intentions as he advanced towards her with a menacing laugh.

Spinning on her heel, she gasped. Another similar figure blocked her exit. Suddenly, it dawned. The man she had followed had led her here on purpose. And for a far darker purpose than she wanted to consider.

As the two figures closed in on her, she spun in a circle, weighing up her options. She would have to fight her way out, that was certain, but which one of the Wren Boys looked the most vulnerable? Even though she was versed in Bartitsu, a form of self-defence similar to that used by the Suffragettes, she'd never tried it in such a narrow space, nor without a stick or pole of some nature. If they both rushed her at the same time...

A shout came from behind the second figure, accompanied by the sound of pounding footsteps. Spinning around again, she saw Clifford sprinting down the alley waving his ex-service revolver.

'Her man's got a gun!' the first Wren Boy yelled over her head. With a violent shove, the other slammed her hard against the wall. Pushing herself off, she kicked out, but too late. Winded, she watched the two Wren Boys dart down another alley as Clifford joined her.

'And next time I'll use it without hesitation!' he roared after the disappearing pair. 'My lady, my abject apologies.' He scanned her face, his own filled with deep concern.

She smiled despite her ribs aching. 'For what? Coming to my rescue?'

'No,' he said earnestly. 'For being so distracted as to allow myself to be bundled into an empty house and locked in. Unfortunately, I had to break the door to get out. We will need to recompense the owner.'

For the first time, she noticed his scuffed shoes, dusty coat and awkwardly held hand. She shook her head. 'Oh, Clifford, someone planned the whole episode!'

31

'But what good would that do?' Back in the slushy snow of the village square, Eleanor took a sip of brandy and swallowed with only the minimal of wincing given her bruised ribs.

Clifford rolled his eyes. 'How about it would keep you safe, my lady? Just for once!'

Knowing his uncharacteristically terse tone was only borne out of concern for her safety, she spoke softly. 'But only by letting whoever is behind all this know that they are stronger than we are. Because that will be the truth if we retreat back to Hennelly Towers and hole up until the Rolls is fixed so we can flee back to England.' Pressing his hip flask back into his gloved hand, she shrugged. 'Are either of us ever going to sleep again if we leave it there?' Gladstone let out a soft whine and leaned harder against her legs.

Clifford shook his head, permitting himself a small sigh. 'I was not suggesting we flee, my lady. Nor abandon the investigation. Only, at the risk of sounding like a stuck phonograph record, that you—'

'That *we* are a great deal more cautious. You're very precious too, you know.' She pointed to his hand, which he was repeatedly flexing. 'Now, tell me that is the result of cracking whoever grabbed you with an absolute wallop across his jaw?'

He bowed. 'Indeed it is, my lady. I administered a "hay-maker" – that being the term for a blow effective at catching one's opponent unawares.'

She gave a mock fan of her face. 'Tsk, Clifford, really! A lady of the manor shouldn't know about such rough and manly pursuits.' Her tone hardened. 'But do make sure you teach me how to do it sometime. Now, as you masterfully knocked the wretch down, you must have got a good enough look to know if you recognised him?'

'Regrettably not, my lady. He was wearing an all-encompassing Wren Boy costume and I was more concerned with finding you.'

'Well, I recognised the Wren Boys blocking my way. At least I recognised their voices.'

'The Gilligan brothers,' Clifford growled.

'Yes. But they obviously had help. More to the point, what were they after with me?'

He shuddered. 'I dread to think.'

'Maybe it was just intended to scare me off investigating?'

'Or to kidnap you. Or worse.'

'Well, it must all be connected with the man we found in the road. And it suggests we're getting close to finding a truth someone doesn't want us to find. Either way, they failed.' She held up a finger. 'Don't say "this time". Because the fact that they will try again is going to be our trump card.'

'It is?' He took in her determined expression and nodded. 'Of course it is. Spoken just like your late uncle, my lady, if I may say. But as we have just mentioned, whoever is behind this has a larger army than ours of only two, so—'

'And an "almost dog" don't forget!' She tickled Gladstone's chin.

'Lady Swift! Mr Clifford!' Miss Breen's voice called from a

passing cart, which seemed to have even more children in than before. 'You'll be after missing the hurling match if you tarry a minute more.' The headmistress gave Eleanor a pointed look. 'And you wouldn't be doing that after swearing to the children you'd cheer for the village, would you?'

Of course, Ellie! The person who had the surest idea you'd be at the Wren Boys Parade was the one person who had her pupils invite you personally.

She smiled, hiding her disquiet. 'Absolutely we wouldn't.' She turned to the cart's occupants, who had crowded to the side to wave at her and Gladstone. 'Boys and girls, is it alright if we follow you to wherever Derrydee is about to be victorious?'

'Yes, miss!' the children cheered.

By the time they reached the end of what looked like a disused farm track, the cavalcade behind them numbered over twenty packed carts and a stream of individuals on donkeys, ancient bicycles, or foot.

'This is more than all the village, surely?' Eleanor said.

Clifford looked around. 'I believe it is, in fact, a testament to the magnitude of this match's importance. The Mullakerney players appear to have galvanised a fair handful of their own supporters to make the arduous journey around the Crag, despite the snow. It likely took them three or four hours to navigate the barely four-mile distance.'

'Well, we'd better cheer extra loud for Derrydee then if the competition is that ferocious.'

Clifford eyed her sideways. 'Ferocious is the very definition of hurling, my lady.'

'Pah! I had to endure years of hockey in a girls' school where winning was more fiercely instilled than any element of the curriculum. And girls pinch. Hard!'

Having parked their jaunting car and disembarked, they joined the gaggle of exuberant men, women and children surging towards a surprisingly green and flat field. Marked out with a wide and enormously tall H-shaped set of white posts at either end, it reminded her of an oversized rugby pitch. Gladstone lumbered alongside, his tongue lolling out with excitement.

She called to the boys and girls jumping up and down on the touchline. 'Who can tell me how one plays hurling, then? I know it looks a little like hockey.'

'For sure, miss,' the nearest said in a horrified tone, 'no one plays at it! It's serious stuff is hurling.'

Another tugged her coat sleeve. 'The men have to whack the sliotar with the hurley betterer through the underneath than the other side, more times.'

'And they can hand pass but not hand run, and snag and slice, but not hand hurl.'

'Thank you,' she said weakly.

Clifford leaned in and whispered, 'All clear now, my lady?'

'As the murkiest peat bog, yes.' She shuffled him away from the children. 'Explain, please.'

'In short, teams number fifteen aside. "Hurling" is the name of the sport and "hurley" the name given to the flattened curve-ended stick you can see the players carrying. It is similar to a hockey stick. The "sliotar" is the leather stitched ball, traditionally filled with cork which can be legitimately carried by hand no more than four steps, flicked up with the hurley and then whacked, or balanced on the hurley for an unlimited time. It can never be thrown by hand, however. Goals are scored by shooting the sliotar through the bottom half of the goal post, which you can now see has a net behind. An "over" is worth only half the points of a goal and is achieved—'

'When the ball's shot over the top. Got it. And there must be a referee, too?'

Clifford's brows flinched as he gestured over her shoulder. 'Indeed. Though I believe neither of us would have correctly predicted who is presiding over today's match.'

'Father Quinn!'

They watched the heavyset, white-haired priest jog across the grass to join the two groups of players clad in knee-length shorts. That he still sported his black cassock, albeit it with the bottom half gathered up to his knees, was incongruous enough to her mind. It gave him the appearance of wearing no trousers at all, since the shorts he may have had on underneath were hidden.

'Really!' Clifford tutted at her stifled laughter, evidently having read her thoughts.

On the pitch, Father Quinn held his arms wide, a ball in one hand.

'Welcome be, neighbours of Mullakerney!' This drew a rousing cheer from the opposing team and their supporters. Derrydee responded with a round of amicable clapping, including Doctor O'Sullivan and Constable Doyle, who were standing only feet apart. Father Quinn then raised his arms and voice. 'Now, let the best team win!'

Whoops and cheers erupted from the crowd, Eleanor included, much to the children's delight.

And then with the blast of a piercing whistle achieved with nothing more than his thumb and forefinger, Father Quinn started the match. Eleanor jerked with empathy as one of the Derrydee players was immediately and unceremoniously felled by his nearest opponent.

'You were right, Clifford. It's positively brutal! Almost as brutal as an English schoolgirls' hockey match!' She winced as a Mullakerney player flew through the air and landed heavily. 'Oh gracious! Whatever is riding on winning this match? Because it can only be a small fortune, surely?'

Clifford shook his head. 'Village pride alone, I suggest, my lady. And, ahem, possibly also the chance for men to indulge in physical confrontation without censure. Though that is a very secondary element of the sport, to be fair. However, even the ancient Celtic Brehon Laws included dictums regarding redress for accidents and penalties for deliberate injuries or death, with the game subsequently being banned altogether in the twelfth century.'

She stared at him. 'The Irish have been playing this since before the eleven hundreds!' Now all the more fascinated, she watched the rest of the first half avidly. What really impressed her, apart from the players' fierce determination to win, was their fitness. They sprinted from one end of the pitch and back as if it was nothing in the bitter December air. What also amazed her was their ability to run at full tilt while bouncing the ball on their stick and still managing to dodge the opposing players trying to bring them down. Eleanor had cheered herself hoarse by the time Father Quinn whistled the players to a halt.

By now, both teams were a man down due to injury, with several players on both sides hobbling or holding their shoulders. Once again, what really caught her attention, however, was the referee. She nodded to Clifford, and they slid off to a quieter patch of grass.

'Not bad for a man I clearly owe an apology to. I ignorantly assumed he was about as physically fit as an elderly tortoise. He's been charging up and down the pitch tirelessly.'

'Indeed, my lady.' He nodded to the headmistress as she paused in walking past. 'Luckily for both sides, Miss Breen, you have an excellent referee in Father Quinn.'

'For sure,' she said. 'Though it'll be eating himself up not to be in the team. He used to play in his seminary, so he told us.'

She strode on.

'And looking like he's not lost more than a few ounces of fitness despite his advanced years!' Eleanor whispered. 'Certainly fit enough to dispatch a man in a barrel of water.'

'Though the other males on our suspect list I would not preclude in that regard either.'

With that sobering thought ringing around her head,

Eleanor went to investigate the surprisingly respectable-looking wooden structure housing the facilities for women spectators. Ringed by a decorous straggle of bramble bushes, she felt for her butler, as the men's facilities were nothing more than three panels of old wooden fencing erected a short distance from the sidelines.

Grimacing at the memory of the far more basic sanitation – or lack of it – she'd encountered on her world travels, she re-emerged to find three brutes in Derrydee players' colours blocking her exit. Each held a hurling stick with thick scarves pulled up to their eyes and heavy brimmed hats pulled down low adding an extra air of malevolence.

She kept calm and folded her arms. 'Three of you? Against just me? Hardly sporting. Which I thought was what today was all about?'

An angry voice made her breath catch. 'Sport is not in play here! This is a game that needs end. And now!' Father Quinn stepped around the three men and stood facing them.

What's going on, Ellie?

He addressed the Derrydee players, who were looking as surprised as she was. 'Let me warn you now, you'll only get your hands on the Englishwoman over my dead body!' He paused, then took a step forward. 'And welcome you'll be in hell with the blood of a priest forever fresh on your hands!'

For a moment the three men hesitated, then with a shared look of horror, they turned and sprinted in different directions.

She let out a deep breath. 'Father, thank—'

But the priest strode on towards the pitch without even turning back to her.

'Interesting...' she mused aloud, staring after him.

'Indeed, my lady.' Clifford stepped around from the other side of the bramble bush and released his grip on Gladstone's muzzle, which was tucked tightly under one arm. His other hand held his revolver, cocked and ready.

She nodded. 'And, if I may say so, a more than successful execution of a brilliant idea.'

He slid his gun into an inside pocket and ran a gloved finger around his tightly buttoned coat collar. 'Aside from my disgraceful lurking beside the ladies', ahem, rest area, indeed it was.'

'Oh relax! No one saw you, you're far too stealthy and cat-like for that, even encumbered by a portly bulldog. But thank you for breaking your rules and lurking so scandalously close to make sure I was never in danger.' Her eyes were bright. 'Come on though, our plan worked. We hoped if I appeared to go off alone, it would prompt someone to show their hand and try again. And it did! And it shows that whoever we are up against can definitely mobilise more than just the Gilligan brothers because I don't think this time it was them. And what an extra bonus! I didn't expect it to result in Father Quinn revealing he's on our side! As it seems he is, yes?'

Clifford nodded. 'However, who else is? And more perti-nently, who isn't?'

'And even more pertinently, will we find out before whoever it is tries again? This time successfully? Which is what you are trying *not* to articulate, I know.' She groaned. 'This is definitely the most difficult of all the unpleasant matters we've tried to solve. So, I say we stay for the second half and then leave amid the safety of the rest of the village. And I think I was wrong before. At least partially. Outnumbered as we are, I think Prudence and Patience might have to be our companions. At least for a while. Let's beat a partial retreat to Kiltyross. In the main town, we may be safer and gain some time to think clearly.'

He hesitated, his face grave. 'A welcome suggestion, would it not be an almost certain re-enactment of a very unwelcome event.'

She threw her hands out questioningly.

'My lady, with the Rolls disabled, we are reliant entirely on the perilously slow pace and capriciousness of our mule. Or our stamina for trekking the entire snow-covered distance to Kilty-ross. To say nothing of the roads being cut off so there will be no passing traffic if we did try. Except one truck, I predict, which would certainly happen along.' He swallowed hard. 'The very one upon which the man we watched being buried took his last, and fatal, journey. The Gilligans' water truck! My lady, I doubt we would get a yard further than he did before they caught up with us.'

She nodded slowly. 'And we suffered the same fate!'

32

A relieved croak broke out of Eleanor as Hennelly Towers came into view. Clifford's lips twitched.

'It appears you left your voice behind on the sidelines of the hurling pitch, my lady. Along with your decorum.'

She flapped a hand. 'What was I to do? Derrydee won a hard-fought victory over their opponents. I could hardly have just applauded politely and offered a "I say, well played, chaps!", could I? Although I confess, I didn't quite understand the final score of 1-24 to 0-19?'

Without replying, he halted Mullaney and checked that they were unobserved. They'd kept in the midst of the other carts leaving the hurling pitch, but everyone else had since turned off into the village, leaving them on their own. Jumping down from the jaunting car, he disappeared into the snow-laden undergrowth. Appearing a few moments later, he climbed back in and they set off again.

Alright, Ellie, if he wants to be enigmatic...

Back at Hennelly Towers with Mullaney installed in a stable with fresh straw, Clifford made sure the doors to the house were all still securely locked from the outside. Once inside, he then bolted them again. Meanwhile, she changed out of her wet clothes and then prepared her own bath to warm up while Clifford was busy with dinner. Once out of the bath and into fresh clothes, she slid into one of the hard-backed wooden chairs in the smaller of the two kitchens. She raised an enquiring eyebrow at his tut.

'My lady, I will be but a short while longer creating a suitable mountain of comestibles to tame your hunger as I completed the greater part of the preparations this morning. What was left of it,' he muttered. 'If you would care to wait more appropriately in the drawing room?'

'No, I wouldn't, thank you.' She pointed at the floral apron tied over his smart black waistcoat and starched white shirt. 'Unless it's because you don't want me to see you in that pinny, in which case it's a bit late. Besides, Clifford, it's still Christmas and...' she ran her finger along the dark grain of the tabletop, feeling embarrassed, 'I enjoyed making the festive decorations together. And helping with the pasties and pies for yesterday's Christmas lunch at the village hall.'

'Ah, that was helping, not hindering?' he teased. 'Very well then, if the mistress insists. Perhaps, however, you might be gracious enough to write whilst I deal with the cooking as I feel we need to...?'

She nodded. 'I know. Things are looking a tad... tight.'

He produced a small bottle from the cupboard and, without asking, poured them both a generous measure. He raised his glass. 'Please excuse the liberty, my lady, but I can think of no one – except his lordship – I would rather be in a "tight" situation with than yourself.'

Her eyes welled as she clinked glasses. 'Thank you, Clifford. And I can't think of a greater compliment. Although,' she continued after she sipped the soft nutty sherry, 'I don't much like the look of those withered stringy vegetable fellows you've got there.'

Without replying, he chopped them finely and popped them into a small pan of boiling water. He reduced it to a simmer for a minute or two and then poured the liquid into a tall, silver-handled glass and slid it across to her.

She took a sip and peered at the pale, yellow water. 'I say, that's odd. Earthy with a hint of sweetness. Nice, though.'

'It is mallow tea. Mallow, or "withered stringy vegetable fellows", as you called them, is a medicinal plant prevalent in this area. It is a most effective tonic for a severely mistreated throat.'

'So that's what you were doing charging off into the bushes on the way home? I thought you were...' She bit back a quiet chuckle as he steepled his hands over his nose in horror. 'How about then, Clifford, you tell me what culinary masterpiece you're conjuring up while we work out how to "unstick" ourselves from this tight spot we've got into?'

'Suffice to say, it is a menu you have never yet eaten, my lady.'

'I wouldn't be too sure.' She tried to peer past him at the bubbling pans. 'There can't be much I didn't try in all my years of travelling. And we're only in rural Ireland, not the depths of remotest Himalay. Come on. What is it?'

'It is, my lady, ready.' He spooned some from the nearest pan into a bowl. 'And served with salted herb scones.'

Cheered that he perched unbidden on a seat, albeit without any food of his own, she peered at her meal. 'Oh, delicious! Buttered leeks, celery, chicken, parsley and' – she leaned forward and sniffed – 'chive, maybe? What's the sharp tang?'

'Several jovial measures, as your cook always refers to it, of Worcestershire sauce substitute, the genuine article not being available.'

'It's sublime, thank you.'

She tucked in, pen at the ready. After a few mouthfuls, she paused.

'One thing that's been bothering me about all this is, why wait until the village festivities to try and kidnap me, or whatever those men were attempting to do?'

'Because the locals were distracted, perhaps? And, more importantly, so were we. And with the confusion of crowds and costumes, it made for excellent cover.'

'But that's the puzzle. Whoever is behind this isn't scared to be recognised by the villagers.'

'Evidently. Sadly, I am minded to believe Derrydee may be in the grip of a gang of some sort. And a gang that wants us out of the way. Possibly permanently.'

She finished the last of her broth, wishing she could manage more. Clifford busied himself at the oven before returning with her second course. Gladstone's nose twitched in his sleep before he jerked awake so hard his front half tumbled out of bed.

'You've squashed Tomkins, you great lump,' she chided gently as he lumbered over and stretched his neck to see her plate.

'Master Gladstone, ahem,' Clifford said firmly, pointing under the table. 'Her ladyship's potted salmon rissoles on seasoned cabbage dressed with a butter and dill extraction is not for bulldogs already sporting an unwieldy girth.'

'Although mine won't be any better after devouring this amazing feast, for which I'm very grateful. I'll dutifully plough in while you carry on now.'

'As you wish. My thoughts keep returning to our previous assessment that finding the gentleman by chance in the road set off a chain reaction that has led directly to today's unsettling events. And yet, despite our best efforts, we have drawn a blank following this line of thought.'

'Gracious! You mean, you now think it wasn't by chance that we found him?'

'No, I am still convinced it was by chance. After all, only the staff at Hennelly Towers knew our estimated time of arrival—'

'Which was fearfully behind, as it turned out, since we got hopelessly lost.'

'Temporarily displaced, I believe we finally agreed on.'

'When we'd stopped squabbling, yes.' She smiled. 'But what were you saying?'

'That only the staff here – who in the event were not actually here – knew of our arrival time. And as we said, we never arrived at the prescribed hour, anyway. Thus, it is unlikely in the extreme anyone would wait in the road with a body, and when we failed to arrive, wait a further half a day and then dump it in front of us just as we approached.'

'So where does that get us?'

Pausing the conversation while she devoured another mouthful, Clifford paced out of her eyeline. Only the telltale soft beat of one hand tapping the palm of his other let her know he was still in the room.

'Done!' She pushed her plate away.

He appeared at her elbow, holding another plate out of her reach. 'Too full for the next course, perchance, my lady?'

'Never! What is it?'

'Toad-in-the-hole, Dauphinoise potatoes, honey-glazed parsnips, and onion gravy, if that is acceptable?'

'Absolutely!'

He placed the plate down where she eyed it eagerly.

'Clifford, you've gone to all the bother of wrapping the sausages in delectable bacon first!' She took a mouthful. 'And adding mustard, sage and rosemary too, I think, to the golden-brown batter they're nestled in.'

'A pleasure, my lady.'

She took another mouthful. 'You know, as there's no topping, I've never understood why it isn't called "upside down" toad-in-the-hole. I mean normally—'

'Of course!' He clicked his fingers. 'Upside down. Bravo, my lady! Just as you have alluded to the concept of the pie having been reversed, we need to do the same and consider every event the opposite way to our previous approach.'

'Brilliant.' She seized his fountain pen and pulled her notebook over. 'I've no exact idea of what you're talking about, but I'm all ears.'

He gathered his thoughts. 'Contrary to what I thought before – that finding the gentleman half-dead in the road was the catalyst for all that followed – I now believe it may actually have been receiving the invitation in England.'

She gasped. 'In that case, if it was the invitation that triggered these events since we arrived, and as Miss Breen sent the invite, despite her denial, she may be the killer!'

'Possibly, my lady. Shall we, however, list the events that occurred following the invite so we can come to a possibly more considered conclusion?'

She nodded contritely. 'Agreed. So, having received the invite, accepted it and arrived in Ireland, if we hadn't found our poor friend in the road, we would have come straight to Hennelly Towers and discovered the staff had fled. But neither of us believe the story about the ghost and I cannot fathom why anyone would make that up.'

'The only rationale I can think of, other than the one we came up with earlier, is that the ghost was fabricated to drive us back to England.'

'But what was the point of the killer inviting me here and then trying to get rid of me almost immediately?' She threw up her hands. 'Someone seems to badly want me here but at the same, doesn't. I wish they'd make up their mind!'

'Is it two people, or the same person, one wonders?'

'Hopefully two. Because if it's one, they are a confirmed lunatic!'

'Moving swiftly past that disconcerting theory. Event number three. The Rolls being disabled.'

She nodded. 'Well, if the invite was indeed the catalyst, not us finding the man in the road, then whoever did it was making sure that, having been invited, we were forced to stay. Which doesn't make sense if the ghost – and fire – was intended to do the opposite and drive us away! And having mentioned the fire, why would someone have burned down the gatehouse and not the main house if they were trying to drive us away or harm me?'

'Because it would be significantly more risky, my lady. And harder. Hennelly Towers itself is almost entirely made of stone. The gatehouse had wooden beams, window frames and door lintels, amongst other features.' He rubbed his chin. 'Actually, the timing of the fire, my lady, if it was deliberate, is telling. Since, if it was designed to drive us away, its occurrence *after* the Rolls was disabled made it impossible for us to do so. Literally. We would have been forced to make our withdrawal like Cervantes' *Don Quixote* and his imagined highborn Dulcinea riding Mullaney across the peat bogs of West Ireland.'

She groaned, reminding herself to find out later who on earth Dulcinea was. 'So, the only thing we have been able to ascertain is that there are either two "entities", as you called them, warring here, or one entity at war with itself!' She slapped the table. 'Well, that hasn't got us that much further. However, I don't intend to sit around waiting to be picked off by whatever entity it is that seems to want me gone or dead! One thing is certain to my mind now.'

He cocked his head. 'And that is, my lady?'

'That there only seems to be one certainty in all this mystery. There is some sort of link between Hennelly Towers and Ballykieran Abbey. Something to do with the man who had the abbey built, and maybe' – she gestured around – 'this place as well.' She took a deep breath. 'I don't know how that relates to what we've just discussed, but I intend to find out before we attend another funeral – ours!'

33

As they neared the end of the tree cover, Clifford paused the cart and darted ahead for another check.

'No prints or tracks of any kind, my lady. Save for a badger and a family of rabbits having passed recently.' He steered Mullaney right with a cluck of his tongue and a wiggle of the reins. They'd left before the crack of dawn, feeling their way in the half-light. They dared not take any known paths to the abbey, so they were following a route that provided the most cover and, hopefully, wouldn't be so snowbound as to make progress impossible.

Once they'd been forced to leave the safety of the woods, however, the vegetation had consisted only of the hardiest of scrubby grasses and a peppering of spiky bushes, all cloaked in winter's coat.

Nothing, therefore, Ellie, to disguise a jaunting cart and passengers. We'll just have to take our chances on this open stretch.

On top of this, the embankment they were now on was not the flat, wide ridge she had imagined it from afar. Instead, it was perilously narrow and steeply sloped, threatening to tip them into the frozen riverbed below without warning.

'Take your time, sir,' Clifford called softly to Mullaney, before turning to Eleanor. 'Fret not, my lady. Mules are more sure-footed than any creature you will ever have encountered.'

'Even scallywag butlers?' she teased to ease the tension. 'What happens when this bank runs out, though?'

'We will emerge just shy of the turning we are aiming for. Unfortunately, anyone keeping a look out where the track joins the main road would see us immediately from that point onwards. Hence, we will need to hide the wagon and our noble steed and continue, hopefully less conspicuously, on foot.'

They crept on, the mule and jaunting car struggling in the heavy snow with Mullaney losing his footing several times but regaining it quickly. Sitting on the narrow wooden plank that masqueraded as a seat, Eleanor was frozen to the bone. And by the time Clifford coaxed the mule to a halt, frozen to the seat as well.

'Here, my lady,' he said in a low voice. 'This needs to be our disembarkation point, I would suggest.'

With the cart and Mullaney hidden and tethered in the bushes with a nosebag of carrots as a bribe, Clifford picked up Gladstone and whispered into one of his stiff pig-like ears. 'Yes, Master Gladstone, another unwise and unladylike mission is on today's unpredictable agenda. Or an "adventure", as our mistress would describe it.'

'Well, Clifford,' she said, pointing up the road, 'maybe our adventure just got more unpredictable. And worrying.'

The telephone line that normally looped its way to the village lay in the shallow ditch alongside. The pole, however, was still standing.

He frowned. 'Mmm. Not felled by the weight of snow, which can be formidable despite its delicate appearance.'

'Which means someone has deliberately cut it, haven't they?'

Fighting just to walk in the deep snow, she groaned as she fell face down a third time. Struggling back up and brushing her clothes off, she steeled herself for the climb up the steep slope to the abbey. Rallying the depths of her stamina, she forged on, panting over her shoulder, 'Onwards, Clifford. Unless you need a rest on account of carrying Gladstone? No, of course, you don't.' She looked up toward the abbey again. 'At least it's the one place we can guarantee the person we wish to see will be home.'

Stopping besides her, Clifford glanced at her soaked green tweed trousers and streaks of mud coating her sleeves.

'Though not expecting a visitor in such a sorry state, perhaps?'

'Oh, stop fussing. I've got in this mess on purpose,' she lied, waving at her clothes. 'There's no way the Mother Superior can refuse us shelter like this. It would be a sin.'

He arched a brow. 'A sin? My lady, the Mother Superior is a *nun*. Bound by her vows.'

Eleanor took a deep breath and started up the slope. 'Well, I vowed we wouldn't come away without getting what we came for. And I'm not breaking that vow either!'

'Child!' The diminutive Mother Superior's intense blue eyes peered through her spectacles in disbelief. 'What could have possessed you to venture here in this?' She waved at the snow-covered world beyond the doors of the abbey. 'Did you not feel God's guiding hand telling you to stay at home with this fierce weather he has bestowed upon us?'

'A good question. And one I shall answer.' Eleanor unbuttoned her coat and shrugged it off into her butler's hands, which she knew would be waiting. 'If, that is, I might prevail on your time for just a few minutes?'

The Mother Superior looked her over slowly, her gaze running from the snow-caked boots into which Eleanor's soaked trousers were tucked and up to her dirt-streaked cheeks.

'No, child, you may not.' She half-turned on her heel. 'Since a few minutes will be insufficient to restore the strength you will need when you leave to repeat whatever foolhardy journey brought you here. This way.' She nodded to Clifford and then seemed to take in the snow-covered bulldog. 'All three of you.'

'This really is too kind,' Eleanor managed through chattering teeth as she hurried to keep up with the Mother Superior in the bone-chilling stone passageway. 'Especially as this is probably not the time you would normally pause in your, umm...'

'Horary,' Clifford whispered in her ear from behind.

The Mother Superior raised her hand without stopping. 'Sustenance is required and thus it is our duty.' She marched through an arched door and waved them in. 'Our calefactory is considerably less chilly, as its name suggests.'

Eleanor stared up at the low vaulted ceiling, wondering what exactly was a calefactory. Three of its stone walls were obscured by bookcases, the fourth with a lit fireplace, the only hint of heating she'd seen in the abbey. The bookcases were unsurprisingly filled with leather-bound tomes of religious texts. But on either side of the fireplace, shelves held ink bottles, women's shoes, brushes and tins of polish.

Clifford obviously guessed her bemusement. 'My lady, a "calefactory" might also be referred to as a "warming house". It is an important area for the preparation of learning materials, the storage of precious scripts and the one place of sufficient warmth to allow shoe polish to be applied.'

The Mother Superior nodded. 'It is also where we afford

ourselves a moment to unfreeze our bones!' She produced three embroidered chapel kneelers that she placed on the only other nod to comfort Eleanor had seen in the abbey – a woven tapestry rug, filling the central area of flagstones. Gladstone made a beeline for it and sprawled himself out inelegantly.

'Tea, Reverend Mother.'

Eleanor smiled gratefully to the same novice sister who had opened the door to them.

'And toast! With honey and bubbling hot pots of cheese. Too gracious, really.'

As Clifford took the tray, the young nun blushed and hurried out. Perched on her kneeler, Eleanor curbed her natural instinct to dig in, waiting head bowed for the Mother Superior to say grace. When the words came from her butler she winced, realising it had probably been her duty to do so.

Why doesn't life's awkward social situations come with an instruction manual, Ellie!

'Eat,' the Mother Superior said as Eleanor raised her head and unclasped her hands. 'Sister Bernard is in charge of our boisterous herd of goats and always produces a fine batch for dipping, among other nourishing purposes.'

Eleanor savoured a mouthful of toast dunked in the cheese. 'And it's wonderful, truly.' Clifford nodded, having barely nibbled the edge of his first undipped slice. She hesitated. He had rightly pointed out on the way up to the abbey that stealth might be a better approach. If she charged in like an out-of-control rhinoceros and asked the Mother Superior what she really wanted to know, it was likely the nun would clam up and throw them out on their ear. He'd put it a little more diplomatically, but she knew he was probably right. *The trouble with this softly-softly approach, though, Ellie, is you have to sit there with a fixed smile on your face talking nonsense. However, you agreed, so let's just chatter on, I suppose.* She nodded in the direction the novice nun had gone.

'Is her full name Bernadette? Or Bernadine, perhaps?'

The Mother Superior's eyes narrowed behind her spectacles. 'Neither. "Bernard" is her vowed name, in veneration of St Bernard of Clairvaux, in France. She was brought up there before dedicating her life to Our Lord. It is not unusual for Benedictine sisters to take the male name of the saint to which they feel the strongest link. St Bernard was instrumental in reinvigorating the Benedictine monasticism in the eleven hundreds.'

Eleanor scrabbled for more conversation. 'Do tell me the incredible story of the abbey. I think you hinted at it before.'

The Mother Superior looked up sharply from her tea. 'I believe you may already know it was built by the original owner of Hennelly Towers?'

'We had guessed because of the stained-glass window in the abbey being similar to the one at the Towers, yes.'

'Well, his name was Feargal Gallagher. He was quite the eccentric by all accounts. His relatives came from Kiltyross originally but moved to Dublin. Feargal made his money in the Dublin property boom of the 1780s, so they say, and got out before the bubble burst, unlike many unfortunate souls. He returned to the area and had what is now called Hennelly Towers built with the fortune he had amassed and which, sadly, for him, eventually turned his head entirely.'

Eleanor leaned forward. 'In what way?'

'His vanity swelled to the point your house, Hennelly Towers, could no longer contain his sense of his own importance. He had a much larger, more palatial palace built for him and his family. On his death, the house was put to a far more worthy purpose' – she waved a hand around her – 'as an abbey.'

'Fascinating. But surely his family should still be living here?' Eleanor busied herself with more toast in the hope the nun would continue. She did.

'There was no family. Despite it being their first night in the new home, the man had to attend to business in another town.

On arriving back the following morning, he found his entire family had been taken by our Lord in the night. The tale tells that a disgruntled servant who Feargal had dismissed just before leaving for his business appointment that evening crept back into the house and murdered the whole family while they slept in their beds.' She pressed her hands together. 'God rest their souls.'

'Oh my,' Eleanor muttered. 'Then what became of Feargal?'

'He furthered the tragedy by taking the stewardship of his life, which God bestows upon us all, with his own hand.'

'Suicide,' Eleanor said quietly.

'Yes. In the letter they found with him, he left the building and grounds to the Benedictine nuns. At the time, we strove to do the Lord's work on the other side of the Crag. All he asked was that we prayed for his, and his family's, soul, which we would have done automatically. Since there was no mention of Hennelly Towers in his suicide note – and he had no surviving relatives – it was sold by auction and bought by the then Lord Hennelly, who renamed it "Hennelly Towers".'

Clifford cleared his throat. 'His lordship's distant second cousin, my lady.'

Eleanor's brain was whirling. 'I can't tell you how precious any information about even the remotest or long-deceased members of my family is, Reverend Mother. Thank you, that means the world.'

'No trouble, child. The mind and heart require occasional sustenance also.'

As the conversation had unfolded, Eleanor's mind had come into sharp focus. She tried to keep her voice neutral.

'Actually, I thought you were going to say another name as you neared that part of the tale. Not that I know how to pronounce it correctly, since it's Gaelic. But "Stiobhard" or "Ó Cinnéide" was the name I expected to hear.'

The Mother Superior's expression hardened. 'For why?'

'It's inscribed in the stained-glass window I asked you about the last time we were here. And I also noticed it was inscribed in a similar window in Hennelly Towers.'

The Mother Superior's voice was icy. 'A word of advice, child. Your sharp eyes would be better used to appreciate the wonders our Lord has bestowed on us. Like today's weather!'

'Absolutely. But someone in the village told me that his surname means "Sea Warrior", I think it was. Perhaps all Irish names mean something?'

'I preferred your honest approach last time you were here,' the Mother Superior snapped. For a moment, Eleanor thought the conversation over, but then the nun continued. '"Stiobhard" is Gaelic for "Stewart" and "Ó Cinnéide" is Gaelic for "Kennedy". And as to their meaning, Stewart means "Guardian of the Hall" or "Keeper of the Estate" and Kennedy "Helmeted-chief" or "Ugly Head", some say. Now, is that all you wish to know, because duty calls?'

'Actually, there is another thing. Are there any Stewarts or Kennedys in Derrydee, do you know?'

The Mother Superior's tone was terse. 'One Stewart, no Kennedys.'

'And this Stewart, are his family builders? Or glass workers, perhaps?'

'No. They've been farmers for generations.' She rose stiffly. 'My time is being called elsewhere, child. I trust you are warmed sufficiently to leave?'

'Yes, thank you.' Eleanor rose too and held the nun's firm gaze. 'One last question on names, though. What was the name of the poor man we brought to your door for help that night? The man who subsequently died here in the abbey?'

A haunted look flashed across the Mother Superior's face. 'Our time is done.' She waved Eleanor out. 'May God bless your return journey.'

Eleanor stood her ground. 'That's unlikely unless someone

finds the courage to speak out and break this wall of silence. Silence brought on by fear. Until then, when I leave, I am heading for exactly the same ungodly fate as the man who died here that night. I know that. Just as I believe you do. And just as I believe, despite your protestations to the contrary, that you know the man's name.'

Clearly shaken, the Mother Superior patted her habit down with a jerky hand, then gratefully accepted the pristine handkerchief Clifford held out. She dabbed her eyes, then looked into Eleanor's. 'The man you brought here, and who died here, was... Ronan Hennelly!'

34

'I came here wanting to find a connection with my family. Even a tenuous one. And instead, I actually met one of them... after a fashion. Ronan Hennelly.' She tried to shrug off the wistful shroud tightening around her shoulders as she climbed back onto their jaunting cart. 'Or "Cousin Ronan" as I would have called him if I'd had the chance before he died, poor man.' She shook her head. 'I think that's the hardest part about learning who he was.'

'My lady, you did all you could.'

'No.' She smiled. 'You're wrong. *We* did all we could. As we shall continue to do.'

His relief at her having reconciled the worst of her grief was clear in his face. He produced a hip flask from somewhere she was convinced was nowhere but thin air. 'Perhaps this might be the spirit?'

She accepted it readily. She was still warm inside from the calefactory, but the insidious cold was already penetrating her clothing after ten minutes back in the cart.

'Port, Clifford? It was whiskey last time.'

'I felt it more appropriate on this occasion, my lady.' She handed it back, and he magicked it away again.

In front of them, Mullaney seemed to have an unerring sense of direction on the return trip, perhaps the prospect of a warm stable guiding him across the frozen landscape.

After a few minutes of silence as Eleanor mulled over her thoughts, she let them tumble out aloud.

'So why, Clifford, if Ronan was still alive, didn't he inherit Hennelly Towers rather than me?'

His brows flinched. 'Because he was disowned and disinherited, my lady.'

'Oh gracious! Whatever did my errant cousin do that was so awful?'

'Perhaps what he *didn't* do might render a shorter answer. His lordship favoured reading snippets of the letters he received from Ronan's father, Lord Hennelly, to me. Why, I am not sure.'

'Because you were his voice of reason, naturally. Just as you have quietly become mine. But go on.'

'Initially, the letters bore only countless tales of wild and boorish behaviour which had landed Ronan in significant trouble. But mostly only with his family as the police were forced to turn a blind eye, given his father's title and standing in the community.'

She grabbed the rail as one wheel hit a rock hidden in the snow. 'Far from excusable though his behaviour sounds, Clifford, he was probably going mad kicking his heels out here in what must have felt like the deathly dull doldrums.'

'Our assessment exactly, my lady. Hence his lordship strongly advising Ronan be engaged in an endeavour to suit his natural interests and aptitude.'

'But to no avail, I'm guessing?'

'No. Only a matter of a few months later, Lord Hennelly received a visit from the police again. Ronan's misdemeanours had escalated to such an extent that the officer informed him that when they tracked Ronan down, a permanent place had been reserved for him in Maryborough Penitentiary. An institution which has long held the dubious accolade of being Ireland's harshest prison.'

'But, surely, the threat of being incarcerated in that awful place would have been enough for Ronan to change his ways?'

'It seems not. When he turned up at the family home, he was served with an ultimatum. Give himself up to the police and renounce his wicked ways and his father would do all he could to mitigate his punishment. Or be disowned and disinherited. To Lord Hennelly's disbelief, Ronan left without a backward glance. Lord Hennelly was furious and did indeed carry out his threat. He also warned every member of the family not to help or harbour Ronan, who was now, as far as his father was concerned, just another fugitive from the law.'

Eleanor winced. 'That was pretty harsh.'

He nodded. 'True. But Lord Hennelly felt betrayed by his own, and only, son. And he had his family's reputation to think of. Moving the tale on, Lord Hennelly passed away more than a decade later, by which time his lordship was the only surviving relative left to inherit Hennelly Towers. Which, of course, he subsequently bequeathed to yourself.' She stopped counting on her fingers as he added. 'Ronan disappeared sixteen years ago.'

'And no mention was ever made of him again?'

'He was never seen or heard of again, my lady.'

'But why then did he suddenly surface at Uncle Byron's funeral?'

'Why indeed? And then why again here, just as you arrived?' Her butler's already rigid shoulders stiffened.

'You're thinking he might have wanted revenge on the family?'

'There is that possibility. Or perhaps he simply wished to get his hands on the Hennelly estate, which he could long have considered he'd been wrongfully denied.'

'Maybe he only recently discovered that I'd inherited Hennelly Towers?' She frowned as she heaved her heavy bulldog to one side and tried to rub some feeling back into her legs, which had already gone numb from Gladstone's weight and the cold. 'Hang on, though. If he'd been disinherited, then removing Uncle Byron and then me wouldn't have helped him, would it?'

'Possibly not in law. But maybe in his mind, it would. Or perhaps he knew, or hoped, he could bribe or threaten an official who was in a position to then reinstate him as the heir?'

'But actually, there was no financial trust included with Hennelly Towers, was there? It's basically a white elephant made of rambling stone, isn't it?'

'Yes, but Ronan was probably unaware of this, as the family's financial difficulties only occurred some years after he left. His lordship, however, was aware of it as I mentioned. On inheriting Hennelly Towers, he made provision for the staff to be retained with their salaries paid through an agency here in Ireland, plus a fund containing enough for necessary repairs. The latter, though, I cannot be certain have been completed. Quite disgraceful.'

'You can help me sort all that side of things out later.' An arctic gust blew over them, making her gasp. *Assuming we survive, Ellie, because if the killer doesn't finish us off soon, the elements might!* She shook the thought out of her mind. 'There is one thing we know for sure, though. Ronan can't have been the ringleader if our theory about the village being in the grip of a gang is correct.'

'Because?'

'Because he was already dead by the time every trouble-some event from the Rolls being disabled onwards occurred. And at the Wren Boys' Parade and hurling match, the Gilligan brothers, I'm pretty sure, weren't acting on their own initiative.'

He nodded. 'They are not the sort to have thought to disable the Rolls with the artful finesse of removing the ignition leads. It is such an intricate piece of engineering, a whack with a hammer would have rendered it such far more easily and permanently.'

'Which is much more their style, I agree. So, they were acting on someone else's orders. Someone far more intelligent.' She frowned. 'So maybe Ronan's penchant for crime led him to being a gang leader elsewhere, and he had decided it was time to return home and claim his throne, as it were. But maybe there was already a gang here and Ronan lost.'

'But why then would he have the newspaper clipping of you so well secreted in his jacket collar? And why rent a hotel room in Kiltyross and hide the key?'

'The Mother Superior,' she muttered.

He looked at her oddly. 'Go on, my lady – Mullaney!'

Her eyes shot to the mule whose head was thrown back, a wild look in its eye, its front legs scrabbling for grip. A split second later, the whole cart slid down a dip hidden by the snow and upturned. She was hurled into a snowdrift, Gladstone landing on top of her, winding her.

Scrambling upright, she hauled the wide-eyed bulldog out of the drift. Clifford, who had jumped clear, was already steering Mullaney onto safer ground. She joined him, crossing her fingers the mule wasn't lamed for his – and their – sakes.

Luckily, he seemed unharmed and unshaken. But by the time they'd rescued the jaunting cart, checked that it was also undamaged, and got going again, the insidious cold had not only penetrated their clothes, but their bones. And what little light there was under the leaden sky was fading fast.

We were lucky, Ellie. If one of the wheels had shattered, or one of Mullaney's hooves been injured, we'd never make Hennelly Towers before dark. And would we find it then?

She glanced at Clifford, who was obviously thinking the

same. He caught her eye and cleared his throat. 'So, my lady, you were saying?'

She dismissed the grim thoughts from her head.

'The Mother Superior. She said I couldn't rely on what I'd seen through the stained-glass window at the abbey because it distorts things. Which made me realise we've been looking at this whole thing through a distorted lens as well.'

He nodded. 'Much as we realised we had initially taken the wrong approach in thinking that everything was a chain reaction to our finding the man we now know was Ronan Hennelly.'

'Exactly! In fact it was the other way around. The invite was the trigger for a series of malicious events that had been pre-planned.'

'And your new insight, my lady?'

'That all the people on our suspect list, I owe a sincere apology to. Don't you see? They've been on our side all along! Think about it, Clifford. They've welcomed us, fed us, helped us whenever we ventured into Derrydee, and embraced our presence at all the festive events.'

'Hmm. Your conclusion, therefore, my lady?'

'That the whole of Derrydee was too scared to tell us the truth. They lied and warned us off for the same reason. To protect us.'

Clifford took a deep breath. 'Does that apply equally to Doctor O' Sullivan?'

'Yes. I think now that he, and the Mother Superior, lied about not knowing who Ronan was to protect us. And I think the doctor insisted Ronan died of natural causes because he knew if we got involved, we'd be in danger.'

'Mmm. And Father Quinn did, as we said, risk his neck to save you. Unless his apparent heroics at the hurling match were staged to throw suspicion off him?'

She nodded. 'Possibly. But he had no idea you were there

and armed. If he did, he's a finer actor than many I've paid to see at the picture house.'

'I concur, my lady. And Constable Doyle?'

'Maybe even he was just trying to protect us. You found that pool of oil near Ronan's body. We think it's from Doyle's motorbike. And we could still be right.'

Clifford tilted his head. 'A contradiction to your reasoning, therefore, surely?'

'No. Because what if he was there trying to *save* Ronan, not kill him?'

'I see.' He rubbed his chin. 'Then perhaps Murphy and Smithy's seemingly suspicious arrival during the gatehouse fire can be explained in a similar vein?'

'Yes! They could have been quietly patrolling out of concern for our safety and were too scared to intervene directly while the fire was being started. But then reappeared once the coast was clear to help do all they could.'

'And Miss Breen?'

'Maybe she never sent that invite. Maybe she's telling the truth. And maybe she was trying to warn us when she offered to meet us before Midnight Mass, but was warned off herself.'

Clifford digested this for a moment. 'Which just leaves... Ronan?'

Eleanor grabbed the rail again as the wheels bumped into a dip and then back out. 'Suppose after he disappeared as the deplorable black sheep of the family, he continued with his criminal life as you would expect. Think about it. If Ronan was an accepted member of the criminal classes, if not a ringleader in one gang at least, he was in a prime position to find out.'

'To find out what?'

'That an attempt was to be made on Uncle Byron's life.' She pushed on past the wobble in her voice. 'We know it was orchestrated by a gang leader because the person who actually planted the poison told us. But suppose Ronan wasn't behind that awful plan to kill Uncle Byron? Perhaps he went to Henley Hall to try and *stop* Uncle Byron's death, but arrived too late. Perhaps, despite being disowned, Ronan was still willing to risk his life to save his family?'

'Then why steal a newspaper clipping of you, my lady?'

She hesitated. 'Clifford, I don't believe anyone is entirely bad. Or necessarily good, for that matter. We are all human. Including Ronan, I'm sure. Despite his chosen path in life, suppose he missed his family? I would,' she said quietly. 'Suppose he broke into Henley Hall to feel close to his family? To feel part of it, just for a moment. Why, otherwise, look through the family albums?'

Clifford nodded slowly. 'And while doing so, he discovered that his lordship actually had a niece he did not know of. A niece who he now feared would be next on the killer's list. So, he took the newspaper clipping of you so he could recognise you and—'

'Save me, where he'd failed with Uncle Byron. Which is why he turned up here on discovering somehow that I had been invited for Christmas.'

'But the murderer was too smart for him, despite his having tried to return without anyone's knowledge?'

She nodded. 'Exactly. Which meant Ronan had to escape. But he only got as far as that stretch of road we found him on before he was caught. And killed.' She sighed. 'Poor cousin. We can only hope while he was unconscious, he wasn't suffering.'

Twenty minutes later, with the last of the light gone, they edged past the gatehouse ruin, now just a black ominous shadow, and reached the main building. Climbing stiffly off the jaunting cart, Clifford stabled Mullaney and trudged across to the front entrance with a solitary oil lamp, accompanied by Eleanor and an exhausted and grumpy Gladstone. He unlocked the door, his brows knitted.

'My lady, if we are correct, the only remaining question is why a ruthless killer seems determined to eradicate the last of the Hennellys.'

Inside, she shook the snow off her coat. 'I believe I know the reason.' The oil lamp threw a ghostly shadow on the walls. 'And they might have succeeded with Uncle Byron,' her voice hardened, 'and poor Cousin Ronan, but they've failed twice with me already.'

The shadow spoke. 'Then third time lucky!'

35

A familiar balding domed forehead stood in the doorway to the cellar.

Corcoran!

In the flickering light of the oil lamp, he bared his stained, yellowing teeth in a grotesque grin. 'I'll not be bothering with tugging on the old forelock since your days of being the lady of the House of Towers just ran out, so they did.'

The penny dropped. She gasped. 'You're not Corcoran at all! You're the gang boss who's got the whole village living in fear!'

'And town!' he said sharply. 'I own Kiltyross as well. And thank you for your flattery.'

'None intended,' she said coldly. 'Despite everything, I'm nothing but glad I came here. The people of Derrydee are wonderful.' Her eyes flashed. 'How did you get in? And what did you do with the real Corcoran?'

'Your man locked the place up real secure, so he did. But the real Corcoran "volunteered" the information that there is a hidden way in through the cellar there. And don't worry yourself, he's still alive. I sent your old retainer fleeing with the rest of the staff and took his place. Seeing as neither of you had ever seen him, it was easy to do.'

The fake Corcoran took a step over the threshold. He wore an expensive fitted dark-blue wool suit instead of the previous wrinkled shirt and button-beleaguered cardigan. In his hand was a revolver. Behind him, the grinning Gilligan brothers, armed with shotguns, shuffled in.

Clifford stiffened, but his tone remained as impassive as ever. 'Bravo, Mr—?'

The man bowed. 'You can call me O'Donovan. It's as good a name as any.'

'Bravo, Mr O'Donovan. But why the charade?'

'Why? To allow me to keep tabs on you, of course.'

Clifford clapped slowly. 'A round of applause for your fine acting, then. And cunning, no less. I assume you made up the story about never coming into the house since a child because if you had, I would have known immediately that you'd never been in service here?'

He gave a mock bow. 'Spot on, Mr Clifford. And I knew that from reading the letters you sent dear old Corcoran. You really are every bit as I imagined.'

'Only you *did* come into the house,' Eleanor said. 'I saw a lighter on a shelf upstairs, which I had assumed the staff used to light the lamps. But Clifford found another one at the scene of the fire. Only it was the same lighter, wasn't it?'

He shrugged. 'A careless moment on my part.'

She shook her head. 'I should have worked out you weren't Corcoran when you sent us off to Kiltyross on the truck. You told us the wrong place to wait, and that there was only one truck a day coming back, when there were obviously more.'

Clifford raised a finger. 'Plus, at no point did Murphy or Smithy ask after Corcoran while we were tackling the blaze. Not, as I thought at the time, to spare a lady's sensibilities, but because they knew the real Corcoran had fled with the other staff.'

She nodded. 'And Sullivan never actually said it was Corcoran's body they found in the gatehouse after the fire, now I think back over his words.' She curled her lip in disgust. 'And that's why Miss Breen was trying to tell me not to mourn! It's all been one big sham. Like the imaginary ghost. That wasn't to drive us out. It was to keep up the ruse of why the staff had fled, wasn't it?'

Clifford frowned. 'But why, Mr O'Donovan, having artfully set yourself up as the fake Corcoran to spy on us, did you then arrange your own death?'

O'Donovan grinned. 'Because your mistress has a far sharper brain under that bonnet of red curls than I imagined. I was smart enough to realise she'd soon cotton on to me. And that you would as well. And if I'd disappeared, it would only have made you both poke your noses in all the harder. So, I set up the pretence that my poor old soul had been tragically taken in the gatehouse fire.' He laughed. 'The idea tickled me too, so it did.'

She purposefully turned away from O'Donovan. 'That explains why there was no second body in Murphy's pub then, Clifford.'

He did the same and nodded. 'And why, my lady, there were only two sets of footprints approaching the scene of the blaze.' He inclined his head at the Gilligan brothers. 'And three sets leaving. Mr O'Donovan's being the additional set.'

So obvious now, Ellie! 'So, whose body was it they found in the burned-out gatehouse, Clifford? Assuming one was there at all?'

'Sadly, my lady, that of your cousin Mr Ronan Hennelly, I conjecture. The man drowned by the disgraceful reprobates in this room.'

'Hey, this isn't a cosy chat over tea between the two of you!'

O'Donovan shouted. 'I'm in charge here. And you might think yourself smart, woman, but you paid your respects to an empty coffin!'

She tried to keep her voice even. 'So why did you murder Ronan?'

He cocked his head. 'Come now, I heard you as you came in the door there. You know why.'

She nodded. 'He got in the way of your plan to lure me here... and then murder me.'

Already certain of the answer, she asked anyway to buy them some time. 'So, how did you drown him?'

O'Donovan snorted. 'I knew Ronan from before he disappeared. We vied to be King of Derrydee and Kiltyross back then. I won and he fled! Then I found out he'd returned. Somehow he'd found out you were coming here for Christmas, I think. Anyways, I knew he would have no choice but to flee again once he realised I was on to him. If he wanted to stay alive long enough to save you, that was. And that road was his only route out. We found him quick enough and encouraged him into a barrel on the back of the lads' truck.'

She stiffened, but caught Clifford's eye and forced herself to relax. *Keep a level head, Ellie, it's not over yet.* O'Donovan was still talking. 'Then that old fool Doyle turned up, trying to do right by his uniform. But it was three to one, and he knows I've the other police in the area in my pocket, so he fled.'

The Gilligan brothers laughed. 'Once he'd wrestled his motorbike back up!'

So that's why there was such a noticeable patch of oil! Her voice was icy. 'Let me finish the tale. Once he was dead, you dumped him in a ditch. But you couldn't even do that properly because he wasn't dead and crawled out into the road with the last of his strength.'

'Alright!' O'Donovan snapped. 'So what? Once I found out you'd stumbled along at the wrong moment and played the wretched Samaritan card by taking him to the abbey, I returned to finish the job.'

We must have been tailed to the abbey. 'So, it was you I saw on the other side of the stained-glass window?'

He nodded. 'And I saw you. No mistaking that shock of red curls, however distorted the view. But the nuns played hide and seek with Ronan. Just when I was driven to getting nasty, O'Sullivan appeared with the grand tidings that he'd finally died, anyway.'

So the Mother Superior was protecting Ronan by locking him in that room so deeply buried in those winding corridors.

O'Donovan shook his head ruefully. 'I should have remembered how hard it is to kill a member of your family. It's like none of you want to die!'

The Gilligan brothers guffawed at the joke, but stopped at O'Donovan's scowl.

Eleanor gasped. 'I... I was right about that as well. It was you who orchestrated my uncle's death!'

O'Donovan rolled his eyes. 'And just like Ronan, the trouble he gave me! You don't think I got rid of the old buzzard the first try? Pah! That's why I had to get help in the end to poison him. And one of the reasons I lured you here where I could control the process better the second time around, as it were.'

She saw Clifford's jaw tighten and his eyes glance sideways at the Gilligan brothers. But other than that, his face failed to betray the emotions she knew would be coursing through him.

O'Donovan's yellowed teeth shone in the flickering oil lamp again as he grinned at her. 'So, Lady Swift, now you know who sent you that soon-to-be-fatal invite. Me.' His tongue flicked over his bottom lip like a snake watching a rabbit. 'But I warrant you still have no idea why?'

She took a deep breath. 'Maybe not. But I'm sure I can guess. The only reason you could have for killing off the last of my family – including me – is to get your hands on what Ronan never could. Hennelly Towers. With no one left to inherit it, it would be sold at public auction and you could pick it up for next to nothing. Just like Lord Hennelly did after its original owner, Feargal Gallagher, committed suicide, leaving no heirs.'

O'Donovan nodded appreciatively. 'Fair play to you. But you haven't guessed why I really want this pile of worthless stones, have you?' His eyes lit up with an eerie glow. 'You see, neither the first – or the last – of the Hennellys knew what I know. That it contains a fortune within its walls! A fortune hidden away by the fool who built it. One he planned to transfer to his new home but never did.'

'Of course!' Eleanor's mind was racing. 'Before Feargal could, his family tragically died that terrible night.'

O'Donovan grinned. 'Murdered by a servant, by all accounts! Well, that was what gave me the idea of posing as old Lord Hennelly's servant, Corcoran, you see.'

Her lip curled. 'And did you also originally intend to murder us in our beds?' She shook her head. 'Whatever, I bet after learning about his family's death, the fortune Feargal had amassed and hidden suddenly wasn't at the forefront of his thoughts. He was torn with grief at the death of his family and terrified for his soul, knowing what a sin he was about to commit by taking his own life. And he knew the nuns over the valley had nowhere to carry out their work. So, he left the building to them that is now Ballykieran Abbey on the proviso they'd pray for his and his family's souls.'

One of the Gilligan brothers glanced towards the front door. 'Boss, we should be getting moving.'

O'Donovan waved his gun at him. 'Shut it!' He turned back to her. 'Keep going. I'd like to see you connect the last pieces for yourself.'

She thought for a moment. 'Somehow, you found out about the fortune and...' Suddenly, she was blinded by rage. Catching

Clifford's eye again, she swallowed hard. *If he can stay calm at this moment, Ellie, you can too.* She forced herself to continue, 'And you killed Uncle Byron for it.'

'And it should have worked too,' he said bitterly, the lack of remorse in his voice cutting through her like a scythe. 'When I was a kid, my family had nothing. Most days there was no food on the table, no peat on the hearth. I swore I would be rich one day beyond anything anyone around here had ever seen! Then I overheard my grandfather telling my father about the rumours that the man who built Hennelly Towers and the abbey had died leaving a fortune stashed away somewhere. But they all held the secret had died with him. I swore to myself from that day on I'd crack that secret and find that fortune.' He leaned forward, eyes glinting. 'And when I did, I'd spend every single penny living like the mightiest king ever crowned.'

She laughed harshly. 'A comforting bedtime fairy tale to tell yourself.'

'No!' he barked. 'It wasn't a fairy tale. But I never cottoned on to where the fortune was until just after old Hennelly died. But you' – he jabbed a finger at her – 'you were too close to working it out. You've been up to the abbey sniffing about. It was only a matter of time before you traced it here. To Hennelly Towers.' He spat on the ground. 'You've been a thorn in my side from the moment your uncle croaked!'

Blinking back the tears now burning behind her eyes, she smiled thinly. 'It's been an absolute pleasure.'

'Not for me! You were never supposed to exist! Once Old Hennelly died off, with Ronan disinherited and likely dead, we all thought it only left your uncle, Lord Henley, as an heir. I waited for him to come here, but he couldn't even be bothered to visit the house he'd inherited. Just like an Englishman! Then I dealt with him and found you had inherited! I figured, like him, you wouldn't bother to come over either. But I knew if I just ignored you and marched in and started taking the place apart someone would blag. And then the national troubles really kicked in and it took up most of my time just trying to keep a grip on things.'

Keep him talking, Ellie! She caught the barest flinch of her butler's form in her peripheral vision, and an imperceptible movement of his head. She discreetly nodded back. 'So,' – she smiled sweetly – 'all your plans came crashing down because you hadn't factored in... me!'

He scowled. 'I never knew you existed. But if I had, I'd have dismissed you. Girls aren't supposed to inherit! Your uncle must have been touched in the head.'

It happened too quickly for her to process. But in a blur, Clifford elbowed the Gilligans aside and leaped forward, his fist making bone-crunching contact with the smug face before her. O'Donovan collapsed to the floor.

'For his lordship!' he growled as the Gilligan brothers grabbed him and shoved him back against the wall.

O'Donovan rose shakily, not daring to touch his obviously broken nose, which was spewing blood down his suit. 'Oh, I'm going to enjoy the next part even more than I'd thought. Because now it's time for you to have that accident I planned all along.' His face twisted into an evil grin. 'Don't worry, girl, you and your fool of a man there are due for a little drive. Only in all this snow, your fancy car is going to skid off that icy pass and hit one of those big, nasty old rocks. And then burst into flames. How sad!'

36

With their hands tightly bound behind them, Eleanor and Clifford were bundled out of the house by the Gilligan brothers, O'Donovan bringing up the rear, nursing his bloodied nose. The icy blast that met them cut straight through her. The brothers had given them no time to change or grab a coat and she was still wearing the same frozen clothes she'd left Hennelly Towers in that morning.

'In the car with them!' O'Donovan barked, waving through the darkness towards the barn Clifford had stored the Rolls in.

One of the brothers held up the ignition leads. 'She'll go just fine once we've put these back on.'

'That's right!' the other brother smirked. 'Straight over the cliff!'

In the garage, O'Donovan ran admiring hands around the Rolls' polished walnut steering wheel, as Eleanor and Clifford were each roughly shoved into the back of the car. So roughly, that they banged heads as they tumbled together. Eleanor's only consolation was that they'd left Gladstone behind. 'Don't worry,' she'd told him, 'we'll be back soon.' Whether or not he believed her, she didn't know. She wasn't sure she believed it herself.

One of the brothers climbed into the front passenger seat while the other headed to their car, hidden around the back of the garage. O'Donovan turned and grinned at Eleanor, his bent and grotesquely swollen nose and the blood congealing along his lips making his malevolent expression all the more disturbing.

'Your last ever chauffeur-driven ride, Lady Swift. And with your oh-so-faithful driver trussed up fiercer than whatever fancy roast pheasant you're used to eating, it'll be me driving.' His grim laugh cut her retort dead. 'And I'll do you the honour of making it a ride you'll remember every day you're lying in your ice-cold grave. Which, just to be clear, is waiting at the end of it!'

Even Clifford's usually reassuring presence could offer her no comfort against that image, despite him being sandwiched hard up against her side. For even before O'Donovan had turned back fully to the steering wheel, the Rolls spun clear of the barn and slewed wildly across the snow-laden yard.

Clifford leaned forward, his perfect butler tone as measured and impassive as ever. 'I trust, Mr O'Donovan, you have had the foresight to make the aforementioned grave sufficiently large to accommodate us all. Unless, that is, you intend to drive with more finesse in these conditions?'

'Shut it!' O'Donovan spat.

Despite the crime boss's bravura, it seemed Clifford's words had hit their mark, for O'Donovan slowed down and they made it the full length of Hennelly Towers' drive with only three more slides. The steep slope down to the bottom road presented far more of a challenge though, and they covered it mostly sideways and partly backwards after a particularly violent spin with many muttered expletives coming from the front. Thankfully, Clifford had gallantly leaned slightly forward the minute the car had turned out of the drive to allow his shoulder to respectfully press Eleanor more safely into her seat.

Still with their hands bound, they lurched every which way, alternate groans and grunts escaping with every heavy snatch O'Donovan gave the steering wheel. In the front, the Gilligan brother hung onto the leather door strap with both hands, his brother following gingerly behind in the other car.

On the brief, more level stretch at the bottom, O'Donovan urged the Rolls onwards, the car's tyres crunching along the icy road. Five or so minutes later, he swung the car right onto the main road. In the back Eleanor and Clifford exchanged a glance.

'The end destination of this farewell tour of yours is...?' she called forward.

'Is far enough and no more,' O'Donovan barked over his shoulder. 'Five-mile point is my favourite part of this road, wouldn't you know. It's just about driveable up to there and then it's completely snowbound.' He sniggered. 'You won't be the first to have lost concentration and driven clear over the edge. Doesn't need too much height. There's the perfect welcoming crop of granite just below. And, of course, the car will naturally catch fire, burning its occupants to a crisp if they are lucky – or unlucky – enough to still be alive.'

Eleanor silently chewed over what their captor had inadvertently let slip.

Five miles out from Derrydee, makes it about how far from here?

Clifford gave three quiet coughs as if clearing his throat.

Three miles roughly, then. Even at this slip-slide speed up a slope, which sounds less steep than the one down from the house, we've not got long.

She nudged Clifford's side discreetly and shifted her legs sideways, which he copied. After waiting for another lurch of the car to make it seem natural, she turned her upper body so that she and Clifford were at a slight angle to each other. Her numb fingers could now just reach the ropes bound so spitefully tight around Clifford's wrists. Forcing herself to work calmly while chipping in with her butler's distracting entreaties to O'Donovan, she traced the knots and set to work on loosening his bindings as best she could.

But in the wildly sliding car, her best efforts fell short all too soon.

'Here!' O'Donovan growled darkly, slewing to a halt.

In the headlights, she could make out the line of roadside undergrowth on the right. But on the left, there was only an abyss.

The other car parked next to them and the two brothers manhandled Eleanor and Clifford out onto the road.

'Now,' O'Donovan said, grinning maliciously, 'in the front. Both of you.'

While he was talking, Eleanor's sharp ears had pricked up. In the lull of the wind, she was sure she'd heard something out there in the dark past the light thrown by the cars' headlights.

O'Donovan cocked his head as if he'd heard something, too. Quickly, she turned to Clifford.

'Such a dashedly bitter wind from the north-east up here, Clifford. I don't much care for it.' She tipped her head imperceptibly in the direction the sound had come from. Then, flopping backwards, dug her heels in against the side of the car and addressed O'Donovan and the brothers. 'Nor the lack of manners, you savages! I'm a baronetess, you know!' Increasing the petulance of her tone, she stamped a foot at her kidnappers who were staring at each other in confusion. 'You're not lord of the manor yet, O'Donovan!'

Clifford, taking his cue from her, jumped backwards and flattened his back against the car as well. 'Absolutely! You'll get your goons here to apologise to her ladyship forthwith, O'Donovan, or I shall give them – and you – the thrashing of your lives!'

O'Donovan gawped at them both in disbelief. 'You're not serious?' His eyes narrowed evilly. 'You're going to be sorry you messed with me!'

He nodded at the brothers and all three of them advanced menacingly towards them.

'That's far enough!' a voice called from the dark. 'Drop your weapons and turn around. Slowly.'

Murphy, Ellie!

O'Donovan and the brothers froze. For a moment, no one moved, then another voice called out. 'We mean it!'

And Smithy!

O'Donovan motioned for the brothers to lower their weapons. Slowly, all three turned around to see Murphy and Smithy standing in the road ahead of them, oil lamps in one hand and a pistol apiece in the other, jaws set hard.

'It's over,' Murphy called calmly, taking up a defensive stance with Smithy.

O'Donovan glared at the two. 'You've one chance to go back to the village. OR ELSE!'

'I wouldn't agree with that, actually,' Doctor O'Sullivan's educated voice answered as he stepped into the pool of light. As smart as ever in his neat green suit, in place of his leather medical bag, however, he too held a revolver. He nodded to Eleanor as he strode to join the other two.

One of the Gilligan brothers pointed at the gun in the doctor's hand. 'Boss, that's one of ours. They've raided our bloody arms' stash at the yard!'

O'Donovan shrugged. 'No matter, boys, we're still in charge here.' He threw his arms wide. 'I've more men with more guns, you know that. And they'll be coming after you three.' He grimaced. 'You'll be begging them to kill you instead of what I'm planning.' He nodded at the brothers and started to raise his gun.

'I really wouldn't do that,' Murphy said as calmly as before.

From the darkness, the last man Eleanor expected to see stepped out, revolver at the ready. 'Your other men are under lock and key, O'Donovan,' Constable Doyle said. 'At least the bulk of them. And they squealed as to your plans without much persuasion. Those we haven't got yet are being flushed out with dogs as we speak. And if you and your men don't drop your guns right now—'

'Then what?' O'Donovan snarled.

The chain of defiance started by Murphy, Smithy and the doctor grew as more armed men emerged from the dark, faces set in grim determination. Eleanor recognised many of them from the village, including Sheeply Walsh, the farmer who'd towed the Rolls. Doyle stepped forward to stand eye to eye with O'Donovan.

'You can force me to turn a blind eye when you kill one of your own kind, like Ronan Hennelly,' he said grimly. 'Especially when I thought he'd come back to cause trouble as of old.' He shook his head. 'I tried, but I wasn't prepared to lose my life saving the likes of *him*. But this!' He gestured at Eleanor, then at Clifford. 'This is not going to happen as long as I'm still breathing. Nor while any of the good folk of Derrydee are either.'

Eleanor blanched as Kathleen appeared with another lit lamp and marched over to stand next to her father. It seemed certain there was going to be a bloodbath. And then Clifford casually stepped forward and with a now free hand swung a haymaker at the already broken nose in front of them. With the wail of a snared animal, O'Donovan collapsed to the ground for a second time. Eleanor quickly turned to the Gilligan brothers.

'Your boss is finished. Are you really going to fight on without him?'

The brothers looked at each other, hesitated, and then both dropped their guns to the ground. The villagers surrounded them, Murphy and Smithy tying the Gilligans' hands behind their backs. Meanwhile, Doyle slapped a pair of handcuffs on the now semi-conscious O'Donovan and dragged him to his feet. He shook his head, blood spraying his suit and the ground.

'Lady Swift,' his tone was mocking, 'it seems the luck of the Irish is with you tonight, not me. But, know this.' His voice darkened. 'I'll be back to claim that fortune. If not in life, then in death. I'll haunt your wretched House of Towers for all eternity till I do!'

As Doyle led him away, Murphy and Smithy took a Gilligan brother each and followed the constable to a waiting cart. Meanwhile, Doctor O'Sullivan strode over and cut the rope still binding Eleanor's hands.

'Everyone, thank you,' Eleanor called out, her voice equally shaky from emotion and cold. 'I don't know what else to say.'

'That's easy.' Doctor O'Sullivan scanned her face. 'Say nothing. Instead, get yourselves back to Hennelly Towers before you succumb to hypothermia or shock. Since indomitable is not the same as invincible.'

Clifford offered his left hand to Dr O'Sullivan. 'Thank you, Doctor. I have been trying to persuade her ladyship of that for years.'

She laughed shakily. 'But you must all come back to—'

Doctor O'Sullivan shook his head. 'There's a few as were injured in the skirmishes when we were rounding up the other members of O'Donovan's gang. And there's still a couple out there that gave us the slip. Although, now we've got the ringleader, I don't think they'll give us any trouble. So, unless you need anything in the way of medical assistance from me, be off to get out of those clothes into something warm as soon as you can and rest. And listen to every word of sage advice your man here has to offer.'

Clifford held up a finger. 'On that note, Doctor, you don't happen to have an ear trumpet about your person? Hard of hearing so oft befalls her ladyship on that score.'

With a final call of 'Thank you!' and 'See you all in the pub in the morning!' Eleanor allowed herself to be led back to the Rolls.

As they gingerly set off back to Hennelly Towers, she slumped in her seat. 'Well, Clifford, I don't know about you, but I fancy a hot bath and then something fortifying to eat – and drink!'

Back at Hennelly Towers, Gladstone gave them the lickiest welcome ever and was soon ensconced in the window seat alongside Eleanor and Tomkins. Clifford poured her a generous measure of port and then, at her look, one for himself. He raised his glass.

'If I may propose a toast, my lady?'

She shook her head. 'Actually, no.' She smiled mysteriously as he arched a brow. 'There's something we need to do first. One last adventure!'

A pained expression passed over his face. 'Really, my lady? To date, I rather felt we'd had an overabundance of such on this supposed holiday?'

She shrugged. 'Possibly, but there's always room for one more. You see, O'Donovan was wrong about him finding the fortune in life. Or death.'

His brow furrowed further. 'My lady?'

But she was already heading for the stairs...

In the small alcove on the landing, Clifford peered through his pince-nez.

'They are, aren't they?' she breathed.

'Indubitably, my lady.' He straightened up, eyes bright with curiosity. 'The names you asked the Mother Superior about whilst we warmed ourselves in the abbey's calefactory are indeed those inscribed on the stained-glass window here. "Stiobhard" and "Ó Cinnéide".'

'As they are on the only original stained-glass window at the abbey. Thank goodness they left it as a mark of respect for the man who bequeathed the building to them, I assume.'

Clifford tapped his pince-nez against his palm. 'Hmm. "Stiobhard". Mother Superior was most confident of its onomatology.'

'Whatever that is?'

'The study of the formation and history of names. Of places or people. However, "Stiobhard", the lady was sure means "Keeper of the Estate".'

'Well, dash it, that's no help! The estate here might not be as big as Henley Hall, but it's still too huge to scour every inch of.'

'Ah, but remember the second of the names' meanings?'

'Umm, guardian of... of...'

'The hall.' Her butler pointed down to the stairs. 'My lady, to the Great Hall!'

Downstairs, she ran her hands over the first of the five door frames, then stepped back to peer up at the coat of arms as Clifford examined the next one along. A few moments later, with the last one also offering no clue, she sighed.

'I was so sure we were on the right track.'

'Uncharacteristically defeatist, if I might be so bold. I'm sure we are in the correct room, at least.' He paced a few steps away and back, tapping one hand in the palm of the other as he muttered. 'Guardian of the Hall? Guardian—'

'Clifford!' she cried, her words tumbling over each other in her eagerness. 'It's not the doors that are guardians of the great hall. The other name!'

'"Ó Cinnéide", my lady.'

'Which means?' She hurried over to the regiment of armoured suits against the wall.

'Helmeted-chief.'

She tapped the nearest one. 'Or... "ugly head".'

He joined her and stared at the helmet. 'It looks perfectly normal.' After a moment, he shrugged and reached out. But as he lifted it up, he paused, his brows knitted. Then his eyes widened.

'Good lord, my lady!'

37

Eleanor looked around in contentment. Breakfast had been devoured in fine style among fabulously raucous company and, to her delight, not in the snug but in the main bar.

'A woman in the pub proper?' she whispered in Murphy's ear. 'Won't you get into trouble?'

He shook his head. 'My pub. My rules. Besides, this is a one-off. Like you. Anyway' – he pointed out Constable Doyle among the crowd – 'the local constabulary are present in case your man cuts up rough. We've seen first-hand the damage he can do!'

She laughed and glanced over at the policeman who was downing a pint with impressive speed. 'Like all of you, Doyle did an amazing job. But to be the one to actually face and hand-cuff that terrible man can't have been easy. I've tried several times to tell him how impressed I am but it seems I really did upset him when we first met.' She glanced over at the policeman again. 'Every time I go near him, he just slides away without looking at me.'

She jumped in surprise as Murphy slapped the bar, doubling over with mirth. 'Forgive the lack of blarney dressing it up, but you are the most unusual lady to ever walk this earth! Certainly, the blessed earth of West Ireland. Have you not even enough conceit to see what your looks do to men like Doyle? And most of the others in this room?'

As he spoke Doctor O'Sullivan threaded his way through the crowd to them.

She shook the thought of Doyle being a secret admirer out of her head and smiled at the new arrival. 'I think I owe you an apology, Doctor O'Sullivan. I thought—'

He raised a hand. 'That I was only interested in issuing a death certificate in the name of Lady Swift? Because you noticed the back seat of my car was suspiciously wet?' He laughed at the look on her face. 'I saw you from the abbey and wondered what you were doing. As it happens, I'd visited a couple of patients before coming to the abbey and my bag and coat were quite soaked through.'

She grimaced. 'Well, in my defence, I did suggest to Clifford that might have been the reason.'

He laughed. 'And you also concluded I was up to no good at the hotel in Kiltyross among other things, perhaps?' For the first time, a smile played around his lips. 'I was actually following you to try and keep you out of trouble, as it happens. I thought you'd spotted me at Flannery's workshop but I wasn't so sure if you'd seen me at the hotel or not. Just in case you had, we assigned Murphy to the job after that.'

She laughed. 'Well, he wasn't that much better at it. I spotted him watching us round the back of the church.'

Murphy shrugged. 'You are one tough lady to follow, let alone to try and keep safe.'

'I know. Only don't get into that with Clifford, will you?' she whispered.

Smithy appeared, looking for a refill. While Murphy obliged, she thanked him too. 'Not only for the night of the fire, but also, of course, last night. And for taking Mullaney in until the staff and Corcoran – the real Corcoran this time – return.'

Murphy lifted the bar and came around to her side, ruffling Gladstone's ears as he did. 'Now, you're sure we can't persuade you to stay for New Year?'

Smithy nodded enthusiastically. 'We've the fiercest party planned, you know.'

She shrank back in mock horror. 'And that's supposed to be tempting! I saw Derrydee's definition of partying on Christmas Day.' She nodded at her butler where he was standing his usual respectful two steps off. 'Even Clifford's normally infallible mind was no use to us until way after lunchtime.'

'Ah, fair play to him, though,' Murphy said, 'he got that fiddle to sing until almost dawn.' Pretending to cover Eleanor's ears in gentlemanly fashion, he hissed to Clifford, 'Though there was a line of tiddly women went home disappointed you hadn't played their—'

'My lady, ahem!' Clifford stepped to her side, running a horri-fied finger along his collar as the nearest villagers broke into peals of laughter. 'If you still wish to make the ferry tomorrow morning, we need to leave soon. Or perhaps you have had a change of heart?'

She shook her head. 'Much as I'd love to stay longer, I feel New Year at home in Henley Hall might be a safer place to be than Derrydee Village Hall!'

Before she could leave, though, a vaguely familiar face blocked her way.

'Lady Swift, I think we met before, like.'

She winced. 'Yes. I'm terribly sorry. We rather rudely invaded your home, didn't we?'

The man who she'd spoken to in the low thatched cottage where Clifford had spotted the Gilligan brothers shook his head. 'And thankful I am. Like everyone else here, those brothers of the devil had been demanding money and food off of me and me family for as long as I can remember. And now, finally, it's over.'

Eleanor tried to keep her face neutral. From what she'd seen, the poor man and his family had barely enough to keep body and soul together. How anyone could prey on such people made her blood boil.

Outside, there was another sea of eager faces who were joined by the entire pub which emptied behind her. The three lines at the front, however, were enough to make her grateful for the pristine handkerchief Clifford slipped into her hand. Miss Breen's pupils stood smartly scrubbed, their faces aglow, holding aloft a paper banner above their heads written in wobbly coloured-in letters: *Thank you, Baronetess Lady Swift. Derrydee will miss you.* Below was an even wobblier drawing of Gladstone.

As Eleanor pressed the handkerchief to her mouth, Miss Breen stepped around, every inch the headmistress. But she and Eleanor caught each other by surprise as they both reached for the other's hands.

'All the thank yous in the world be laid at your feet, Lady Swift,' Miss Breen said. 'You inspired our menfolk to stand up for the village and finally bring down that monster. That's a lesson they'll never forget! Fancy it taking a single woman's spine to remind them all they had one longer than the main street and back between them.'

'Oh no, several women's spines!' She beckoned the hovering Kathleen over and slipped a hand through her arm. 'I realised last night the moment Murphy, Smithy and the others appeared that between the two of you, you were the voices that persuaded them.'

'For the children's sake,' Miss Breen said firmly. 'They couldn't be brought up in fear any longer.'

'And the adults too,' Kathleen said with a new air of confidence. 'My da's the salt of the earth. He didn't deserve more years of living hell on account of worrying about me.'

'And you should be very proud of him.' Eleanor smiled as Kathleen hugged her. 'Your father is—'

'Too handsome for the likes of Derrydee,' Murphy whispered in her ear, having snuck up on them.

'Actually, I was going to say a delightfully cheeky rascal!'

'I'll take that as well, for sure.'

'And if Kathleen was my daughter, I'd be the proudest parent ever.'

'Ah, don't be giving her ideas.' Murphy chuckled, stealing his daughter away for a hug of his own. 'There's a kitchen's worth of washing up to be done after you brought the whole village in for eating. And she needs to keep her strength up for taking over my pub when I'm too old.'

'Or lazy, more like, Da!'

Clifford coughed and waggled his hip flask at Eleanor. 'Apologies for interrupting, but a little fortification to keep your strength up, my lady?'

She stared back blankly. 'Strength for what?'

'For attending the official ceremony arranged by the Derrydee Village Committee.'

Her eyes widened. 'Official what?'

'Relax, my lady.' His eyes twinkled. 'Your speech is perfectly memorised, of course?'

'... and Lady Swift has generously insisted that once the treasure of Hennelly Towers is sold, all the monies raised will go to the village committee to administer fairly to those in need.'

A tremendous cheer erupted from the crowd, forcing Eleanor to seek refuge in her handkerchief once more.

'... and so, as the Head of Derrydee's Village Committee, it is my honour,' Miss Breen continued in her best school teacher voice, 'to pass to you in return, Lady Swift, the greatest treasure our village possesses. Eighty-nine doors open to you forever with the fiercest of welcomes awaiting in each and every one!'

'Though you'll be wanting to make sure to wear your thickest underneaths if you come again in a winter like this!' a male voice called over the cheering. Clifford closed his eyes in horror, shaking his head as she laughed and stepped forward.

'Thank you. To everyone. And I sincerely hope that the final sum from the treasure will be sufficient to ensure for many winters to come that every Derrydee family will have enough for a proper daily meal and a proper fire.'

What Clifford had discovered on lifting the helmet in the great hall was that it was actually made of gold hidden underneath the base metal. The weight had given the game away. However, it seemed that many of the gold helmets must have been sold off by Feargal to pay for building the new house, (now the abbey). Nevertheless, Clifford informed her, there was still enough left to raise a princely sum for a village as small as Derrydee.

As the cheers continued to ring out, she shouted her thanks again and then gratefully stepped back out of the spotlight.

A quarter of an hour later, Clifford waved his pocket watch under her nose. She sighed. It was time to go – in fact past the time to go – but she was finding it hard to tear herself away.

Murphy snuck around to her side.

'And, don't be worrying, Father Quinn couldn't be here, he agreed readily enough. There'll be a proper grave and headstone for your man Ronan Hennelly. *Inside* the churchyard this time.'

Clifford slid a piece of paper into the undertaker-cum-publican's hand. 'If you could ensure the headstone bears her ladyship's precise inscription?'

'Why for sure.' Murphy unfolded the paper and smiled as he read aloud. 'Family First. Last. And Forever. Whatever the name. No matter the history. Sleep well until we meet again, Cousin.'

The Rolls bumped along the rutted road out of the village as they rode in silence. Gladstone, tired out from a morning snuffling up sausages and cuddles from the children, snored sprawled out on the back seat, his now inseparable friend stretched out beside him. They'd debated whether or not to take Tomkins back to Henley Hall. Obviously Gladstone had taken a shine to him. And in truth so had they. And Clifford had pointed out that none of the staff had taken the cat with them when they'd left, so it was unlikely they'd miss him on their return. But Tomkins himself had made the decision for them, by jumping in the Rolls as Clifford started to pack and refusing to leave.

It had started snowing again, but only light flakes that danced playfully around the car. As they passed the spot where they'd found Ronan, she rubbed her face with her hands.

'You know, Clifford. This so-called holiday has been anything but! I'm exhausted. And emotionally wrung out, in truth.'

'But hopefully a tiny piece of the hole in your heart has been plugged, my lady?' he said gently.

She sighed. 'More than a tiny piece. In the strangest way, I feel like I'm leaving home. To go home.'

'Precisely as it should be.'

They carried on in amiable silence until their progress was interrupted by the sight of Father Quinn and the Mother Superior standing by the turning to the abbey. Slowing the Rolls down, Clifford shared a puzzled look with Eleanor.

'Whatever can it be now?' she whispered.

As she stepped out of the car, the Mother Superior came forward to meet her.

'There you be, child. I just wanted to wish you God's blessing on your journey. If you ever decide to put your bound-less energy and fortitude to even better use' – she glanced down the road towards Derrydee – 'then there is always room at the abbey for those who decide to dedicate themselves to God's work.'

She smiled. 'Thank you, Reverend Mother. I'll keep that in mind. One never knows.'

The Mother Superior nodded. 'Indeed, my child, only He does! Now, I believe Father Quinn wishes a word.' She walked around the Rolls and leaned in the window to talk to Clifford. At the same time, the priest approached Eleanor and held his hand out.

She went to shake it, but then realised he was holding some-thing in it for her. Mystified, she accepted it and unwrapped the small tissue parcel.

'Oh gracious.' She stared up at him. 'It's... it's Ronan's St Christopher's medal.'

Father Quinn nodded, a smile playing around his lips. 'It is that. The one I think you believe I'd stolen from him?'

She felt her cheeks redden. 'I'm so sorry, Father. I—'

He raised a hand. 'No need. Correct you were in the abbey when we first met. I was the only one with him when he passed away. And he did speak.' He held up his hand again. 'It is alright. I am not about to breach the confessional. His last words were not a confession, we had already taken care of that and it will remain between himself and me. No, afterwards, he gave me this medallion and begged me to pass it on to you to keep you safe where he'd failed with your uncle.' He looked into her eyes. 'St Christopher, you see, is not only the patron saint of travellers like yourself and Ronan, but also the patron saint of... sudden death.' He smiled. 'The problem was, I realised that if I did pass it on to you, O'Donovan and his men would believe Ronan gave it to you himself. And, most likely, believe he told you in the same breath who his attackers were. Therefore, sadly, I felt it was too risky to fulfil his wishes. Until now.'

She smiled at the priest through her tears. 'Thank you, Father. I'll treasure it forever.'

The monotonous rhythm of the windscreen wipers had sent her into a trance. Her reverie was broken by the rustle of a paper bag.

'Mint humbug, my lady?'

She stared down at the medallion she still held. 'Sorry, I got lost in my thoughts. How long have we been going?'

'It is about half an hour since we left the Mother Superior and Father Quinn.'

She popped the sweet into her mouth and winced. 'Ow!' Her hand shot to her cheek.

Clifford glanced at her enquiringly.

She grimaced. 'I think I'm getting toothache.'

He nodded to the medallion.

'What? You're not telling me St Christopher is also the patron saint of... toothache!'

He nodded again. 'Indeed he is, my lady.'

She shook her head as the car finally turned onto a better road and they picked up speed.

'In that case, let's hope he works his magic in time for New Year's Eve. Because I intend to eat and drink for two.'

'Only two?' Clifford's eyes twinkled mischievously. 'Uncharacteristically defeatist, my lady! However will our local shopkeepers survive?'

Laughing, she held her cheek and pointed down the road. 'Drive, you terror. I need another festive holiday to recover from this one and I know just the place!'

A LETTER FROM VERITY

Dear reader,

I want to say a huge thank you for choosing to read *Murder in an Irish Castle*. If you did enjoy it, and want to keep up to date with all my latest releases, just sign up at the following link. Your email address will never be shared and you can unsubscribe at any time.

www.bookouture.com/verity-bright

I hope you loved *Murder in an Irish Castle* and if you did I would be very grateful if you could write a review. I'd love to hear what you think, and it makes such a difference helping new readers to discover one of my books for the first time.

I love hearing from my readers – you can get in touch on my Facebook page, through Twitter, Goodreads or my website.

Thanks,

Verity

www.veritybright.com

facebook.com/veritybrightauthor
twitter.com/BrightVerity

HISTORICAL NOTES

THE POTATO FAMINE (1845–1852)

When Eleanor and Clifford visit the hotel in Kiltyross, Clifford alludes to the potato famine. A terrible time in Irish history, a disease – blight – attacked the leaves and roots of the potato plant, one of the main – and in some cases almost only – sources of nutrition for a large portion of the population. The disease decimated successive crops for five years causing widespread famine. At the time England ruled Ireland and their misman-agement of the situation is generally agreed to have worsened, rather than improved, the situation. Around one million people starved to death, with a further million emigrating, mostly to America.

IRISH WAR OF INDEPENDENCE (1921–1922)

Eleanor and Clifford have to contend with some anti-British sentiment, most seemingly from Constable Doyle, when they first arrive in Derrydee. This is not surprising given the British and Irish had recently been at war with each other. There had always been strong resistance to British rule in Ireland and in 1921 this became open warfare. The following year, with neither side being completely victorious, the warring sides agreed to split Ireland into a new, independent Irish state in the south and the north would remain under British rule, which it has to this day.

IRISH CIVIL WAR (1922–1923)

Not everyone in Ireland was happy with the division of Ireland into North and South. Subsequently, those supporting the split and those opposing it started a civil war that lasted another year. The provisional government of the Irish Free State that had been established in the south at the end of the War of Independence emerged triumphant and the division remained when the war ended in 1923. In *A Lesson In Murder*, Eleanor meets Miss Munn, a PE teacher who wonders, given the divisions, if she is now Irish or British?

WATER IN RURAL IRELAND

Eleanor and Clifford are puzzled how the man they find in the road (Ronan Hennelly) came to drown miles from any lake or river. In the 1920s (indeed until the 1950s), most rural areas in Ireland had no mains water, only water pumped from wells like the one Eleanor and Clifford used in tackling the blaze at the gatehouse. Hence the need for a water delivery service like the Gilligan brothers. When I visited my relatives in West Ireland, they still had no mains water and drew all their water from a hand pump.

ELECTRICITY IN RURAL IRELAND

Unlike Henley Hall, Eleanor and Clifford find Hennelly Towers is without electricity. Like water, there was no mains electricity in the 1920s in rural areas. Households relied on candles or oil lamps for light. Heating relied on burning mostly peat as they did in Miss Breen's school. (My West Ireland relatives still used peat they cut themselves to heat their home.) Cooking again used peat and was done over an open range.

PEAT – A THOUSAND YEARS OF USE

The Irish have been cutting and burning peat for a thousand years. Peat bogs chiefly consist of rotting vegetation such as leaves and plants. Some vegetation in peat is over ten thousand years old. The peat itself is a layer of soil underneath the bog. This is cut into 'bricks' using a special spade. The bricks are then dried and used rather like you'd use logs on a fire.

IRISH PUBS

Opening Hours

Originally, ancient Brehon law (sixth to seventh century) insisted public houses were open twenty-four hours a day and could never turn down a thirsty or hungry traveller! Unfortunately, for the customer if not the publican, this law fell into disuse. However, when Eleanor and Clifford arrived in Derrydee, the law still insisted that a 'bona fide' traveller could have a drink and a meal outside licensing hours if he or she was more than three miles from home. Also, as Eleanor and Clifford found out, on a Sunday you were not allowed to enter a pub between two and four p.m. (the so-called 'Holy Hour') but if you were already inside, you were welcome to stay and carry on drinking.

Women

When Eleanor tried to enter Murphy's pub by the bar door, she was politely told to enter by the snug. It wasn't until the 1960s that women were generally accepted in the main bar in pubs. This didn't mean that Irish women never drank. On the contrary, they simply sent their husband or son out to bring a tipple home from the pub for them. The snug has died out in a lot of Ireland, but in Britain I'm still sometimes directed to the snug when I have my dog with me.

Bodies

One can't blame Eleanor for being a tad surprised when she spots the body of the man they found in the road (Ronan Hennelly) in the cellar of Murphy's pub. However, after the Coroners Act of 1846, it was common to take a body to the nearest pub as it was the only establishment with a room cool enough (the beer cellar) to slow decomposition. Autopsies were also often performed there, with the Act decreeing a dead body had to be brought to the nearest public house for storage until further arrangements were made. It became common for publicans to have marble tables in their cellars for autopsies and the preparation of the bodies. This legislation was not removed from the statute books until 1962, and the dual role of publican and undertaker is still common in some parts of Ireland.

ST STEPHEN'S DAY AND THE WREN BOYS' PARADE

Eleanor doesn't have the best experience at the Wren Boys' Parade, but they don't normally involve attempted kidnap. Clifford's description is, as ever, very thorough, so there's little to add. The parade is always held on St Stephen's Day.

HURLING – THE REAL IRISH SPORT

As at the Wren Boys' Parade, Eleanor doesn't have the best experience at the hurling match. But then again, it's always been something of a rough and tumble as Clifford explained. What's not so well known is that it was also one of the most successful sporting stands against foreign rule ever. In 1918, the ruling British forbade anyone from holding a hurling game without seeking permission first from the authorities. This was partly as hurling was seen as a display of 'Irish nationalism'. Instead of there being no hurling games the following Sunday, there was a match held (without permission) in every parish in Ireland at exactly the same time. Over fifty-four thousand people played, and over one hundred thousand watched the matches. After that, the British quietly dropped the idea of insisting written permission was sought before a match could be held and hurling has remained Ireland's most nationalistic sport. And, like Father Quinn, many priests have refereed or managed teams, with bishops often being the ones to start the match by tossing the ball into play.

IRISH WAKES AND FUNERALS

When Miss Breen tells Eleanor not to grieve for Corcoran, she's saying this because she knows he hasn't died in the gatehouse fire, it's all been rigged by the crime boss masquerading as the old retainer. However, Doctor O'Sullivan is right when he tells Eleanor that the Irish tend to celebrate the life of a departed loved one as well as grieve for them. The body would usually be displayed for at least a day and a night in the family's front room in an open coffin (closed if the body was disfigured in death).

During this time, anyone who knew the deceased would call at any time of the day and night without the need to let the family know they were coming. Sometimes they'd sit all night next to the coffin. The wake I attended was slightly different in that the family and friends all gathered together the day of the funeral and held a very noisy, boozy wake filled with as much laughter as tears.

ST CHRISTOPHER

The religious medallion Eleanor is given at the end of the book is a St Christopher medal. St Christopher is known as the patron saint of travellers and children. He is also, less known, for being the patron saint of bachelors, storms, epilepsy, gardeners... and, yes, Clifford as ever is right – toothache! Oddly, although one of the best-known saints, he isn't actually a saint at all, as he was never canonised.

ACKNOWLEDGEMENTS

Huge thanks to my readers who continue to give me wonderful feedback and to the fabulous team at my publisher, Bookouture.

Made in the USA
Monee, IL
04 March 2023